CRAG BANYON.
HE'S JUST SUPER.

When Minus, the city's newly minted superhero, shows up at Banyon Investigations looking for help tracking down his archenemy, Banyon's first instinct is to tell his prospective client to take a flying leap. Supervillains are notoriously unforgiving types, and so when it comes to dealing with them Banyon has a firm business policy that consists of three pillars: truth, justice and running away. Not necessarily in that order.

But the hero is a sad sack, and the office elf wants Banyon to take the case, and none of the really good bars in town are open, and so, caught in a weak moment, Banyon relents. Big mistake. Soon our plucky P.I. is caught up in the crazy chaos that comes hand-in-glove with the larger than life superhero biz. If he's lucky enough to survive the thrilling flights, dizzying heights, Spandex tights, bare-knuckled fights, and a doozy of a demented ex-girlfriend, Crag Banyon might live just long enough to make it to his own funeral.

BANYON INVESTIGATIONS.
WHERE A HERO IS A SANDWICH.

FLYING BLIND

A Crag Banyon Mystery

JAMES MULLANEY

James Mullaney Books

Cover art: Scotty Phillips

Cover design/layout: Micah Birchfield

Interior design/layout: Rich Harvey

Editor: Donna Courtois

To Phil Anderson,

physical therapist extraordinaire,
who never gave up on our mom
when nearly everyone else did.

You gave her back to us.
Eternal thanks.

FLYING BLIND

1

The sleazy motel was the high-class variety that rented rooms by the hour but could have gotten away with five minutes in most cases, including maid service.

Not that there was anyone on nightshift duty who functioned in the traditionally accepted role of chambermaid, at least not as it is recognized either by polite French society or by impolite aficionados of motion pictures of the slobbering pervert genus.

The maid in the case of the Happy Hobo Motel was a middle-aged ogre with a stump of soggy cigar clamped between his pursed, blubbery lips and an overflowing laundry cart of hopeless dreams and impossible-to-remove stains parked at his side.

The squat mound of muscled lumps stood at the ready with a spray bottle of Spic and Span in one stubborn, hairy hand like some seedy Minuteman, and he schlepped from room to room as doors steadily popped open and shame-faced patrons who had briefly occupied the grimy quarters scurried past him with their eyes and -- after the preceding injudicious minutes of wanton frivolity -- libidos low.

It takes a fairly substantial commitment for non-sociopaths to snuff out every last vestige of self-awareness and self-loathing. Personally, I've found that the copious application of alcohol works reasonably well, albeit temporarily, for the former but is total crap for the latter. In point of fact, most mere mortals aren't up to the challenge of eradicating that pesky five-letter bastard known as shame, no matter how much booze they try to drown it in. Still, I figured most of the cocky good-time Charlies I'd watched come and go at the Happy Hobo Motel over the past few days probably thought they'd successfully put a bullet in the brains of the little bugger, only to realize the instant they stepped out of their rented room and came face-to-face with a bland, nonjudgmental ogre that shame is harder to kill than the gamboling vermin that were even now hitching a ride back home in their boxers to surprise the missus for Valentine's Day.

You're pretty far gone down the ladder of moral degradation when you can work up even one ounce of shame in front of an ogre. The upmarket ones dine at the nearest sewer and sleep in a pit of their own filth. The one on night duty at the Happy Hobo was cleaner than most. He at least looked like he was hosed down pretty regularly and shoved into a relatively unpolluted, bright red quadruple-X staff T-shirt by motel management. But in his watermelon-sized heart he would always be filthier than a Guatemalan Burger King. Still, every single one of the motel patrons who passed him averted their eyes, suddenly finding the cockroach deposits near the baseboard the most fascinating flecks of offal in this seedy backwater of what used to be considered the civilized world.

I'd decided days ago that if you want to rev up the engine on the old shame jalopy, having a hooker octopus on your arm more than did the trick. In point of fact, the one I saw coming out of room 202 was on her fourth trick of the night. As she slapped her way down the hallway she busied herself by reapplying lipstick, checking one cell phone for messages, texting on another phone, pulling a wedge from her pantyhose and curling one suction-cup limb around the arm of the head of the local department of public works. As the DPW director's invertebrate inamorata passed the ogre, her final free limb slipped a couple of bucks into the gruesome mook's T-shirt pocket.

I got the whole transaction on film with a couple of clicks, courtesy the camera I'd strategically hidden under my folded trench coat which I'd sat on the counter beside me.

I'd been surreptitiously snapping pictures of the Happy Hobo Motel clientele for the previous three glorious nights, and if my telephoto lens and I had been an unscrupulous blackmailing duo, I could've sunk a Kodak well into the deep pool of local politicians, business leaders and assorted movers, shakers and late-night gyrators I'd seen skulking around the joint over the course of the past half-week. Just a couple of the juicy shots I'd taken and I could have retired to Borneo as a wealthy, if unprincipled, king.

I'm not that far gone yet, although I am pretty far down the ladder of moral degradation. Not much of a surprise there. I'm a P.I. Yeah, don't snap your wrists vigorously applauding my miserable vocational selection.

Despite my position circling the drain at the lowest shit stratum of the Yankee Doodle caste system, I actually don't take photos of perverts for the sheer joy of it. Ordinarily, I don't even do it for the dough, but times had been tight the past couple of months, so when the dame had come to my office the previous week weeping Niagara waterworks about her husband's suspected extramarital monkeyshines, I was forced to bite the bullet and take the case. Hey, sue me for having to pay the electric bill.

I'd followed the creep for most of the previous three days. I figured for sure that I'd hit pay dirt the very first night when Johnny J. Johnson -- mild-mannered bank manager by day, skulking degenerate by night -- had arrived in the parking lot behind the Happy Hobo. The hornball banker had shut off his headlights halfway down the block and ran silent-ran deep until he coasted into a parking space tucked away in a hidden spot behind the panel truck that went with the one-hour sea horse groomer's out back.

Johnson, like everybody else who ever dallied their rocks off at the Happy Hobo, had signed in under an assumed name. There was no super sleuthing in uncovering that particular fact. I gave the twenty-something dame behind the front desk ten bucks, and she flipped me the hotel register and, subsequently, the bird when I told her she was easier to buy than a Moxie and a pack of Marlboros from a bus station vending machine.

"I ain't got no idea who you are, but I hate you," the bangled and orange-headed babe had snapped through a wad of angrily popping gum.

"There's always an abundance of that going around," I'd assured her. "Get in line behind my ex-wife, a string of irate floozies, more bill collectors than you can shake an empty checkbook at, and, frankly, myself at the moment."

The register was loaded up with enough Smiths to shod a John Ford movie. I found out that first night that Johnny Johnson's nom de infidelity was J. Smith. Clearly the CIA lost out on a top man when Johnson's high school guidance councilor steered him away from "international goddamn genius spy" and stuffed that banking brochure in the cover of his geometry book.

I was tempted to change his phony name to something plausibly phonier, like a twelve character-long Polish eye chart with three W's and a dearth of vowels. His wife was already the suspicious type, and I didn't need her to grow mistrustful as well of the shady P.I. she'd hired, thinking erroneously that I was making bullshit up just because her husband showed all the originality of a goddamn Michael Crichton novel.

"You have a pen?" I asked the young girl who was loitering behind the motel's cash register and glaring at me from deep inside her raccoon eye shadow.

"Pen rental's five bucks," she said.

Her jeans were so tight I could see Hamilton's profile gasping for breath in her front pocket on the last of my folding money I'd already slipped her.

"I can't imagine that I can persuade you to roll that into the original bribe just for old time's sake, given everything you and I have been through these past thirty seconds?"

Her mouth gave birth to a bowling ball of pink Bazooka which exploded like a rancid-smelling gunshot. "Five bucks."

I shrugged and pulled my camera out from under my trench coat, successfully snapping a shot of the register before the dame could yank the book away.

"Pictures are twenty!" she snarled as she swept the register under the counter.

"They are also worth a thousand words," I confided. I snapped one of her. "I'll start the ball rolling on that one with 'repulsive' and get back to you on the remaining nine hundred and ninety-nine. They, like you, won't be pretty."

That had been day one and, thanks to the mystifyingly oversensitive younger generation, there was no returning in person to the Happy Hobo for me after that.

Fortunately, the Happy Hobo Motel was the old-fashioned three-tier U-shaped kind of dump with all three floors thoughtfully equipped with open hallways, each with a railing overlooking a slimy pool occupied by one of those lagoon creatures that were so popular among suicidal research expeditions back in the 1950s. This one looked like he was about ninety. He'd emerge from the depths of the 8-foot mark wearing a dripping cardigan, shake his fist at passing cars, pick up the paper from the stand on the corner, then submerge back to the depths of the deep end where I'd seen the dim glow of a reading lamp switch on.

I'd staked out a post directly across the street from the Happy Hobo, which afforded me a view of every door in the entire joint. How a motel with such a sterling reputation as flypaper to debauchery and a perfect perch to observe the nocturnal commissions of duplicitous other halves didn't result in at least one good, public rolling pin beating per night was a testament to the inappropriate level of faith a good chunk of the wedded segment of the population still applied to a couple of crummy tin rings and a scrap of yellowing paper on file at city hall.

Night three of my thrilling observation of Johnny Johnson -- banker, philanderer, soon-to-be alimony pauper -- found me sitting with the rest of society's pathetic castoffs on one of the stools in a shabby downtown restaurant that was a real-life version of Edward Hopper's "Nighthawks." That's the painting of the corner restaurant at night with the big plate glass windows. You'd know it if you saw it. Don't be too impressed with my seemingly vast knowledge of fancy-ass art. I only know the name of that particular painting because my secretary is the prize-winning dingbat who bought it after those museum thieves who stole it back in '99 dumped it in a local pawn shop by mistake after a series of amazing sitcom screw-ups. Doris, the moron queen of my office staff, might have accidentally stumbled into the find of lifetime if she'd realized for two seconds what she'd managed to luck into. Instead, she'd immediately turned around and gone on *Antiques*

Roadshow with her ratbag mother in tow to get the most famous heisted art in the USA appraised by professional sissies on Public TV. Yeah, *that's* her. My goddamn cup runneth over. If you want the worst secretary on Earth to ruin your business too, you're welcome to her, assuming you can pry her out from under the hairdryer she parks over her bleached head in that fingernail salon she calls the reception area at the world headquarters of Banyon Investigations, Inc.

Thanks to all the work I had to put into tracking down the real thieves in order to spring blubbering Doris from jail, "Nighthawks" is pretty much the only painting I know by name other than "American Gothic" and that other one. The one with the fat, smirking guinea dame the Mole Men burrowed into the Louvre to paint whiskers on last year.

I was the third oil-painted sad sack from the left with the cold cup of coffee at my elbow and the waitress in the powder blue dress, white apron and a #2 pencil jammed up her beehive giving me the hairy eyeball for sitting in her station for five hours three nights in a row without ordering so much as one measly delicious slice of rubbery meringue pie.

"Hey, big spender, you want me to top you off?" snarled the only waitress employed at Bottomless Joe's Diner as she unenthusiastically waved a dented aluminum coffee pot around the far end of the counter.

"Maybe later. I'm still waiting for the analysis to come back from the lab on that cup of lukewarm mud you poured me two nights ago. I'm terrified there was an error in the kitchen and an actual grain of coffee might have mistakenly made its way into it."

She hesitated, holding the steaming pot in the air as she considered the effort she'd have to invest in slogging down the counter, pouring its contents in my lap, then schlepping back to the ancient Mr. Coffee to assault another innocent can of Folger's.

Ultimately, she decided the extra work wasn't worth the momentary joy, and she stuffed the pot ferociously back into the coffee maker and wandered through the filthy silver door to the kitchen. I noted from the corner of my eye that she immediately entered into consultation with the chef, a hulking slob in a T-shirt that looked like he'd used it as a drop cloth when he painted his living room ceiling with bacon grease. She whispered something into his cluster of ear hair and, roughly equidistant between his hair net and the cigarette that dangled from his lower lip, a pair of dull, porcine eyes narrowed.

I'd earlier deduced that the chef was also the owner of Bottomless Joe's owing to the hollered and conflicting orders that emanated from his exceedingly large pie hole, which the waitress grudgingly endured with quiet hostility. Additionally, he wore a name tag which read "Joe," which I was certain was a positive boon for all the food poisoning victims when they finished with their diarrhea and finally got around to filling out the legal forms.

The quiet kitchen consultation of the Bottomless Joe's staff was less thrilling to me at that moment than the sudden activity on the second floor of the Happy Hobo Motel. Across the street a door had just opened and a figure had emerged from room 311.

I snaked my hand to the camera tucked beneath my trench coat folded on the counter and took a few discreet shots.

The room wasn't Johnson's. The banker had disappeared into room 315 an hour earlier, but I had determined by the subsequent lack of commotion around his closed door that first night that it was probably not a lousy idea to keep track of who he might be associating with via secret passages, false doors or yelling through the wallpaper.

The figures who exited the room slunk off in opposite directions, and even before they'd entered their respective stairwells the ogre on sentry duty was dutifully rolling his overflowing laundry cart to the gaping black entrance to their carnal cave.

I was as amazed as I had been a million times already that week that the rotted open hallways that traversed the second and third floors were safe for both the nightly philanderers' promenade as well as the ogre's bulk, which even by blobbish ogre standards made him too damn big for his age.

Not to be out-bulked by anybody else in the crummy neighborhood, Joe from the Legionnaires' disease hothouse that Bottomless Joe's Diner erroneously called a kitchen chose that moment to hove his way through the squeaking silver door, an actual greasy spoon clutched unironically in his size XXX-large catcher's mitt of a hand.

The guy was massive from the waist up, all ponderous potbelly, barrel chest and arms swiped off a comically out-of-proportion cartoon muscleman from a Charles Atlas ad in the back of a funnybook. Just south of his equator, however, his body collapsed into a concave declivity that made his rear end look like a blue jeans pothole that the city had failed to fill in after a bad winter.

Joe marched up to me, the annoying waitress following in lockstep with savage glee, and threw his massive shadow across my more modest and exceedingly less hilariously assembled form.

"Are you gonna order anything?" he demanded.

"Absolutely," I replied. "The moment I arrive at my favorite bar I plan to order up a bathtub full of anything that will help me forget the disgusting odor from this joint which, I realize now, is not in fact the product of the reeking

warm front from the bathroom encountering the putrefy-
ing cold front from kitchen to create a superstorm of stink
over the dining area, but rather is emanating specifically
from you." I raised my dirty mug to congratulate his grand
malodorous accomplishment. "Hail to the stench."

The coal-black dots recessed beneath the eaves of his
supraorbital ridge clouded with slight confusion, and his
menacing spoon lowered just a bit.

"Yeah, well, you wanna stay sittin' here all day every
day, you gotta order something other than coffee," Joe
insisted.

"Forget the java, Joe," the waitress hissed, tugging on
an apron string so filthy it looked like it had been used
to tow a garbage scow up Shit Creek. Even from the side
I could see the loose ends of the knotted apron strings
dangling down in the open space where the guy's keister
should have been. "The creep just made fun of you like
you stink or something. You, with your injury in the line
of duty and everything."

The spoon was back up like a cudgel, and this time I
knew there was no way I was going to be able to remain
on stakeout duty any longer at that particular locale.

"Forgive me for being undiplomatic," I said. "I was
distracted owing to the fact that I had mistakenly assumed
the 'bottomless' in Bottomless Joe's referred to the limit-
less cups of mysterious brown fluid advertised for two bits
on the sign out front, when in fact it is clearly an allusion
to your astonishing and apparent utter lack of anything
resembling a human ass."

I'm not quite sure what was said on their side of the
counter as I calmly shrugged on my trench coat, donned
my fedora and gathered up my camera. The waitress was
shrieking with such deep offense that I realized for the
first time she must be married to the palooka with the void

where his voidance should go.

Joe had fallen into sullen silence, glaring a hole through my head, but as I headed for the door the dame just kept pointing at a framed, yellowed newspaper article hanging on the wall next to a stack of cracked coffee mugs. The photo was of a much younger Joe on crutches and wearing an RCMP uniform, a deep declivity at the back as if each cheek had been removed with a giant ice cream scoop. The headline from the *Calgary Herald* read, No Way! This Guy Loses His *Ass* In Freak Saddle Explosion, Eh?

"Hey, wait!" Assless Joe's wife shrieked like a hysterical teakettle as I opened the door. "You didn't leave a tip!"

I gave her one that was worth far more than the bent penny I'd found in the gutter out front that I'd planned to roll across the dirty counter prior to her meltdown.

"Dine elsewhere," I kindly suggested.

I let the door swing shut on the latest Canuck vocal detonation and vowed to call my congressman to propose we squander trillions on an inadequate fence on that goddamn border too.

It was probably for the best that I'd been chased from the grimy corner restaurant by a demented harridan and her hollow-assed husband. In the three nights I'd staked out the hotel from the counter of Bottomless Joe's, I hadn't learned anything of value about Johnny J. Johnson. I was going to have to alter my preferred modus operandi of doing next to nothing and deploy my second-tier line of attack of doing as slightly more than next to nothing as was possible on an empty stomach and with a mild hangover.

I stood on the sidewalk momentarily as I considered my next move. I longed for it to be a lateral one from the stool at the botulism paradise I'd just vacated to another stool, this one an inviting perch at my watering hole across town. Too bad for me the barkeep at O'Hale's Bar had gone out of town for a funeral and the bastard replacement he'd parked in his stead was not respecting the time-honored nightly O'Hale's tradition of getting me loaded for free while indulging my repeated lies that the next day would at last be the day I finally began making some feeble move in the direction of doing something about paying down my gargantuan bar tab.

The faster I got the Johnson job out of the way, the faster I could resume my more important life's work of slowly dissolving my liver in a solution of watery vodka.

I trotted across the street, careful to avoid the lobby windows of the Happy Hobo Motel and the raccoon eyes of the clown-haired vicenarian shakedown artist who was holding down a rusted and creaking stool behind the front desk.

I'd scoped out the motel in the daylight hours while Johnson was safely ensconced behind his desk at the bank where he wasted the hours between prostitutes, so even in the shadows I had a good sense of the exterior layout.

A large glowing sign with half the letters burned out hung on the side wall and was positioned high enough to be spotted from the highway by amorous pants partiers. The Happy Hobo had been too cheap to shell out for actual neon, so the sign was made with that banned Mexican knockoff called neoneon, the only differences between it and the real thing being that it was a little cheaper, incredibly toxic, and very faintly buzzed "La Cucaracha" rather than the more traditional nothing.

An alley cut along the entire back wall of the joint, and a row of telephone poles slung with sagging wires ran alongside the narrow road. I circled the hotel and counted off windows until I reached the spot below room

315. An unwelcoming light glowed dimly beyond closed curtains.

Johnson hadn't been as careful as the rest of the army of deviants along the rear of the Happy Hobo Motel who had buttoned up their windows with more care than they had their trousers. There was a sliver of bright yellow on the left-hand side of Johnson's window where the curtain had not been pulled completely closed.

I'm pretty sure the concomitant glamour of my chosen profession is what garbagemen feel about that reeking liquid that pours out of the backs of garbage trucks every time they screech their air brakes.

Just my pathetic luck, the telephone poles were the old-fashioned, easy-to-climb models with the handles up either side, so I had no excuse to ditch this particular misadventure and strike off to the nearest liquor store. I slung my camera over my shoulder, grabbed the lowest pair of handles and heaved my middle-aged ass off the ground, managing with a series of grunts and creaking bones to do the whole Glen Campbell-lineman number up three floors to Johnson's motel window.

The gap in the curtain was about two inches wide, which would have been ideal if the window wasn't precisely one foot into the domain of suicidal inconvenience.

I hooked one leg around the pole and leaned as far as gravity and semi-sobriety would permit, managing to get the lens of my camera somewhere roughly in proximity to the dirty window pane. I had not yet begun to click when I heard a great rumbling from the alley below as well as an even greater shrieking.

"There he is!" yelled Bottomless Joe's wife, who had apparently decided to take her banshee hash-slinging show on the road.

The rumbling that accompanied the rotten waitress,

to whom I now wished I'd generously donated that bent penny, was the result of a very large laundry cart overflowing with soiled linen being rolled around the back corner of the Happy Hobo Motel by the massive ogre chambermaid in the red T-shirt.

"I see you make up for your husband's missing ass by being one yourself," I called down to the waitress. As I spoke, I quickly snapped a couple of shots of what I hoped was the interior of Johnny Johnson's room and not the motel's bent aluminum siding, which was stained with streaks of rust from ancient, weeping awnings.

"I told you I seen him come back here. And with a *camera*," the bigmouth waitress insisted to the ogre, undeterred. "He's some kind of pervert."

My feet were now firmly planted back on a pair of rungs. I was stuck up the pole but with the way down blocked I was already looking for an alternate escape route. "Tone is everything, sister. I gather from your inflection that you mean that in a negative way and not in the jovial 'I really like that fellow, he is *some* kind of pervert' way, which is the official corporate position of the Happy Hobo Motel. I'm not kidding. It's stenciled on T-shirts in the lobby."

The ogre slammed the laundry cart at a good thirty miles per hour into the rear of the building. Lights snapped out in rooms all over the joint, and worried shadows peered around ruffling curtains searching the night for, frankly, somebody exactly like me. The light in Johnson's room remained lit and I heard nobody moving around inside the only room that was no more than five feet from my elbow.

My new ogre pal marched up to the telephone pole and grabbed onto the bottom two rungs with two huge paws.

Ogres are excellent at hiding in the shadows under bridges, tunnels, and underpasses and then jumping out to *boo!* ten years off your life. They also boo the cash from your wallet and the watch from your wrist. The nicer ones might even let you keep the hand below and the arm above where your knockoff Rolex was attached. Lucky for me one of the major reasons ogres take pleasure in lurking underneath stuff is because they are absolute shit for climbing. It's a whole inner ear thing. I saw it on Nova. Unlucky for me, extreme ogre vertigo didn't prevent the one who'd just abandoned his favorite filthy laundry cart from gripping the rungs at the base of my telephone pole with a pair of hairy gorilla hands and shaking like he was a starving Polynesian islander and my sorry ass was the last goddamned coconut up the tree.

I wrapped arms and legs around the pole and held on for dear life, all the dearer as it was my own that was about to get snuffed out and not some far more deserving SOB's.

"I take back my tip," I yelled down at the dame once the initial round of shaking ceased and the last of the ogre's spent outburst rattled the wires down the line in either direction. "Eat all of your ass-challenged husband's cooking you want. I'm positive your Canadian digestive system won't self-detonate."

"Do it again!" the waitress commanded, and the ogre obediently grabbed onto the telephone pole and began to once more vigorously shake the hell out of it and me.

I felt like a tourist riding a wildly malfunctioning electric bull in one of those contemptible "fun" saloons that put hay on the floor for ambience, unlike serious bars that only use it as a sensible janitorial aid to absorb excess blood and vomit.

By this point I could hear doors frantically opening

and closing on all three floors of the Happy Hobo Motel. Risk-averse lemmings were fleeing for the exits, abandoning caution, most of the clothes they'd worn in, and probably half the marital aids sold in the tri-state area in the past six months.

The mass deviant exodus had not gone unnoticed by the lone sentry who held down the fort in the lobby. At the precise moment the ogre was reaching for the pole to give me another firsthand idea of what it was like to be a can of Dutch Boy latex in the Home Depot paint department mixer, around the corner came tearing the twenty-something dame who'd tried to evilly extort an extra twenty out of me for snapping a picture of the hotel register three nights before.

"What the hell is going on back here?" she demanded. Her shock of hair was blue for the evening, but her eyes still looked like she'd gone five rounds with Jack Dempsey in his prime. She directed her masked gaze up the pole to the pitiable figure clinging thereto.

I'd already figured out my escape route, but I was reluctant to embark upon it as it had about as much chance of ending in my premature demise as being flipped to the pavement and squashed to paste by my new single-minded ogre pal, who had taken a step back when the babe with the circus hair had shown up and was now glaring holes through my forehead with a pair of tiny, recessed ogre eyes.

Stalling was the order of the moment as I, lacking the necessary level of fortifying distilled beverage in my system, worked up the sufficient amounts of nerve and stupidity which would be coequal partners in my great escape and, more than likely, my spectacular demise. Not to mention I'd done the math and figured out that it would help immeasurably to have some aid in my getaway, and unfortunately there was only one way I could think of getting it from the tough audience below.

"I suppose you, the staff of the Happy Hobo Motel, are wondering why I summoned you here," I called down real casual-like to the chick from the desk, the broad from the restaurant, and the ogre from my impending murder. "I'm wondering how it didn't occur to anyone during what I presume was an arduous process of conceiving a name for this impressive monument to the eternal love between star-crossed chiggers and bedbugs that Happy Hobo Motel was clearly inferior to the more alliterative Happy Hobo Hotel. You could have been Triple-H in the tour guides. Of course, some wags, lamentably myself included, would have assumed the H's stood for hepatitis, HIV, and health code violations, but as a general rule you're wise to not pay any attention to people like me. Incidentally, that extends to murder, in case you're interested. I certainly am, for obvious self-interested reasons."

"He's some kind of peeping tom, Bootsie," the waitress volunteered to Blue-Hair. "He's got a camera, eh? He's been taking pictures of your dad's motel all week."

"Ah, so it's a family business, is it, Bootsie?" I called down. "So you're the clown-haired offspring of a moron who couldn't figure out how to string three H words together? Was your mother stupid, too, and if so did that make for a difficult childhood? I'm guessing it would, but unless a benevolent recessive gene kicked in to rescue you from a life of inexhaustible ignorance you probably didn't know why."

As I figured, Bootsie with the blue hair got a look of rage in the sinister interiors of the rings of black war paint she'd smeared around both eyes.

The young dame slapped the panting ogre hard on the shoulder, never shifting her coldly furious gaze from the visage of purely innocent inquiry three stories up.

"Bring that jerk down here," she commanded. She did a little pantomime of holding a pair of invisible rungs and yanking down hard.

I was surprised the ogre got her point on the first try. He immediately wrapped his thick hands back around the lowest metal spikes that jutted five feet up from the bottom of the pole and jerked down with all his ogre strength, which was considerably more than that which he usually expended stripping soiled sheets from stained mattresses.

This time the pole didn't shudder. This time it dropped three feet directly into the ground.

I felt the contents of my chest launch up into my throat, the contents of my throat launch up into my skull, and my brain shoot out the top of my head where it was fortunately prevented from firing like a cannonball straight up into the night sky by my strategically jammed-on fedora. As quickly as the telephone poll sank into the pavement it slammed to a stop, and I was once more clinging onto a couple of metal hooks for all I was worth as every part of me that had previously flown up now rocketed back down into the pit of my stomach where, in a just world, it would have all splashed down safely in about a gallon of cheap booze.

I was up slightly less than three stories now. Down below and closer than she had been a moment before, Bottomless Joe's shrew wife clapped her Canuck hands with glee. Beside her, Bootsie Blue-Hair still wanted to murder me, apparently in her limited mind it being a capital offense for a guy to be incisive. The Happy Hobo's resident ogre grabbed onto the next set of metal rungs and gave a second hard yank.

The world rose sharply around me once again as the

pole dropped further into the ground, this time four feet. The wires that snaked out to the adjacent poles hummed like plucked violin strings and I could see that a couple of them were already straining to the breaking point. I didn't want to be there when the power lines snapped, since getting cooked like a chicken on the end of the world's biggest kabob skewer over a couple of dirty pictures was far too spectacular an exit from this mortal coil for a guy as calculatedly uninteresting as me. Not to mention that it completely undermined the insignificant departure a la William Holden that my liver and I had been painstakingly colluding on all these years.

I could see the ogre reach up and snag firmly onto the next set of rungs. A taut electric line above my head hummed like an anxious kazoo.

The ogre yanked and the pole dropped. The wire overhead snapped with a crack and danced through the air like a hissing black snake. A transformer that had been minding its own business on a nearby pole lost patience with the whole ridiculous dispute and decided to make a point of its disapproval by exploding the shit out of itself.

The bomb blast from the transformer brought a single, brilliant flash of daylight to the dark alley, rattling buildings, setting off car alarms, and shattering a dozen windows in the rear of the Happy Hobo Motel.

The one window the detonation was not responsible for smashing to a billion sparkling bits was the one through which I launched myself the instant the ogre had jerked the telephone pole down for what wound up being the final time.

I'd calculated that the second-floor window was my best chance to keep from becoming dead, which was not how I'd planned to spend the rest of my life. The last yank from the ogre dropped me directly in front of the dark,

dirty pane, and the simultaneous detonation of the transformer gave the cover I needed to nearly break my neck
as I jumped from the pole through window pane.

Shards of shattered glass flew everywhere.

I landed in a tangled heap of arms, legs, and flapping trench coat tails, which is pretty much the generic
type of tangled heap I most often land in, so my highly
trained muscle memory dealt with it in the standard way
by deploying a million bruises and, possibly, a couple of
cracked ribs. It was so dark I figured I could be unwittingly bleeding to death, but I hoped the fact that I had
been very cleverly thickening my blood with a profusion
of scotch for decades would get me to the nearest bus stop
before the onset of crippling anemia requiring emergency
transfusions of vodka.

As I scrambled to my feet, the flash was already dying
outside the broken window.

"Where did he go?" I heard the Bottomless Joe's
waitress shriek.

But the dame from the front desk of the Happy Hobo
had suddenly lost interest in massacring an insignificant
P.I.

"Oh, my God…oh, my God…oh, my God! My old
man's gonna kill me!" Blue-Headed Bootsie cried.

"Do I have to clean this up?" grunted a third voice,
presumably the ogre who was no doubt trying to figure
out how he was going to jam the broken transformer and
a bunch of live wires into his laundry cart.

I'd landed in a supply closet, narrowly missing what I
judged to be a slop bucket out of which jutted a decaying
floor mop. I found the doorknob in the dark, apologized
with overwhelming sincerity when a shouting, angry
voice caused me to realize that I had erred about pretty
much every damn assumption I'd made in the previous

five seconds, found the actual doorknob, and stumbled out into the second story hallway.

I immediately checked in the weak light of the hall to confirm that my camera had made it through all the excitement intact. It had, no doubt owing to the fact that the company had discontinued manufacture of that particular model thirty years before, so it wasn't made from the fragile cobwebs and worthless hopes and dreams that all modern crappy gizmos are comprised of.

I tucked the camera away in my trench coat and patted my pocket. "All I can say is, Johnny J. Johnson, you'd *better* be cheating on your wife."

I actually could have said a shitload more than that, but like an opera virtuoso I was saving my voice for a night of vitally important drink orders.

I snatched off my fedora and used it as a makeshift brush for my coat, leaving a trail of tinkling, glittering glass fragments in my wake as I ran like hell for the nearest exit.

2

Twelve hours later found me a lot less hung over than I had a well-earned right to be and riding the groaning elevator up to my second story offices.

After bravely fleeing my ass out a side door of the Happy Hobo Motel the night before, I'd managed to successfully flag down and board a city bus without anybody trying to kill me, which was a personal record worthy of a Mardi Gras-level celebration.

I'd naturally tried to get loaded at O'Hale's Bar, but the bastard replacement bartender was still on duty and refused service to the joint's best customer. He had even taken issue with what he perceived to be my gross misuse of the word "best," viewing it purely from the perspective of a cynical business transaction and not taking into account my prodigious product consumption and the frequency, duration, and Noel Coward bon vivant-ism of my legendarily celebrated appearances on my exclusive bar stool.

I'd been forced to retreat to my apartment and the cache of booze stored therein, but between the excitement of my evening playing squirrel up a bucking telephone pole and without my aforementioned O'Hale's stool beneath my ass to keep me upright and performing at peak drinking efficiency, I was out like a light before midnight.

And so it was that the bell on the elevator rang without the usual accompanying, comforting knife-like stabbing pain to my occipital lobe, and the doors rolled open without my wanting to wrap a couple of sofa cushions over my ears while I visualized the bloody ax murder of one Mr. Otis P. Elevator.

The door to my offices was unlocked, and inside I found one-third of the crackerjack Banyon Investigations squad already hard at work.

The little elf in the tiny business suit looked up from his typewriter as I entered the outer office of my secretary, the apparently MIA Doris Staurburton. The plate of Pop-Tarts and can of Pepsi at his elbow made my teeth ache at twenty paces.

"Good morning, Mr. Crag!" Mannix cried, with far too much enthusiasm for any o'clock in the morning. "You have a client!"

He nodded excitedly to the closed door to my inner office. Through the white translucent glass I saw a vague blob shifting in front of another, squarer blob. The last time I'd had the piquant unhappiness of coming to work, that square blob had been my desk, and I had an ugly private eye's hunch that it probably still was.

"I already *have* a client," I replied. "I actually got up for the fourth day in a row and followed said client's possibly unfaithful and definitely annoying husband from home to the bank where he works, where I watched him plant himself behind his drab little desk for another drab, long eight hours. I even managed to get off a snapshot or two to commemorate the dreariness. I'm going to have one framed and hung on my office wall as a daily reminder that somewhere out there is a life even more horrible than my own."

"This is a *new* client, Mr. Crag," the elf said. He seemed particularly excited about whoever was using up all the oxygen in my office, but with Mannix it was hard to tell. He was an all-around good egg, but he pretty much always kept the gas pedal of his enthusiasm stomped to the floor mat. Mannix, for instance, was thrilled to see the mailman each and every day, even though our blue-clad USPS hero stuffed half the building's mail down a sewer grate down the block because committing a federal crime on a daily basis in broad daylight was easier than doing his actual job.

"I'm not a juggler. Mannix," I informed my eager elf assistant. "My laser-like focus has to be directed at screwing up only one case at a time. Where's Doris?"

It was clear by his collapsing smile that Mannix had hoped I wouldn't notice Banyon Investigation's gatekeeper wasn't lounging the day away at her assigned sentry post. It was understandable that the elf thought I might not observe Doris' lack of presence, owing to the fact that she generally spent more of the business day buying lottery tickets at the corner pharmacy than she did drying her nails behind her desk.

"Miss Doris called up yesterday morning in tears," the elf explained.

"She wasn't here yesterday either?" I asked.

Neither had I been, but as the martinet who cut the checks for everybody in the joint I had earned the right to avoid my office for however long and far the bender muse kept me staggering at a sprint away from the depressing dump. (Three weeks, five states and two drunk tanks was my current record.)

"Miss Doris is in trouble with the IRS," Mannix informed me, with a somber nod.

"Oh." I returned his somber nod. "Who gives a shimmering shit?"

I pulled off my coat and hat and hung them on the rack in the corner, remembering two seconds after I walked away to turn back around and pull from my trench coat pocket the roll of film from my previous evening's adventure up the caber.

"Be a pal and develop this, would you, Mannix? Thanks."

I tossed him the film, and the elf caught it, but I could see by his lack of characteristic eagerness that he wasn't entirely pleased with me for my total lack of interest in my worthless secretary's Internal Revenue woes.

Ex-North Pole elves blow Jewish mothers out of the water for their ability to guilt trip the hell out of even the most purely guiltless soul. Mannix had in the past managed to rummage through the flotsam of my cluttered psyche and uncover and lightly burnish the tiny remnant of a conscience I'd tucked away for safekeeping under the garbage heap of an R-rated existence of adult language and mature situations. This time, however, whatever was left of my conscience could slumber safely away under a stack of dirty magazines and empty bottles, undisturbed.

"It is an amusing and amazing fact about Doris, Mannix, that for the first three years she worked for me she insisted on pronouncing IRS as one word: 'erse.' This was a human woman who somehow astonishingly made it to adulthood without having any clue the terror those three letters, arranged in that particular, evil order, inspire in the hearts of all non-moron men. However, our Doris has been classified by the World Meteorological Organization as a typhoon-scale imbecile, and so they would only achieve relevance to her if they were stamped on the label on a bottle of cheap perfume."

A pair of purely innocent elf eyes the size of tennis

balls did their best to shame me into giving a crap.

"That isn't very nice, Mr. Crag," the elf insisted. "Miss Doris is very, very upset. She said she's being audited."

"That, Mannix, was an inevitability even a charlatan carnival Gypsy could have predicted with half her Tarot cards tied behind her back. Despite my innumerable warnings, Doris persisted in deducting every goddamn road trip she takes with that battleaxe mother of hers as well as her entire whorish wardrobe as business expenses." I crossed my arms, giving him my best Perry Mason pose. "So, Mannix, is perennially cheating the government of the United States naughty or nice?"

Personally, I thought cheating Uncle Sam out of every last penny the red-white-and-blue bastard attempted to bleed quarterly out of me was the highest vocation on earth, but I wouldn't let my elf assistant in on that fact since I could see as soon as he bit the inside of his cheek in contemplation that I had him over an ethical barrel.

"Well…" he slowly ventured, "I'm sure Miss Doris didn't *mean* to lie."

"Of course not," I lied, meaning to. "We can write that on the cake we mail to her with the nail file baked inside, care of the Al Capone Suite in federal stir. In the meantime and while we're on the subject of dough, I need my bank book. Where do you have it hidden?"

The elf hustled over to a filing cabinet to unearth the item in question.

"Business or personal?" he asked.

The question threw me, since I was unaware I had more than one. "Beats me," I said. "Let's empty them out in alphabetical order."

"Why do you need your business bank book, Mr. Crag?" he asked as he rummaged. Mannix managed my office with the highest level of efficiency, which rendered unnecessary any need for him to rummage, so I knew he was stalling.

"Because the allowance you placed me on, while ordinarily more generous than what I earned prior to your employment here, did not take into account Ed Jaublowski's bastard cousin not respecting the time-honored tradition of me not paying for my booze," I informed my employee. "And since when do I have a business bank book?"

He was flicking his way even more slowly through the files. "I separated business from personal," the elf explained. "I've made you a corporation."

"I already *was* a corporation, Mannix," I explained right back at him. "That's what that 'inc.' has proudly stood for on my official letterhead all these years. Rhetorically, of course. We are assuming momentarily for the sake of argument that Banyon Investigations, Inc. has now or ever has had official letterhead. Okay, no, when I decided to incorporate I technically didn't go to a lawyer or an accountant or anything so prosaic, but in my heart I've been incorporated from the start, which, bear in mind, is what we'll tell Doris' IRS buddies if she sics them on my trail."

"You don't have to worry about the IRS," Mannix assured me. "It's all taken care of. The money is kept separate, which is what you should have done long ago, Mr. Crag. The corporation protects you so that bad men can't sue you for your personal assets."

"What personal assets? There's the shit contents of this office, the shittier contents of my apartment, and a rusted car that I misplaced months ago and haven't been able to find which, if I'm lucky, has been crushed, melted down and recast as something more useful, like a Dumpster or a statue of Spiro Agnew."

I snapped my fingers and he reluctantly, immediately passed the book up to me.

When I opened it, I suppressed the perfectly understandable urge to perform a sitcom double-take. There were lots of deposits, few withdrawals, and an amount at the bottom of the page that wasn't just the string of mocking zeroes which a decade as a humble and perpetually broke P.I. had conditioned me to expect.

Mannix had been running the show for me for ages now, and apparently had been making a far more impressive job of it than even I thought. He was passing up a second bank book, which I assumed contained my personal savings, but I pushed it back into his little hand without opening it, along with the business book. There are some things a part-time boss and full-time reprobate should not know.

For his part, Mannix was delighted to accept both bank books. He stuck them back in their proper file and slid the drawer shut before I could change my mind. He'd sat the roll of film I'd given him on top of the file cabinet, and he quickly scooped it up and headed for the exit before I had time to change my mind.

"Your client is waiting, Mr. Crag," he said, nodding to my office door as he quickly slipped out into the hallway.

The least favorite part of my job was all the interesting people it was my professional misfortune to encounter on a daily basis, but a couple more years of my elf pal managing my finances and I could probably buy the swankiest isolation tank at the bottom of the loneliest abandoned missile silo in the heart of the most desolate desert. It was a consummation devoutly to be goddamn wished, but in the meantime there was the matter of the amorphous blob that had been shifting around anxiously in a chair inside my office for the five minutes I'd been hiding out in Doris' waiting room.

As a general rule when I am confronted by a new client, my first instinct is to sneak off into a crowd unnoticed. Clients are enormous pains in the ass, literally in the case of the case I'd been working on the previous night, as my morning bruise inventory had revealed. But I'd just found out that I'd become a thousandaire overnight, so it was with an ebullient spirit that I threw caution to the wind and threw my office door wide.

The instant the door opened, the guy seated in front of my desk sprang halfway out of his chair in a sort of half-sitting, half standing crouch.

"Mr. Banyon? Hi. Hello."

He remained in that uncomfortable, nervous crouch as I circled around him, and when I got close enough he shoved out an eager gloved hand.

I was full of general rules that morning, but as another general rule I don't like to shake hands with superheroes. I'd once seen a guy have his hand crushed to joint compound by a dame superbroad who'd only recently been doused with those radioactive space waves that hit mild mannered people sometimes and make them go all Hercules heroic. She was new at it and was still trying to get used to her own newfound strength. First she busted his hand and then she ripped the door off his Lexus when she panicked and tried to drive him to the hospital. Chick even forgot she could have flown him there. She lasted about a week in the business before I read in the *Gazette* that some mad scientist had strapped her to a plutonium rocket and crushed her between a pair of comets.

"I don't want to appear rude," I told the guy in the cape who was squatting as if my office chair was a public toilet, "especially if you've somehow managed to squeeze a wallet in that skintight spandex, but how aware are you of your own strength? Better yet, why don't we just pretend we shook hands, delighted in the experience, and move on."

I was the first to move on, specifically to the chair behind my desk. The window at my back advertised Banyon Investigations, Inc. to the street below with more than fifty percent of the painted-on letters more-or-less intact.

"Oh, okay," said my confused wannabe client, sitting back down. He sat on a lump of his cape and had to get back up to smooth it out under his rear before he sat back down again. "I'm sorry if I seem, you know, nervous. It's just I... that is I've never hired a private investigator before. Not that I have anything against your profession," he quickly added, holding up the apologetic palms of both gloves like he'd just committed a faux pas commensurate with using his White House state dinner soup spoon to flick peas at the Sheik of Araby. "I just never had cause, that is, a *reason* to hire one of you. Somebody *like* you. A private investigator. That didn't come out right. Nothing *ever* comes out right. I should just stop talking now."

He laughed one of those mirthless, hyper-nervous laughs of the pathetically self-conscious. The guy could bound tallish buildings in a single leap, but was apparently a complete spaz.

I'd seen him in the *Gazette* the past couple of weeks, and I'd even caught his act up close and personal a few days before when he flew overhead one of the evenings I was staked out in front of the Happy Hobo Motel. Bright yellow body suit, offset with purple boots, gloves, cape and mask. They called him Minus because of the white badge on his chest with the mathematical symbol for get-the-hell-out displayed front and center. His main catchphrase was "you've been subtracted," although "you plus me equals jail" had been catching on lately. He'd used that one after stopping a holdup at an ATM. The stupid slogans on T-shirts and hats were making street corner peddlers a fortune. It made me yearn for the sparkling wit of the halcyon days of "where's the beef?"

The city had decided it was a huge deal that we had a superhero back in town. Daily front page stories in the *Gazette*, the cops bending over backwards to help him out, an upcoming meeting with the mayor scheduled for the next week. The whole schmiel.

The last big superbastard in the whole tri-city area had been one of those nighttime brooders who stalked the downtown rooftops, drove around because he couldn't fly for shit, and cost about a billion bucks in property damage every time he got into a knockdown, drag-out with one of his archenemies. The police budget for crashed cruisers alone was about a million bucks a night with that jerk. He'd been poached seven years ago by a bigger burg. We were strictly bush league.

But now Minus, the biggest thing to hit town since that meteor carrying those furry ice monsters from Alpha Centauri obliterated half of Midtown last spring, was sitting before my desk and giggling like a frightened first grader outside the principal's office, and of course it fell to yours truly -- the goddamn welcoming committee for every freak, lowlife and loser in town -- to put the jumpy bastard at ease.

"The worst insult you can level against someone in the P.I. business," I informed Minus, "is to not pretend that you think he does something entirely else for a living. However, given the milieu we find ourselves in and the evident fact that you want to hire me, we can't both pretend as if I do something that actually contributes to the overall betterment of society, like managing a roller derby rink or piloting a squid boat. So let's both confront head-on the fact that I actually *am* a private detective, you want to hire me as a consequence of that unfortunate truth, and muscle our way, as it were, past all that."

He laughed again, slightly less manically. "Self-deprecating humor to defuse an awkward situation. I like that." He laughed again, *again*. God, what an asshole.

"It helps in these situations if my clients tell me what the hell they want from me."

"Well, here it is. You see, I'm new at this. Bombarded by radioactive...well, no. Can't say. Might put two and two together and discover my true identity. You're a detective after all." Another spastic laugh. He scratched around his purple mask with the tip of one purple finger. "Anywho, I was turned into this, well, let's just face it... this *super* whatever-it-is a couple of weeks back. Most of it was pretty simple at first. Just fly around, catch wrongdoers in the act, turn them over to the police. Not, mind you, that I don't think the police can handle whatever criminal mischief is out there," he added quickly. "Heavens, no. I have infinite respect for the police. They have a...well, let's face it...an *impossible* job on their hands, don't they?"

"Yes, I imagine managing adult onset diabetes is quite a chore. Although I understand the fact that Dunkin Donuts has recently begun mixing insulin into the jelly has eased the burden considerably. Can we fast-forward past the public service announcement? I have an impatient pink elephant waiting to give my liver a flat tire, and I'd hate for him to run off to terrify some other slobbering drunk just because I didn't have the courtesy to get punctually polluted."

He fidgeted in his hard-backed chair, as if trying to get comfortable by resting his elbows on wooden arms that weren't there. He wound up folding his hands in his lap.

"As I say, the criminal element I dealt with in the first few days was a common sort. But very soon a fellow showed up and started *taunting* me. It was grammar school recess all over again. I wasn't--" He waved a hand from mask to knees. "--*this* in school, as you can well imagine. Anyway, I've caught some of his henchmen, foiled his increasingly ambitious plots, but, darn it all, he keeps getting away."

"Your archenemy," I supplied, offering a professionally blasé nod. "There's one out there for every superhero. They crawl out of the woodwork the minute one of you pulls on your first unitard. It's possible you're even responsible in some way for creating him, or him you, albeit unwittingly. I can't find that out for sure unless you're willing to let me in on your secret identity, which you say is a deal breaker. Either way, it's an old story. I'm surprised you've managed to keep it out of the paper." I pulled out a notebook and slapped it on my desk. "He a doctor?" I asked as I rummaged around for a pen.

Minus' eyes widened within his mask. "How did you know?"

I shrugged. "You'd go nuts trying to track down all the evil doctors out there. If they're not poisoning the city's water supply, they're stitching together unholy golems in one of those castles over on Shelley Boulevard. The latter variety won't be a problem for you. They're more just grave robbers with a God complex, so they don't travel in the same circles. It's the megalomaniacal, evil inventor kind of doctor you're looking for."

"Yes, yes!" Minus said, sitting forward in his chair. "Oh, absolutely. That is, frankly, Mr. Banyon, why I'm here. I need *you* to help track him down."

I'd dredged up a stub of a pencil from the back of my drawer. "Did he give you his evil moniker, or is he just anonymous so far?" I got nothing back but silence and a dumb, quizzical look from the guy in the tights. "His sinister name," I explained. "Dr. Lunatic, Dr. Violence, something like that?"

"Oh, I see. *Cohen*."

I glanced up from my notebook. "Your archnemesis is a Dr. Cohen?"

"Well, that's what he told me when he had me strapped to his sun-harnesser. Oh, dear, I'm getting ahead of myself, aren't I? You see, he had this laser ray gun, and I didn't expect it, and…well, the thing packed one heck of a wallop. He knocked me out and when I woke up I was on the roof of the Beecham Building. That art deco twenty-story apartment building over on Holcomb Avenue? You know it?"

"I am aware of that structure's existence," I conceded very slowly.

"Oh, good. It's a lovely building, by the way. I say it every time I drive by. Not as lovely when someone's trying to fry you to death on the roof, but that's neither here nor there. Anyway, it was on the roof of the Beecham Building where he told me he was Dr. Cohen and that he was my archnemesis and that he was finally going to 'eradicate me from the face of the planet' for disrupting a bunch of his schemes. That's the exact phrase he used: 'eradicate you from the face of the planet,' he said. I told him I didn't know he was the brains behind half the schemes he was telling me were his, but he wouldn't hear it. *Very* unreasonable man. He set the sun-harnesser to 'ash' and then left cackling, with me up there waiting for sunrise. I got loose, but the henchmen he left behind weren't what you could call helpful, so I tried looking him up in the phone book, but I had no idea there were so many Dr. Cohens in town. I checked the first few out but, really, Mr. Banyon, I *do* have a life outside of all this." He grabbed both trailing corners of his cape and gave a frustrated flap. "That's why I came to you."

All I had written down so far was a rough black dot from the tip of my pencil which continued to enlarge as I repeatedly tapped the stub on my notebook.

"What did this guy look like?" I asked.

"I'm not sure. I'm terrible at this kind of thing. I always say I better not witness a robbery, because I'd have a terrible time describing the suspects to the police. And now look where I am. I suppose that's why they call it irony, isn't it, Mr. Banyon? Anyway, what did he look like. Let's see. Kind of curly hair. Long. Glasses, I think. Average looking, normal build. You know. He kept the lower half of his face covered with a high collar. He's probably around fifty or sixty. His hair was white, if that helps."

"*Around* fifty or sixty," I said. "So he could also be, say, forty-five or sixty-five?"

Minus gave a long, thoughtful nod. "Yes, I suppose he could."

I looked down at my utterly blank notebook to refer to the copious notes I had completely failed to take. "So I'm looking for an average guy, who's could maybe be, say, forty to seventy?" (Minus nodded emphatically.) "With white hair and glasses."

"Exactly," said Minus.

"I quit," said I. I swept my pencil and pad into my desk drawer.

The superhero's face fell. "What? Why? I need your help."

"There are a hundred other private eyes in the yellow pages," I explained. "The fact is, at the moment I am vigorously engaged in another case which is already seriously impinging on my gross apathy, and what you've got in mind is a time-consuming needle-in-a-haystack on which a newly-minted prosperous P.I. like me wouldn't waste good shoe leather, although I apparently *can* now afford to have my Florsheims resoled."

"*Please*, Mr. Banyon," Minus begged. "It's not just for me. I have another life outside of this one. I don't have *time* for this."

I can't stand to see a grown man beg, which is why I advocated a ballot initiative the previous year that would have strategically draped municipal sheets over all sidewalk indigents. (It lost by one vote, and I was still ticked at myself for not registering. Also, for being passed out drunk in an alley through the second week in November.)

I can stand even less to see a grown man blub like a little sissy girl, and that goes double for a guy who's built like a concrete shithouse. Mainly it was self-preservation that got me to agree to take the case. The guy had gotten his superpowers less than a month ago, and who knew if in that time he'd tested his newly irradiated tear ducts? It'd be my ass the landlord would have in a sling if Minus started blasting hundred-mile-an-hour waterworks through my goddamn office walls.

At least the guy wasn't deliberately manipulating me. I could tell by the rapid gear shift from sniveling to sheer joy that he was on the nauseating level.

"Here's the thing," Minus said, drawing a gloved finger across the end of his nose and giving a mighty sniffle that became a mini-hurricane that yanked half the paperwork off my desk. "Sorry, sorry," he said, snatching up with lightning speed the papers that were fluttering down around him, stacking them and replacing them on my desk. "I'm still getting used to…anyway, I'm sorry." He heaved a relieved sigh. "I'm not rich, Mr. Banyon. That is, *I'm* really not. I mean, the *other* me. Or I never was. But I saw a show once where this supergentleman crushed some coal into diamonds and, well…"

He pulled off his left gauntlet, shook it out over my desk, and a couple of fat, sparkling diamonds dumped out onto my blotter.

I shook my head firmly.

"This is a cash business," I informed him. "On a couple of rare, enjoyable occasions it has been a cask business. It is sometimes a money order business. It is never a personal check business."

"Oh…well…what should I…" Minus gathered up the brilliantly sparkling diamonds and held them in the palm of his glove, unsure what to do with them.

"I assume you want to be unfettered of anything that might connect back to your secret life. Have those converted to American legal tender. Polly Skidmore's Pawn Shop will rip you off more fairly than the other clip joints in town. When you have the folding kind of dough, bring it back and pay the elf in the outer office. He is, at the moment, not actually *in* the outer office, as he's in the basement developing some film for the other case I'm currently risking my neck over, but he'll be back soon. If he's not here when you return and there happens to be a dimwit blonde blubbering about her IRS woes behind the desk out there, do *not* give her the cash, and for the love of God and all that's holy do not flash any of that homemade ice under her nose. I don't care how many city buses you can stack up on your super-fingertip, she'll arm wrestle you to within an inch of your life for just one rock that size, then drag your bleeding carcass to the altar."

"Listen, can I do that later…oh, my," Minus said, suddenly alarmed as he nodded to the ancient analog clock that had been hanging on the wall when I first rented my current offices after they had been abandoned by the professional notary public/amateur furrier who'd stunk up the joint before me a decade ago. "Is that time right?"

"It's possible. Somewhere in the world," I conceded. "But that's unlikely, as it would have to be a time zone that loses seven minutes every five days."

"Oh, dear, I've got to…oh, dear."

He leapt to his feet, misjudged just how far he could leap these days, and wound up planting his head halfway through the ceiling. He flew back down dragging with him shedding plaster, chunks of wood and an apology.

"I promise I'll pay for the damage," Minus insisted. "Once I get these…you know." He scooped up the diamonds that he'd dropped on the floor when he'd accidentally flown to the ceiling and tucked them back in his gauntlet. "May I?"

He indicated the window, and I rolled over in my chair and flipped it wide open. "Knock yourself out," I said. "But before you sweep majestically and homoerotically away, I'll need a way to get in touch with you."

"Oh, I can just meet you here," he assured me, as he rounded my desk and hiked one Spandex-wrapped leg out the window. He planted a purple boot firmly on the rusted fire escape. "What are your regular business hours?"

"I'm a free spirit," I blithely informed him, "and as such have never committed Banyon Investigations to anything so banal as regular business hours. It's only a happy coincidence that this happens to dovetail with my fervent desire to stay the hell away from this depressing dump as much as humanly possible."

The next leg was out and Minus was standing on the fire escape, his masked head sticking back through the window.

"It doesn't matter," he said hastily. "Just shout. I'll come if I'm free. Just try to sound scared. I don't hear regular yelling, like people shouting for a cab or at the dog for making a number two on the living room carpet. But for scared yelling I hear pretty much *everybody* these days. I also do okay for the purely innocent, like kids calling me."

"I think we can safely write off both categories for me," I assured him. "Although I can round up plenty of dames who've claimed I have a lot of growing up to do."

"Oh, don't get me started on the kids," he said, frustrated. "Just between you, me and the lamppost, Mr. Banyon, it's getting to be a bit of a pain in the you-know-where (excuse my French) to keep answering what I think are emergency calls that turn out to be kids wanting me to sign that new Minus action figure from Hasbro or to play on their kickball team at recess. Not that I don't love children. They're our future, after all. But sometimes…" He raised a pair of helpless gauntlets. "I'm stretched enough these days, and sometimes, darn it, with these kids it's just a lot of gosh, golly and gee whiz."

"I can see how it would be," I agreed. "Hey, can we hurry this along? I suddenly would very much like to vomit into my wastebasket."

He chuckled like I was the biggest kidder since Margot hiding in the bushes, and his great sincerity and evident inherent goodness only increased my urge to upchuck.

"Goodbye, Mr. Banyon, and thank you so much."

Pedestrians two stories down were noticing the yellow-clad weirdo with the purple cape loitering on my fire escape. Cars were starting to slam on their brakes as overjoyed drivers hung out windows, pointing and taking pictures with cell phones.

Excited voices were filtering up from the growing multitude.

"*Minus! Hey, Minus!*"

"*Look, it's him, it's really him!*"

"*Goddamn faggot!*" (Evidently not everybody was one hundred percent onboard with our new local hero's sartorial choices.)

Minus offered a weak shrug, pulled his head from my window, bent his knees, and nearly ripped the fire escape from the bricks outside my office when he launched himself into the stratosphere. A couple of bolts sprang loose and at least one smashed through the plate glass window of the ground-floor check cashing joint across the street.

"*Sorry!*" the hero's fading voice hollered down before he became a yellow-purple speck. "*I'll pay for the damage!*" He goosed his speed to sonic boom and vanished in a garishly mismatched streak over the mini-mountain range of downtown office buildings.

I glanced at the clock on the wall, which served perhaps the greatest function at my offices of everything else with the exclusion of Mannix. As always, according to my trusty, inaccurate analog clock, somewhere in the world it was well past the acceptable time to get plastered.

I slammed my window shut and got the hell out of there before the fire escape could come loose and fall on the gawking crowd of upturned faces.

3

Rumor had it that Ed Jaublowski, traitorous proprietor of O'Hale's Bar, was coming back from his out-of-state funeral that morning. My fervent hope was that the deceased family member had had the decency to remain dead and that the mourners weren't chasing an ambulatory corpse around Pittsburgh with pitchforks and torches. That ugly possibility could tack days onto Jaublowski's sentence as a pallbearer, which opened up the terrifying prospect of me being able to walk a straight line and successfully touch the tip of my goddamn nose with my eyes closed for days.

From the outside, O'Hale's was the begrimed paradise dump it always was, but I no longer trusted a formerly trustworthy façade that had been lying to me for days.

The front light was lit even though it was broad daylight, and was crowned by a diadem of pigeon shit. The familiar, crud-encrusted door handle -- always so inviting -- had lost its come-hither luster. It was as icy and merciless as Jaublowski's dastard cousin, the replacement bartender who had interposed cold commerce into the sacred relationship between tavern keeper and penniless rumpot.

When I opened the door and spied Jaublowski finally back holding down the fort behind the bar across the room, I swore for an instant that I could faintly hear the joyous strains of an angel choir, but the blissful heavenly chorus was drowned out by a passing asshole on a Harley Davidson.

There was only one other customer in the joint, sitting over at the bar, and I didn't see Jaublowski's skinflint cousin anywhere.

"Yo, Jinx! You comin' in already, or you just bein' polite and holdin' it open for all the flies in the goddamn neighborhood?" Jaublowski called over to me in what I identified as his friendliest of malevolent snarls.

The barkeep was already sliding a glass of watered-down floor polish in front of my usual stool even before I bellied up to the bar.

"I am astonished, Ed, at how pleased I am to see you back. If someone had told me just last week that I'd ever miss your hideously malformed mug, I'd have assured them that the nightmares I have accrued would last a lifetime."

I downed the booze in one gulp and slid the glass back over to Jaublowski, who filled it on automatic pilot and shoved it back in my direction.

It turned out the poor, dumb jerk's past couple of days hadn't been all that different from the nightmare I'd conjured up in my disgustingly sober brain.

"Gimme a break, will you, Jinx?" the barkeep whined. "I just got back from the worst trip a guy ever took. Great Aunt Tildie -- that's my dead mother's aunt I went to bury -- she must of got bit by a orderly at the hospital just before she bought the farm. Course, we don't find out the dump's been up to its peepers in vampire orderlies for months. They been keeping it quiet 'cause of all the donated blood what's been gettin' stole from the blood bank in the cellar. So, the old broad's semi-dead for a couple of days, only us family don't have no clue. You know, she's in that stage vampires go through…transnational something-or-other. Hell, what's it called, Jinx?"

"Transitional lassitude," I replied, tapping the lip of my empty glass.

Jaublowski gave me an obliging refill and while he was at it he topped off the only other glass that was in service in the joint.

"I told you my pal here was brainy, Mr. D.," Jaublowski confided to the lone other patron in the bar, who was slouching over his booze like a prisoner in the mess hall guarding his tray of creamed corn and sautéed road kill.

The guy turned his hood in my direction and gave a nod, which I wasn't sure was a surly "get lost" or overwhelming gratitude to me for inspiring in Jaublowski the generosity to cap gratis his glass of lighter fluid. It was hard to get the full range of emotions out of him since he was nothing but a bleached skull recessed in the deep shadows of a black hood that hung out over his face like a personal awning. Even a pair of goddamn eyebrows would have helped.

Death used to come to O'Hale's pretty regular back in the day, but not for the skid row companionship or the ambience that fell somewhere between filling station restroom and that Solzhenitsyn feel-good laugh-fest *Cancer Ward*. The personification of man's fear of his own mortality used to check in at the most depressing speakeasy in town in order to claim souls. You couldn't blame him for going after the low-hanging fruit. The clientele wasn't exactly jogging around the block between rounds or doing pushups on the busted pool table, so by the time most people stumbled into O'Hale's for the first time they were already pretty much knocking on Death's door. He just helped them across the threshold with a courteous shove between the shoulder blades.

Jaublowski used to complain about having to call the morgue practically on a nightly basis. He didn't appreciate it when I told him that when a guy lines up bottles in a carnival booth he runs the risk that a crack shot might come along and win all his Kewpie Dolls. Ed Jaublowski hated metaphors, mostly because he didn't understand them.

Death had claimed or chased away most of the old-time regulars. Really thinned the herd. He'd been so effective that I hadn't seen him around the dump in a couple of years. If he was there for the obvious this particular day, I figured I'd better get any awkwardness we might both be experiencing about our situation out of the way.

"Hold whatever boring thought you have rattling around in your head, Ed," I said to the barkeep. I spun on my stool to face the Grim Reaper. "So, are you here for me? If it's yes, let's get it over with before Jaublowski can finish his story, which I'm pretty sure meets Geneva Convention standards for light to medium torture."

"Geez, Jinx," Jaublowski said, pulling his jowls up into a wounded frown. But he clammed up momentarily and took a step back.

Jaublowski's eyes betrayed that he was worried about the deadly weapon the hooded bastard had hauled into the bar, and he wanted to be out of reaping range.

Death had the handle of the scythe he was forever schlepping around with him lying across three stools, with the blade turned down to the floor. Why he carried the thing around with him was a mystery I wasn't interested in solving. He needed only to touch a guy with a fingertip or just brush up against him to send the poor bastard to eternal bliss. I imagined it was all for show. The Grim Reaper had an image to uphold, and being the black-shrouded specter of death with a skull for a head wasn't goddamn scary enough, he had to haul wickedly sharp gardening implements with him on the cross-town bus.

The skull deep within the hood turned toward me once more, and Death shrugged his bony shoulders. "Heaven don't want you and Hell won't take you, Banyon," he informed me. He turned back to slurping his drink.

"Looks like your time's up, Ed," I told Jaublowski. "Don't worry. I'll throw myself on the grenade and take that fatal, final boat ride across the Styx for you. I couldn't bear to live in a world where I have to put up with that cheapskate cousin of yours running things around here."

"That ain't funny, Jinx," Jaublowski said.

The barkeep topped us both off a couple of times over the course of the next few minutes, but he made sure to hustle back to a safe distance outside reaping distance each time he was through pouring for Death.

"Hey, Ed," I said. "Take a break from cowering behind that disgusting bar rag you're strangling to death in both hands and pass me the local phone book, will you?"

Jaublowski was only too happy to hustle to the end of the bar, far away from Death. He pulled the directory from a drawer and slid it down to me.

As I sipped, I idly flipped through the yellow pages. Under "doctors," I found the C's and was immediately, utterly demoralized by the massive number of Cohens listed.

It was no wonder Minus had given up searching on his own. If the guy did have some kind of life outside of superhero work, he'd have no time to slog through all the names on those -- (I skipped to the last Cohen listed) -- *seventeen* goddamn pages.

I was already exhausted as I looked up from the book. "You wouldn't happen to know a Dr. Cohen, would you, Ed? White hair, glasses, supervillain?"

"I went to a Dr. Kaufman for my feet," Jaublowski replied. He was still hiding out as far away from Death as possible, rubbing down the dirty bar with his grimy rag way down by the silent jukebox.

"Save me his number," I grunted. "I'm gonna need him after this."

"Doctors ain't so much the problem," Jaublowski confided. "It's funeral directors. They's all a bunch of greedy bastards. If they was regular Joes like me and you, they'd roll the cost of reburying reanimated corpses into the original package deal. Nope, not these son of a bitches. They let a guy who ain't in the best shape of his life almost have a heart attack chasing an old lady who's turned into a bat, then when you's caught her with a busted pool skimmer in her old attic where she's flapping around the rafters, these funeral bastards make you stake her yourself and then hit you with a whole second bill. Like he didn't notice she was going through that transnational latitude vampire dohilly shit when he was embalming her. *Right*."

Jaublowski was still grousing to a sold-out crowd of himself as I snapped my fingers for the phone. The barkeep continued to yammer away even as he dropped the blower down in front of me and retreated down the bar past the Maginot Line he'd established at the pickle jar, which had been empty of anything but slowly evaporating brine sludge for twelve years.

The first Dr. Cohen was "Aaron B., Cardiologist" over at the Medical Arts Building at Sloan-Frankenstein Hospital.

"Hello, I'm an overweight bartender of indeterminate age with a nacho-clogged heart that I'm afraid is about to explode, and I'd like to schedule an appointment with Dr. Cohen to find out how many minutes I've got left," I informed the receptionist who picked up. I gave Jaublowski a thumbs-up.

"Yes, sir," the dame said. "Can I have your name, please?"

"Not so fast," I said. "I like to know a little about the men I go into small rooms and strip naked for. Does Dr. Cohen wear glasses?"

"Um…no, sir. Why do you--"

"What color is his hair? I'll give you a minute if you have to check."

"Wait a minute," the dame said, dragging out every syllable as the light bulb went on over her head. "Did you call here the other day?"

"No, mine is a freshly minted heart attack. Is it white?"

"What?"

"His hair."

"Dr. Cohen is…well, that is to say, Dr. Cohen doesn't have a lot of… Listen, I don't have time for these prank phone calls, buster. This is a doctor's office."

"My apologies for calling at tee time," I said, hanging up.

Cohen, Dr. Aaron B., Cardiologist. No glasses. Bald as a Titleist soaring majestically into the ninth hole sand trap.

I made four more calls with similar rotten results.

Cohen, Dr. Aesop, Rheumatologist. Glasses, check. Black hair.

Cohen, Dr. Allen, Hematologist. No glasses, red hair.

Cohen, Dr. Alvin, General Practitioner. Glass hair. (The old buzzard was in his nineties and still wore one of those banned fiberglass toupees from Corning.)

Cohen, Dr. Avery, Pediatrician. "At the tone, leave a message stating your child's life-threatening emergency and we may or may not get back to you, but probably not."

Five calls in all, over ten minute's work, and by the time it was over I felt like climbing up on the roof of the skid row apartment building in which O'Hale's occupied part of the ground floor and doing a spectacular swan dive onto the nearest parking meter. I flipped to the last yellow page of Dr. Cohens and saw that there were five Zacharys, two Zeds, one Zeke and a Zeroth. Up above the Z's there was even a goddamn Xerxes.

"You sure you don't want to press just one fingertip right here and put me out of my misery?" I asked the Grim Reaper. I demonstrated the quick route to a welcome eternity of not having to worry about the usual mortal daily horseshit by pressing my own finger to my forehead.

Death's face scowled as much as an expressionless skull is able. "Get away from me, Banyon, you pervert. Anyway, you don't need me. You're doing just fine on your own. The lifestyle you lead will have you on a slab downtown in no time."

He tipped his own glass and the final contents disappeared over his exposed lower mandible. It was a pretty good bar trick for a guy who was basically a walking rib cage wrapped in a black bathrobe. Where the hell all the liquor was going and why it wasn't puddling on the floor I had no idea. If it was dumping into a bucket secreted in his hollow stomach, I'd have to remember to put him second on my list of celebrity drunks I planned to mug if the local temperance league succeeded in collecting enough signatures to get prohibition on the ballot next year. (#1? Lindsey Lohan. No goddamn contest.)

I held the Cohen pages of the phone book between both hands -- A on the left hand, Z on the right -- and bounced them between my palms, but no matter how much I rattled them the right megalomaniac bastard M.D. didn't drop out onto the bar.

There were about fifty more Dr. Cohens on the first phone book page alone, hundreds more on the following sixteen pages, and who knew if Minus' archnemesis was even local, if he had an unlisted number or if he even practiced medicine? Maybe he was a doctor like goddamn Bill Cosby (whose only successful operation was the amputation of my funny bone every time he mugged for a camera). It was time for plan B.

I picked the phone up one last weary time and dialed my office.

I knew Mannix was back at work when the call got picked up on the first ring. When Doris vigilantly mans my office switchboard, it is remarkably similar to a phone ringing in the forest where no one can hear it. (Although in her defense she moves her lips so loudly while reading *People* that it's hard to hear a phone shrieking off the hook two inches from her goddamn elbow.)

I stopped the elf before he got out his whole Banyon Investigations spiel.

"Hey, Mannix, has that new client stopped by with some dough?"

"Not yet, Mr. Crag. You took his case?" he added, and I could practically see his grin through the little holes in the phone's earpiece. "I'm glad. I think he's a nice man. He helps people, just like you."

"Yeah, I'm the world's most selfless humanitarian," I said.

The Grim Reaper choked derisively, and his homely skull mug was suddenly a busted showerhead with whiskey launching out various face holes. Jaublowski was in no hurry to hustle over with his rag to mop up the mess.

"I want you to do something for me," I told the elf. "You know how hospitals and HMOs sometimes put out directories with photos of their affiliated doctors? I want you to go to every medical outfit around town and collect a copy of every one of those directories you can find. Once you get them back to the office, I want you to cut out the pictures of every M.D. named Cohen. I want photo, name and hospital for each. You got all that?"

"Yes, sir, Mr. Crag," Mannix enthused. "Is there anything else?"

"No," I said. "Yes," I quickly amended. "Did you get that film developed?"

"Yes, sir," he answered. "I thought you might want the pictures quickly, so I hired a bike messenger to deliver them to O'Hale's. He should be there now."

The elf was efficiency incarnate. No sooner were the words out of his mouth and planted in my adorable ear than the door to O'Hale's opened and a scrawny bike messenger entered along with an unwelcome and ugly stab of natural light. The sunlight didn't have a chance to warm away the beautiful dank before the door swung shut.

"Mannix, you are worth your weight in Marshmallow Fluff."

I hung up the receiver and nudged the phone to Jau-blowki's side of the bar.

The bike messenger, who looked like an anorexic scarecrow in form-fitting Lycra, was visibly revolted by the atmosphere of O'Hale's. I pegged him for one of those health nuts who aren't embarrassed to remain in a kid's job into their thirties because it's more important to them to waste half their lives charting their resting heart rate and eating just enough withered, organic Whole Foods pigswill to ensure that they shit only a single, dry mouse pellet once a month.

"Crag Banyon?" he sniffed, holding an envelope over his head.

When I signaled to him, I earned the same look of intense disapproval as had O'Hale's matchless ambience.

I continued to get both barrels of silent disapproval as he walked over, and I had no doubt it would have continued for his entire reluctant visit to O'Hale's had Death not chosen the precise moment the bike messenger sidled up beside me to reach over and touch the kid on the temple. The messenger's wires were instantly cut and he dropped to the floor, tongue lolling, eyes bugging, extremities twitching. The whole Three Stooges, slapstick, stone dead repertoire.

"Not that I don't appreciate you saving me the embarrassment of stiffing the punk on a tip and, to a lesser degree, for not killing Ed over there, but some of us are trying to get pounded in peace here," I informed Death.

The Grim Reaper didn't even look down at the body. "Bum aorta," he explained, offering an apathetic shrug. "Their number is up when and where it's up. I'm just doing my job wherever it has to be done." As he clicked his glass to his teeth he glanced over at Jaublowski, who was still down at the far end of the bar and who was now shaking with what I guessed was either joy or the sudden onset dengue fever. "You mortals are always such egomaniacs," Death told him.

Having been given a reprieve from the chair by the great celestial governor, Ed Jaublowki was only too delighted to hustle over to top off Death's battery acid, but the Reaper clamped a handful of bone over the mouth of the glass.

"Not for me," he insisted. "I'm done."

The barkeep cheerily replaced the bottle and happily danced over to the phone to merrily phone the cops about the dead body joyously stinking up his floor.

I shook out the photos the dead kid had pedaled over from Mannix for a quick peek before slipping them back inside the envelope and sliding off my bar stool. I stuffed the envelope in the pocket of my trench coat and thanked Ed -- who was on hold with the local PD -- for the buzz.

"You happen to be going to the north side, Banyon?" Death asked.

I shook my head. "West."

"Too bad. I've got an actuary over on Piedmont who's due to trip on his shoelace on a flight of stairs in about twenty minutes. The moral of that story will be to not carry your lucky math class compass from sixth grade around in your breast pocket all your life. Anyway, I figured we could share a cab. Oh, well."

He hauled up his scythe and slung it against one shoulder. It seemed like it weighed a ton, and the guy looked exhausted. And not just because he was an ambulatory skeleton shuffling around in a black bathrobe. There were fine cracks in his pale skull where human worry lines and crow's feet would go. I decided seeing Death again after a couple of years that there might be worse careers than P.I. Shoving guys down flights of stairs from 9 to 5 every day for eternity might seem like fun on paper, but might not be the barrel of laughs the brochure at the unemployment office made it out to be.

"If that's a look of pity, Banyon, I'll scythe your goddamn head off."

Then again, maybe Death was just an asshole.

We headed for the door, but an angry voice chimed in at our backs.

"Hold it there, pal, where do you think you's goin' without payin'?"

For a terrible instant I had flashbacks to the previous week of the tyrannical reign of Jaublowski's miserly cousin, but it was the Grim Reaper whom Jaublowski had nabbed trying to booze and cruise.

"You let *him* go," Death said, aiming his scythe at my purely guiltless mug.

"Jinx and me has got a arrangement," Jaublowski said. "C'mon." He rapped his knuckles on the bar, palm up, awaiting payment.

I left Hell's grim Tyrant fishing in his robes and flicking quarters on the bar in front of Ed Jaublowski, who with the immediate threat of confronting mortality lifted had suddenly reverted back to his lovable, foul-tempered cheapskate SOB self.

The Grim Reaper leaned his scythe up against the bar and was digging furiously around his pocket lint for a few more pennies.

"Booze costs," Jaublowski was insisting. "I already called the cops for this mess you left for me to mop up, I can just as easy tell 'em when they shows up that you stiffed me an' have your bony ass hauled off to jail. I ain't rich. I just got back from havin' to chip in twice to bury some old bag I didn't even know. You know, come to think of it I should charge you for *that* too. If you'd done your job right first time around--"

At the risk of inviting a haircut down to my Adam's apple, I felt another twinge of sympathy for Death as Jaublowski launched right back into his tale of funereal woe, picking up in the precise spot he'd abandoned boring ship a half-hour before.

As I slipped out into the sunlight, I wondered how long it would be before the Grim Reaper wouldn't be able to take the bartender raconteur any longer and wound up tossing himself on his own scythe to welcome the sweet relief of silent oblivion.

4

I managed to banish Dr. Cohen and the whole Minus archenemy mess, along with Ed Jaublowski's double-dead aunt, as well as death -- both with and without a capital D -- from my mind on the bus ride to the West Side.

I knew going in that I had to keep my head down because of all the gang trouble in that area lately. The *Gazette* was running daily articles about elaborate dance routines and show-stopping songs breaking out up and down the fire escapes and alleys all over the West Side. The cops had even formed a special task force three months before to deal with the sharp spike in serenades outside Puerto Rican girls' windows.

Captain Krupke, the head of the new cop squad, had been quoted in the paper Mannix had picked up for me a couple of days before. Krupke had been a moron beat cop when I'd been on the force, and he was nothing if not consistently stupid.

"There seems to be a story developing on the West Side," the cop had informed the *Gazette*. "Rest assured, we will work day and night to make this area safe for decent people to walk down the streets without having to worry about violent choreography breaking out around them. Also, time permitting, we'll look into all the daily muggings, stabbings, shootings, overdoses, increased Eskimo Mafia activity, and that crack house that burned down with the five dolphin Cub Scouts in it. I feel pretty," Krupke added.

Vicious gang dancing was up 1000% since Krupke came on the case, and there was at least one innocent citizen sung to death in a liquor store every couple of days.

On this day, it was still early enough in the afternoon that the gang members were home gargling with lemon juice and stretching their hamstrings for that night's turf war, so I didn't have to worry about pulling out my gat to warn off any punk snotnoses who might mistake middle-aged me as a soft target whose wallet they could harmonize from me at the mouth of some dark alley.

Johnny J. Johnson's townhouse was part of an urban renewal project from the 1970s, meaning a bunch of worthless dumps had been pumped full of my hard-earned tax dollars and loaded up with Yuppie pod-people for the alleged betterment of all mankind. It would have been more cost-effective and healthier for the overall gene pool to load them in rocket augers and launch them through the Earth's mantle as a main course peace offering on Mole Man Thanksgiving. Call me goddamn Squanto.

It said a lot about my current #1 client (none of it good) that I could see *Jerry Springer* playing on her living room flat screen through the parted curtains next to the stairs. Johnson's wife was on the phone, and when I rang the bell she glanced up from the chair where she was sitting across from the TV.

The dame held up a finger like I was some unwelcome pest there to offer door-to-door salvation and just kept right on yapping. If I smoked, I would have used my lighter to set fire to the building, but instead I cooled my heels for five minutes before she finally wound down her marathon blab-session, hung up and roused herself from her chair.

"Mr. Banyon," served as both welcome and apology, and was delivered on ice so thick I could have skated into the front hallway on it.

She ushered me into the living room.

She hadn't bothered to turn *Springer* off, although when we entered the room she did nudge the sound down as a courtesy to her tiresome hireling. Some flabby tramp was on the screen screaming in full-throated silence at a large ball of indifferent fur that was squatting on its haunches on the seat of a chair. The caption read, "My Werewolf Boyfriend Is A Two-Timing Dog!"

Gwendolyn Johnson slid onto the couch like a pat of butter negotiating the smooth terrain on a stack of lopsided flapjacks. She stretched both bare arms languidly across the rear sofa cushions, and her long legs glided from the equally long slit up the side of her ankle-length dress as she crossed one perfect gam over the other.

I don't know from designer gowns, but I knew enough to figure out the outfit she'd slithered her pretty little derriere into wasn't off the Woolworth's markdown rack.

The neighborhood might not be the greatest, but it was only the best for the banker's wife. From what little I'd seen of her, Johnson was plowing all the dough he earned into the wife who'd hired me to prove his infidelity. She wore only fancy outfits, even while lounging around the joint watching crappy daytime TV, and she sported more jewelry than a Tiffany's display window. The set of fresh rocks around her neck would have been enough for a down payment on a real house in a decent part of town, but wearing it was more fun than living in it, even if it meant risking her slender neck every time she strolled down to the corner market for a yogurt smoothie and a copy of *Cosmo*.

You couldn't blame Johnson for indulging the little woman. The dame had all the curves of a dangerous stretch of mountain highway. One wrong turn and you're over the cliff. She had a rack that entered the room two minutes before she did, and a caboose that drew a cheering crowd every time she pulled out of the station. Her blonde hair was long and straight, and whenever some wayward locks slipped in front of her right eye she'd tilt her head back, exposing her porcelain neck, and give a little wiggle of her shoulders in order to coax the disobedient strawberry strands back in line.

I might have fallen for her too, and had my heart bust wide open like a dropped sack of wet flour, if not for the eyes. Gwendolyn Johnson's eyes were as blue and beautiful and mysterious and inviting as a Caribbean lagoon, and she could turn on the come-hither warmth as easily as flipping a switch. But the same could be said about a bug zapper, and in my first meeting with her I'd seen enough calculation in those eyes to know that any man unlucky enough to be drawn to them would eventually wind up getting dumped out of the tray and into the trash with the rest of the fried mosquitoes.

"Sit," she commanded imperiously from her Sears & Roebuck sofa throne.

She was apparently used to men -- or at least one man in particular -- responding to her commands like well-trained cocker spaniels.

"If it's all the same to you, lady, I'll stand," I replied, as I peeled off my trench coat and hat and dumped them on the end of the sofa. "Your tone suggests the possibility, however remote, that the wingback you're directing me to could snap shut and swallow me whole. And, lest you think I'm coming on to you in some ham-fisted way, that's not dirty pirate talk, I mean all of me."

It was evident by the sour look on her sculpture-perfect face that she wasn't used to brooking insolence. "Show me your report, Mr. Banyon," she commanded, leaning forward and tapping an efficient, impatient finger to the glass surface of the coffee table.

"I don't do written reports," I informed her. "Not that I could even if I wanted to, since I apparently lost my one and only pen and I haven't yet stopped by my insurance agent's to steal a new one. Besides, I prefer to dazzle my clients with incredible feats of memory." I glanced around. "Where did I leave that goddamn envelope?"

She located it for me under my trench coat, and I pulled out a bunch of eight-by-ten glossies which I fanned out like a game of Kodak solitaire.

I'd marked the borders with a pencil I'd bummed off a bum on the bus. I made sure I laid them out according to what day they were taken.

"Day one, two, three and four," I said, indicating the four distinct batches of photos. "Yes, they are so identical they could have been taken on the same day. That's because your husband's day is as interesting and varied as the movement of hands around a clock. Not the second hand, mind you, because that has real, visible movement and at least gives an indication of the passage of time. He's more like the hour hand, where you can stare at it for what seems like forever and realize at what you thought was the end of five hours that only twenty minutes has passed. Yes, he's just that boring."

Each day's photos showed Johnny J. Johnson exiting the front door of the townhouse I had just entered, Johnson arriving at the bank, Johnson sitting at his desk beyond a glass partition that opened on the bank lobby, and Johnson leaving work at five.

"This," Gwendolyn Johnson said, stabbing a finger

tipped with blood-red nail polish on the last few photos in the first row. "What's he up to there?"

She was pointing at her husband's arrival at the Happy Hobo Motel, recorded for posterity by me through the window of Bottomless Joe's Diner.

She'd informed me when she came to my office to retain my incomparable services that she had followed her husband to the motel a couple of times the previous week after he'd broken his routine for the first time in eight years of marriage and failed to come home immediately after work. She hadn't been able to dig up anything more than I had, which was why she'd enlisted the aid of a pro.

The bottoms of the first three rows of photos were essentially identical. The only thing that changed was the color of the sticking-up hair of the girl desk clerk who, in a just universe, was rotting in a jail cell at that very moment for participating in the assassination of a perfectly innocent telephone pole. Her hair went from orange to green to blue, and I was grateful for the absurd follicular transformations which at least proved to the banker's wife that I wasn't trying to pull a fast one, since nothing else about the monotonous day-to-day existence of Johnny J. Johnson seemed ever to change.

"The first two nights were the same," I said. "He checked in -- alone, as far as I was able to ascertain -- and checked out a few hours later, at which time I trailed him back to your loving embrace. Incidentally, if you want those particular photos, I charge extra. Since I was getting nowhere, I decided to shake things up last night by nearly getting myself killed, possibly by broken neck, rampaging ogre, or electrocution. In the process of my near demise, I managed to snap those beauties."

I indicated the last couple of photographs at the bottom of the third stack.

The pictures actually were beauties, considering the less than ideal circumstances under which I'd managed to take them.

I'd held the camera lens close enough to the space in the window that I was able to capture a pretty good representation of the interior of Johnson's motel room.

When he wasn't shoving telephone poles into asphalt as easily as the rest of the world sticks a straw in a McDonald's Shit Shake (it was bad for the clown, yeah, but that new fecal truth in fast food advertising law was hitting Taco Bell worst of all), the Happy Hobo's staff ogre actually did a pretty okay job keeping the rooms far less revolting than they had an assignation obligation to be. Johnson's room was tidy, with ugly art glued to walls that were painted a hideous orange. There was an open closet, a nightstand, and a bed that had seen more action than Patton's Third Army and Michael Bay combined.

I got part of the open closet where Johnson's suit was clearly hanging on a hanger next to his dress shirt. It was too bad that Johnson wasn't like every other philanderer, since the half of the room I'd managed to nab on film was ordinarily the most interesting. The other half of the room was blocked by the close-up of the ugly green curtains and God only knew what the banker was up to over near the unseen writing desk. If he was as fascinating an individual as I'd thus far witnessed, probably writing goddamn thank-you cards to everybody with more than twenty-five bucks in their money market accounts.

"Where is he?" Gwendolyn Johnson demanded.

"You see this very large piece of curtain-like fabric that's blocking fully half of the motel room?" I said, pointing to the ugly green stripe that bisected the photograph. "It is, in actuality, a curtain that is blocking half the goddamn room."

"Well, who's he got in there with him?" she snapped.

"Nobody, as far as I've been able to ascertain. On Tuesday night, I came back after I'd followed him home and managed to sneak into the room he rented. I couldn't find any hidden passages to the rooms on either side or upstairs and down."

"What about phone records?" Gwendolyn Johnson asked. "I don't see a phone. If there's one somewhere behind that--" She dropped onto the image of the motel curtain a red talon that could have been used to harpoon baby seals. "--maybe he's going there to use the phone. Maybe he's calling a bookie or something."

"Maybe," I admitted.

"Well," she said, nodding emphatically. "That's it then. I want to know who he's calling. Did you find that out?"

"Okay, first off, do you have any idea how hard it is to get phone company records? I *do* know a dame who works there, but she hates my guts pretty much all the way from my duodenum to the uppermost part of my descending colon. Although she does have a soft spot for one of my kidneys. That particular organ also has a reciprocal soft spot for her -- or, more accurately, *from* her -- since she once hit me in it with a piano stool. Okay, that's first. Second, I can see by that starving hyena look you're giving me that you're not going to take no for an answer, but before I waste my time and your money, have you checked to see if he's been blowing through your savings?"

I'd given her the homework assignment when she'd come to my office five days before. If Johnson was mysteriously spending vast sums of cash, I might not know where the dough was going but I'd at least know he was up to something other than renting a room to take a quick nap on the way home from work every night.

"He's not spending any more than the weekly allowance I give him," she said. "He must be cutting back on lunch to pay for that motel room. They're always hitting everybody up at the bank for birthday gifts. He must not be chipping in any longer. He's not draining one dime from our savings, I *guarantee* you, Mr. Banyon."

I trusted her guarantees about as much as I believed the Jane Hathaway accent she affected to hide the West Virginia twang that surfaced like the protagonist in some folksy adage playing fiddle in a swamp while unwittingly sitting atop some surprise twist that completed the homespun aphorism. Probably a gator.

"I'm not taking another dirty picture until I see your savings," I insisted.

She knew I'd pinned her down. I could see it in her pretty, frigid peepers. For a second I knew she was considering firing me on the spot, but then she stuffed the luckiest hand in the land down her cleavage and pulled out a bankbook, which she slapped wordlessly onto the glass coffee table.

I picked up the book, did a quick scan on the final pages, placed it back down, and scooped up my coat and hat.

"I quit," I announced, for the second time that day.

I almost made it to the door, but the dame was a track star in high heels.

"Stop, Mr. Banyon," she insisted, sliding around in front of me and propping one hand against my chest.

"I've been astonished twice by bankbooks today, lady. The only thing yours has going for it is the performance art it takes to produce it, but I've seen better acts in strip clubs and at least they've got a crummy complimentary buffet while they rob you blind."

I had the door open an inch but she kept her body between me and escape as she slammed it shut with her rear. "Stop. Just stop right there. That's just our joint account. That's the only one Johnny has access to. I can pay you. Here."

She rummaged one-handed down her knockers safe and produced a scrap of folded paper. She quickly handed over the money order, which I noted had not been issued by the bank her old man worked for.

"That should cover your services for the past four days as well as keep you on the case for the time being, shouldn't it?"

It was an awful lot of zeroes for a broad with a balance of $11.37 in the joint account she shared with her cheating husband.

"Possibly," I said, knowing at a glance that it would cover her for another month for the kind of low-rent service I provided. "Billing is my assistant's purview. I'll place this in his capable, miniature hands. In the meantime, it might be a good idea if I get those photographs back. For $11.37 I didn't give two shits if you stuck them to the fridge with a gold star for your husband to discover on his way to liberate the mayonnaise, but if I'm staying on the case it's probably not the best idea to leave evidence that you've hired a P.I. lying around the living room."

We returned to the parlor, where I gathered up all four stacks of photos and tipped them back into the manila envelope.

On the TV, the flabby floozy was running backstage in tears as her cheating werewolf significant other was tearing the throat out of a stagehand while Jerry Springer teetered on the edge of the stage where he was helplessly rising and falling repeatedly on the malfunctioning hydraulic legs he'd recently had installed.

I noted that Gwendolyn Johnson glanced at the screen, and for a sliver of a second the ice in her eyes melted.

The fat dame on *Springer* was being cheated on by her

hirsute spouse. And maybe for a moment there was a tiny bit of human empathy from frigid Gwendolyn Johnson. I figured I'd test just exactly how deep her compassion actually went.

"You don't happen to keep a flask of Seagram's stashed down your knobs?" I asked.

Clearly the milk of human kindness did not plunge very far below the surface.

Six seconds later, I was back out on the front steps with the manila folder in my hand and the displaced air from the slammed front door fanning my ass.

"Get back to work!" the dame's angry voice shouted through the closed door.

The afternoon was growing long, and the customary sounds of police sirens were rising over the West Side to compete with the punctuation of the odd gunshot. I could hear a bunch of punks harmonizing around a nearby corner, and a couple of gang members came spinning into view engaged in frantic neoclassical ballet.

The whole world was going to hell thanks in large part to generations of parents who'd been turning a blind eye to kids who were dancing and singing while they were still in junior high. Goddamn permissive society.

I left the gang problem to the worthless cops, who were probably half of them secret singers and dancers themselves, and headed up the sidewalk in the opposite direction for the bus stop.

5

When I returned to my second floor offices I was greeted by the familiar sight of Doris not sitting behind her desk in the outer room not doing the work she was supposed to be doing but never did since she was never there. I'm a huge fan of consistency, which is why I do a consistently lousy job paying her.

The real shock would have been if Doris had been sitting in front of her dusty typewriter trying to figure out how to get her hair uncaught from the carriage. Again. (Yeah, no kidding. It's happened eight times. The last time, I just tossed the dust cover over her head and left her there over the Fourth of July weekend.)

My trusty gal Friday had once gone missing for so long on her annual pilgrimage to Dollywood that I'd arranged with Maybelline to get her mug pasted on the sides of every carton in an entire shipment of mascara along with the accompanying slogan, "Have you seen this moron?" Therefore, the fact that she'd failed to show up again thanks to her current tax woes wasn't a shock. I calculated there was a better than eighty percent chance that at that very moment she was curled up in the crawlspace above the laundry room in that dump of a house she shared with her hag mother, while an IRS agent and the moldy old biddy who'd spawned her were attempting to coax her down with a tube of lip gloss lashed to the handle of a croquet mallet.

So, Doris being among the missing was A-okay, but the fact that the outer room was bereft of any heartbeats at all was still worrisome at first blush. The last thing I needed now that I wasn't completely dead broke was for Mannix, my financial savior, to suddenly pick up Doris' rotten non-work habits. It turned out, however, that where my faithful assistant was concerned, I needn't have worried.

Usually it's the stink of failure and desperation that assaults my delicate nose whenever I arrive at work, but that late afternoon it was paint fumes. After I'd hung up my hat and coat, I tracked the source of the stink to an elf on a ladder that was propped open in the middle of my office floor.

"Hello, Mr. Crag!"

The little guy put so much enthusiasm in announcing my name that he nearly teetered himself and a gallon of white flat latex off the top step.

I grabbed the base of the ladder and held it steady.

"Watch it," I warned. "If you bust your neck, I'm back in the P.I. poorhouse, which is worse than the regular poorhouse since it's impossible to hide booze there without some broke gumshoe sniffing it out."

In my absence, Mannix had dragged drop cloths over most of the junk in my inner sanctum. He had patched and spackled the hole that Minus had head-butted into my ceiling and was just putting the finishing touches on repainting the whole mess.

He was having a hard time negotiating the paint roller, pan and paint bucket, and he not only didn't object when I took the bucket away from him and placed it on some newspapers he'd spread out in the corner, he thanked me like I'd just donated enough blood, bone marrow and drool to save every last sick puppy in Toyland.

"How much did you go out of pocket on all this?" I asked.

"Not a lot, sir," he vowed. "It was no trouble. Mount Brando Hospital is right next-door to Home Depot."

"There is a Home Depot next to everything in this world, and on at least two others that I know of, Mannix," I explained. "There are Home Depots on giant balloons floating amongst the clouds and there is a Home Depot peddling no-melt toilets at the fiery heart of Earth's core. It isn't a question of a conveniently situated retail location, it's a matter of the bastard in tights who *made* the hole in my ceiling paying to *repair* the hole he made in my ceiling. Did the schmuck bring by any dough yet? And by 'schmuck' I mean 'asshole,' since I'm cleaning up my language for your benefit."

"No, he hasn't," Mannix said. "I'm sure he'll be along. He's a nice man. He's been saving people's lives, stopping all sorts of naughtiness and catching bad men all over the city for weeks."

"Except *I* get stuck finding the Cohen that got away," I said. "Speaking of which, did you manage to track down all those doctor directories?"

"On your desk," the elf brightly offered.

While he scampered down the ladder with his roller in one hand and a nearly empty pan of ceiling paint in the other, I attempted to locate my desk underneath the white tarps that were draped over everything and which made the dump look like it was being haunted by the ghosts of vintage Kmart office furniture from the *Welcome Back, Kotter* line.

Mannix had removed all the junk hanging on the walls, lest a stray drop of paint forever mar my yellowed

P.I. license or the miniature rendering of Dogs Playing Poker which Doris found hilarious and which she'd hung up without my permission one day to cheer the joint up and which within a week was entirely invisible behind the thousand spitballs I'd launched at it while bored from the hollowed tube of my missing pen.

The stack of frames I felt up underneath the tarp that covered my desk seemed to have gotten a lot naughtier than Mannix had anticipated and had reproduced under the covers. I pulled out a brand new, handcrafted frame.

"Is it okay, Mr. Crag?" Mannix asked hopefully. "I wasn't sure which picture you wanted. If you want, I can replace it with one of the others you took."

In the frame the elf had assembled on the little work-bench in the basement where he worked part-time as the building's janitor, Mannix had slipped a perfect eight-by-ten photographic rendering of Johnny J. Johnson sitting behind his depressing gray desk in his depressing gray suit at the depressing gray downtown central headquarters of the Panhandler Federal Ameribank.

Not every elf is as guileless as Mannix. Some are downright duplicitous bastards. But the ones who are good are so solidly decent to their cores that you've got to watch every word you say around them, lest as a result of their inability to detect sarcastic nuance you wind up with a framed photograph of some loser from a nothing spouse-cheating case hanging on your wall for all eternity. This, lamentably, was what was about to goddamn happen to me and my big mouth.

"You said on the phone you wanted to frame only one of the photos," Mannix said. "I can make some more frames if you want to hang up more of them."

"One is one hundred percent more than enough," I assured him. "Let's just momentarily tuck it away for safekeeping. I want a drop of paint to despoil this exactly as much as I want to use Doris' inspiring 'hang in there, kitty' poster for target practice."

I shoved the picture of the dead-eyed bank drone plodding through his dead-end job back under the corner of the tarp with the rest of the trash from my walls.

"While we're on the subject of the Johnson case…" I began. I pulled out the money order Johnson's wife had given me and handed it over to Mannix. "Make sure this is the real deal. I trust that dame about as much as I trust all my deadbeat clients."

"This is more than she owes so far," warned my scrupulously honest assistant, who wasn't satisfied moonlighting as the building's janitor and had taken on a third, unpaid job as my goddamn conscience.

"If we need to refund anything once I'm through, you handle it. Just don't tell me about it, as reimbursements to nuisance clients gives me polio."

I heaved the tarp halfway off my desk, doubling it over the pile of frames, and sat down in front of the research material Mannix had kindly laid out for me.

The elf had collected all the physician directories from around town, just like I'd asked. He'd cut out all the Dr. Cohens, alphabetized them and laminated their mug shots in a single, bound scrapbook for my perusal. He'd managed to do it all in about three hours, plus make me a frame and patch and paint the ceiling in my office.

"Do you realize, Mannix, that in an amount of time equal to what it took you to do all this, Doris could have had the nails on both hands and forty percent of one foot painted, all without lifting her ass from her chair? Just something for you to consider when I finally get around to doing performance reviews around this dump."

Mannix only ever seemed to get sarcasm when it came

wrapped around a compliment. The elf blushed and quickly collapsed and folded up the ladder which was about ten feet too tall for him. He hefted it up and hauled it into the outer room.

I found a black Magic Marker in the back of my top desk drawer and set to work on the Drs. Cohen compendium Mannix had compiled for me.

Too many of them were far too easy to eliminate. It was possible a lot of them weren't wearing prescription glasses in their photos, but many of them were bald, many had black, red or blond hair, some had the courtesy to be dames, and not very many at all had white hair like Minus had described.

I started to mark out the face of each dud with an X, but the Magic Marker died halfway through the first line of the first X. I found another marker that was completely dry and wouldn't even write one line. I found a third that was yellow and wouldn't have been too visible on the laminated page, but since it was all I was left with I used it. I thought it maybe worked to complete the X I'd only half-finished in faded black on the very first Dr. Cohen, but when I tipped the page every which way in the light to confirm that I was definitely not seeing something that wasn't there, I tossed the latest worthless marker in the trash with the others and opened my yap to holler out to Mannix.

I didn't even get a chance to inhale when everything around me suddenly started blowing all over the joint as if a hundred Mexicans armed with leaf blowers had materialized around my desk in a circular firing squad to take me out for the capital hate crime of racially insensitive accuracy.

I caught a flash of yellow and purple zipping somewhere to my left, and before I could bravely dive for cover under my desk, the squall stopped as abruptly as it had begun and I was as ecstatic as all hell to discover that it had dumped out in its wake a goddamn superheroic jackass in yellow tights and purple Underoos.

Minus was standing before my desk in the middle of the room amid the dying blizzard of settling papers. His purple cape fluttered and settled, as did the paint-splattered drop cloths that Mannix had spread around the room.

"I'm sorry," said the Savior of the City. (An afternoon edition of the *Gazette*, which someone had left on the bus I'd taken back from the West Side, had referred to him by that brand-new appellation five times in one article alone. Clearly I was not the winner of that weekend's write-in contest with my entry, "The Spandex Shithead.")

Minus made a feeble attempt to nab a few sheets of falling paper from the air, but he was clearly too distracted to care all that much about the colossal mess he'd made of my pristine workspace or about the intense emotional trauma he'd caused me as a result of said mess, all of which would be massively reflected in his bill.

"We need to set some ground rules about open windows," I said. "Here's the first one that comes to mind: stay the hell out of mine."

"I *am* sorry, Mr. Banyon," Minus said. "It's just… it's *him*. Dr. Cohen."

He was breathless and panting, but I figured it wasn't due to exertion since here was a guy who had tossed an eighteen-story building into the sun last Friday when some arch-fiend had been using the elevator shafts as two-way portals to bring down an invading army of Moon Men. Little green bastards.

"You found him?" I said. "Good. You owe my assistant for spackle and a bucket of paint. Consider us square. Just don't break the sound barrier on your way out or you'll be paying for all the broken windows in the building, too."

"No, no," he insisted, sweeping majestically and urgently forward. "He's taken over a building downtown. I just got the cries for help. You've got to come with me."

I frowned and fished my business card from my wallet.

"See here, where it says 'private detective?'" I asked as I held it up for the perusal of his super peepers. "It doesn't say anything about me being in the business of saving the city from archvillains. Don't read it too intently. It's my only card, and I don't want to have to replace it because you singed it with your laser vision."

"You don't understand," Minus pleaded desperately. "I told you I've met him before, but I'm also the only one who's *seen* him, and even then I've never seen his whole face. And he keeps getting away before anyone else gets a look at him. I'm new at all this, Mr. Banyon, and I'm not a detective, so please don't take this as if I'm trying to tell you how to do your job, but if he gets away again, doesn't it make sense for you to have seen him too to help you track him down?"

"Actually, your logic is unassailable," I agreed. "But you're assuming that I'm working for you when I haven't seen a single shilling to retain my services."

He did that absentminded thing morons sometimes do and smacked his own forehead with the palm of his hand. The shockwaves cracked the plaster on one of my office walls, creating a deep fissure from floor to ceiling which was, unfortunately, just wide enough to lose me my security deposit while simultaneously not being wide enough for me to escape pain-in-the-ass clients through.

"I'll pay for that," he promised. "I'll pay for *everything*."

He whipped off his gauntlet and shook it out over my

desk.

I don't have a clue how much dough dropped out. I had a hard enough time trying to figure out how he'd fit so many tight rolls of bills inside his glove without giving myself the added challenge of trying to count the loot as it fell out. A couple of rolls landed on the paint-spattered drop cloth I'd folded off to one side. They rolled to join the rest of the cash directly in front of me on the half-exposed side of my desk.

Greed can do ugly things to a man. Lucky for me I didn't need to be greedy, since I now knew that I had enough dough in the bank already to purchase a top-of-the-line pre-owned Winnebago or an off-season trip to the swankiest fleabag resort on the most mosquito-infested island in the Caribbean.

Unfortunately for me, years of prodigious alcohol consumption had not yet managed to snuff out the few remaining brain cells in which dwelled the pesky dregs of my professional ethics. As much as it would have pleased my arid liver to give him the heave-ho and strike off for O'Hale's, I'd given the bastard my word. It also didn't help that it looked like he was about to turn on the goddamn waterworks again, and I was reasonably certain that my policy didn't carry flood insurance.

"Let's be clear on this one point," I informed him with a sigh. "I am *not* a sidekick. I'm mostly a solo act, but when required by necessity I'm the headliner who *has* a sidekick. Mannix!"

My proof bounded obediently into the room from his all-important post of jamming one pointed eavesdropping ear against the crack in the door.

"Yes, Mr. Crag?" my elf assistant snapped. He flashed a pointy-toothed smile and a supportive nod to the sad sack superhero Spandexing up our midst.

"Draw up a contract," I said. I swept my hand over the loot on my desk. "And do your best to stuff this paltry retainer in my burgeoning bank account."

The elf produced a contract and a pen from the ether like a Vegas magician and offered them to Minus, who signed the contract in our presence on the edge of my desk. He started to return the pen to Mannix, but I snapped my fingers.

"Give me that," I said. "My pen's been missing for days and I just sent three deceased markers to the morgue. I don't have anything with which to draw mustaches on jerks in tights flying around the front page of my daily paper."

The big-shot hero handed over the pen and I dropped it in my desk drawer. Mannix took the contract and hustled it out into the next room.

Minus was pulling on the gauntlet in which he'd stashed the rolls of cash when he suddenly cocked an ear to a sound that nobody but he could hear. His face instantly bunched up with the earnest look of selfless souls who can't bear the thought of not pitching in and coming to the aid of the frightened and downtrodden. (I gave our mismatched buddy shtick about twenty minutes before I completely hated his guts.)

"Off into the wild blue yonder!" Minus shouted, puncturing the air with a raised purple index finger.

(I was wrong. Five seconds.)

"What the hell are you hollering at?" I asked.

He glanced around inside the confines of his purple mask and sheepishly shrugged the shoulders of his cape. "It's something I say sometimes before I take off. The kids seem to enjoy it."

"Not being five, I can't say I experience a kindergartner's frisson when some maniac starts bellowing gibberish two inches from my ear. If you do that again, you'll be processing coal into diamonds for a month to afford my new rates."

"Sorry…it's just…sorry." His shoulders sank for a moment, but when I headed for Doris' office he raised an awkward finger and pointed to the window, which was still open in order to air out Mannix's paint fumes. "I thought we'd…it's just there's kind of an urgency to all the yelling I'm hearing. That way."

"Yeah, fine, whatever. But I never save the day without my Lycra trench coat and magic fedora," I informed him.

And, just like that, he was gone and back in a blur, my paperwork was blasted through the wind tunnel once more, I mentally tacked an extra ten percent onto his final bill for a refiling fee, and he handed me my hat and coat which he'd dashed out at hyperspeed to collect from the other room.

After I'd put them on, he hustled me along, out the window and onto the creaking fire escape. Some of the bolts seemed about ready to go, so it was my turn to hustle him along to get me the hell off the metal deathtrap before the entire structure came loose and wound up crushing the sidewalk aficionados of food poisoning who were suicidal enough to patronize the For the Halibut Fish Market on the ground floor.

"Take some of that dough and make sure my life insurance is paid up," I yelled through the open window to Mannix, who had just reentered my office to collect the rolls of cash on my desk. "And while you're there, steal me a handful of their free pens."

The last thing I saw in my office was the look of beaming pride on my little assistant's face.

A steroid-pumped arm wrapped around my back and

grabbed me up under my armpit, my feet left the comfort-ing, wobbling metal landing of the busted fire escape and I was suddenly nose-to-nose with the grimy, crumbling brick wall of my building.

Two seconds after my Florsheims left the fire escape, we cleared the roof line. The famous Banyon Building dropped away beneath my dangling toes, and the ugly cityscape exploded around us in its full, dramatic, pan-oramic glory.

"If you've got an extra minute and if I'm not dead when we're finished, let's fly over my ex-wife's place," I hollered over the wind, which picked up as soon as we broke free of the protection of my building's wall. "On a completely unrelated matter, I'll need to first stop by the airborne Home Depot to pick up some cinderblocks."

Minus wasn't listening to my terrified semi-disin-genuousness. As soon as we were above the rooftops, the indecisive crybaby was transformed into a lantern-jawed pillar of virtuousness and purpose. The readers of the *Gazette* might have seen him as the Savior of the City, but I suddenly saw him as the exact kind of asshole who gets everybody around him killed while the bullets bounce off his own chest.

I wished more than anything that I'd put on my bul-letproof Sears suit that morning as the Shithead in Spandex banked east into the dying daylight and soared majestically into the greasy, sclerotic heart of the city.

6

There is no way to fly through the clouds with another guy clutching onto you like a Prada handbag without feeling the need to swing by Bed, Bath & Beyond to register for the wedding on your way for that all-important tutu fitting.

It was my crummy luck that my worthless city hadn't wound up with somebody like Lady-Girl, that wannabe actress in L.A. who got hit with a super-powering dose of radioactive spray-on tan. Sure, she was always too late to stop every mudslide or earthquake because she always accidentally flew in the wrong direction and had to stop in Seattle or Okinawa for directions back, but at least she had the decency to fly around spilling out of a bikini. (Although knowing me, if we *had* gotten a dame it would've been somebody like The People's Female, a Russian import who immigrated to New York after the Iron Curtain fell. That dame had all the sexiness of Khrushchev on a John Deere tractor, plus an extra four hundred pounds, all jammed into a bright red miniskirt with a yellow hammer and sickle plastered on the gigantic ass. Goddamn Chernobyl.)

Two things Minus had going for him were that he was a lot quicker than the cross-town bus and there weren't any winos passed out on his back seat. After we'd taken off from my building, I barely had time to get oriented before we were coming down fast over a large blue building in the middle of downtown.

I recognized it as the Telecommunications International & Telephone Service Building even without the giant T.I.T.S. plastered on all four sides. (A hilarious acronym that had cost stockholders about $1,000,000,000 in feminist lawsuits.)

The updraft nearly wrenched my hat off, and I had to slap it down hard as we cleared the edge over a massive T and touched down lightly near the roof access door.

A flock of startled pigeons flapped up from somewhere behind the sticking-up shed into which the door was set, and the suddenness of the feathered rats' desperately fluttering wings all around us nearly knocked me on my ass even before the roof door burst open and a couple of palookas opened fire with a pair of Tommy guns.

I'm a lover, not a fighter. More accurately, I'm a runner-away-er and a hider. Fortunately, the guy my suicidal conscience had stupidly forced me to accompany into a landlocked, rooftop reenactment of Iwo Jima was a living, breathing Kevlar vest.

"Stay behind me," Minus commanded, shouting back over one massive shoulder.

"That is, at this moment, pretty much the penultimate place on the planet I want to be," I yelled over the hail of screaming lead. "However, as it happens the very *last* place I'd rather be is in front of you, so, yeah, I'll probably goddamn stay back here."

Bullets zinged around me far too close for anything remotely resembling anybody's definition of comfort, particularly mine, which in the very first entry in my personal *Webster's* involved booze, a bar stool, and broads, in that precise order, and which in no later meaning encompassed in any way whatsoever me having my ass blown out from under me by some archvillain's Chicago typewriter-wielding henchmen.

The gunfire tore through the air for an eternity that in actuality was probably all of about ten seconds.

Stray rounds tore chunks from the surface of the roof and ripped apart the ledge at my back. Windows shattered in the Walter Matthau Building across the narrow street. Great sheets of glass tore away and plummeted from sight like huge sections of a calving glacier cracking and dropping into the sea. I could see panicked office workers diving for cover and running for their lives as desks were blown to pieces and vitally important computer solitaire games were blasted apart, to be forever lamented and unfinished.

Through it all, Minus strode forward in all his heroic glory into what in two seconds of cowering observation I had become reasonably certain was either the most pathetic ambush ever concocted or, more likely, a diabolically clever trap.

"What makes you think--" Minus began, after I'd screamed this aforementioned suspicion into his ear.

He didn't have a chance to finish, as at that moment the two goons with the machine guns abruptly ceased firing. They'd lured Minus into their trap like a hungry spider ensnaring a fly or Rosie O'Donnell ambushing an unsuspecting hickory smoked ham at Safeway. Once the moronic Savior of the City was close enough, the goons tossed aside their worthless guns and whipped out a pair of sleek, black customized weapons that looked one hell of a lot less worthless.

From what I could tell, the guns were pretty evidently the impressive handiwork of a Nobel-worthy mad scientist. The goons pulled the triggers and there was a bright yellow ray from the barrel of each weapon, as well as a terrifyingly loud accompanying *WHOOP!* which I sincerely hoped hadn't triggered an unanticipated biological response which, frankly, it should have in the hearts, minds, and shorts of any sane human being.

Minus took the full blast of both rays directly in the dash symbol on his major league, Barry Bonds-enhanced pectoralis majors. A great glowing yellow pulse enveloped his body and he was blown right out of his purple boots and sent tumbling end-over-ass back across the roof.

In times of great stress, adrenaline and instinct can make the human body accomplish amazing things. Just ask any drunk who's managed with Herculean effort to remain moderately upright and accurate in front of a urinal after a three day bender.

The pair of bastards framed in the doorway hadn't been aware of my mere mortal presence behind the joker in tights they'd just blasted to hell. In the split-second during which their peanut brains were trying to tell their trigger fingers how to react, I charged.

I caught the half-open metal stairwell door with my shoulder and slammed it for all I was worth (which, until that morning, I'd have assessed at about a buck and a quarter, including my spring wardrobe and a couple of metal fillings). The door swung hard into the wide-open faces of the pair of goons, and I heard the twin clangs of a couple of foreheads being rung like a pair of church bells at midnight on Christmas Eve.

My body was coursing with fresh testosterone mixed with Jaublowski's stale booze as I flung the door open wide and charged like Custer into the little shed to finish the pair off before they could regain whatever senses a couple of professional henchman-for-hire might possess. Turns out my incredibly brave and moronic leap into the unknown was justified only for dramatic purposes.

I saw at a glance that the first goon was out cold. He was lying back against the wall of the shed, a red welt the size of a nectarine already blossoming on his forehead. I didn't see the other one right away, and my entire body braced for the blast that would put me through the wall and send me sailing like a wind-tossed plastic Safeway bag over the downtown rooftops.

Turns out the other one was taking a concussion catnap as well. Goon #2 had enjoyed the added misfortune of tumbling down the staircase to the top floor landing of the uproariously-named T.I.T.S. Building. By the look of the way his arm was twisted behind his back, the bastard mook's shoulder was dislocated.

First order of business was disarming the pair of them and trussing them up with their own jackets like a couple of rodeo calves. Next up, I pulled the magazines from their Tommy guns and dumped the weapons down the top floor garbage chute.

I'd pocketed the crazy ray gun of the one upstairs, but the handgun of the goon who'd fallen downstairs had busted apart like a Tinker toy. Beats me if it could be slapped back together on the fly, so just in case I scooped up the pieces and sent all but one sailing twenty-two stories to join the machine guns in the basement trash heap. The lone piece I held onto got stuffed in my pocket with the machine gun magazines.

I didn't see any other henchmen as I snuck around the hallway, but that didn't mean there weren't a hundred more armed gorillas on their way.

Self-preservation should have been the order of the day, and I am generally the majordomo in charge of saving my own ass. With the one weapon -- the brainchild of mad Dr. Cohen, M.D. -- that I'd manage to salvage, plus my own piece tucked away in the holster up under my armpit, I had a shot of getting out of the joint with the majority of my limbs relatively intact. Except I also had an elf with a pair of Bambi eyes the size of tennis balls back at the office who would guilt me from now until doomsday if I bailed without saving the guy who had everybody else in the city but me on his to-be-saved list.

Space age gun in hand, I raced with enormous reluctance back upstairs.

Minus was out like a light. His barrel chest was rising and falling, so at least he wasn't off lollygagging on a cloud somewhere tuning up for the all-harp orchestra after leaving me bound to the terrestrial bliss of holding his goddamn bag of golf clubs.

I momentarily abandoned the Savior of the City, whose bulletproof hide had somehow become my supreme good fortune to rescue, and ran to the edge of the roof.

I'd heard sirens closing in while I worked on the unconscious goons.

The call had obviously gone out over every squad car squawk box. The city's finest had roused themselves from napping on their steering wheels, ditched their crullers, fled their mistresses' apartments and otherwise abandoned their traditional work posts to converge en masse and clueless on the telephone company building. I looked over the ledge in time to witness about a hundred cruisers squealing to a stop.

I tossed the boys in blue the gifts of the busted gun part as well as the machine gun magazines. I took very small comfort in the fact that at least three weapons in the building could not now be used to blow my pretty head off.

I raced back over to Minus, who was beginning to roll groggily in the pebbles that had gathered around his melon head. He opened his eyes briefly, seemed to lock momentarily on my own, and managed to gurgle out a few worthless words.

"Do you have…account…what's going…"

And, almost as soon as they had switched on, the lights went back out. His eyes rolled back in his head, and he was once more booking a flight to that faraway land where assholes in tights store their happiest daydreams. (I didn't know him all that well, but I figured it probably wasn't the one with the Golden Gate Bridge.)

"I'll give you a goddamn account of what's going on," I told the unconscious behemoth. "Banyon Investigations is never again taking on more than one pain-in-the-ass -- known outside the business as 'clients' -- at a time, that's what's going on."

By the time I'd finally managed to drag him back across the roof to the stairwell, I'd winnowed that one-client-at-time rule down to zero.

I pitched him down the staircase on the assumption that he was only unconscious and not depowered, but with the sincere hope that I was wrong.

I was disappointed to find that I wasn't, and that he survived the tumble down the cement stairs without a single bruise or compound fracture.

It was another hellish five minutes of grunting and sweating to drag him into an office and stuff him and the boots he'd been knocked out of into a closet for safekeeping.

I'd done all I could do for the great hero who, two days before, had saved a jet full of kittens and Hummel figurines from crashing into St. Brat's Orphanage and Organ Donor Facility, but clearly didn't have sense enough to duck.

I left Minus where I hoped Dr. Cohen's men wouldn't find him, and I pulled the fancy-ass laser gun from my trench coat pocket as I ducked back into the hallway.

The top floor appeared empty. It was after quitting time, so most of the regular office staff would have gone home for the day.

Little nodes extended from some of the ceiling tiles, concealing the hidden black eyes of security cameras. I figured nobody was manning the monitors downstairs once the building had been taken over, since I was able to skulk along the hallways all the way to the far side of the twenty-second floor without anybody murdering me. Just in case, I made sure I gave all the cameras the finger on the quite sensible theory that I wouldn't have the opportunity to do so in person once my head was blown off.

I took the stairwell on the opposite side of the building from the one in which the ambush had taken place. Super-villains have a habit of engaging in linear thinking, and the straight line down from the roof entrance might have led right into the welcoming, steroid-augmented arms of a dozen more henchmen outfitted with high-tech guns.

By the time I reached the fifteenth floor without encountering a single goon, I realized that Dr. Cohen was no different from every other run-of-the-mill megalomaniacal medical fiend. He'd clearly made the mistake that a lot of arch-bastards do and blithely assumed that his scheme to murder his nemesis would succeed without the need to supervise his sociopath subordinates. And actually, he wasn't so far off the mark, since I figured a couple more blasts from his patented ray guns and Minus would have been reduced to a handful of perfect dental work floating in a puddle of melted testosterone. But in this case, the villain hadn't counted on the hero being a dithering dick-head who was so pathetic that he'd had to hire a private eye to do half the goddamn work he was too incompetent to handle himself. So three cheers for the useless Savior of the City. The mayor could stab yet another medal onto his gigantic, Triple-D chest, assuming some Czechoslovakian cleaning woman on a quest for a can of Comet cleanser stumbled across the great hero stuffed upside-down in the broom cupboard upstairs.

Other than the cautious scuffs of my own Florsheims echoing like thunder off the stairwell walls, the first noise I came across was on floor thirteen.

A ton of chatter filtered through the closed metal door. A chorus of female voices was nattering away like a Mormon nightmare on Superbowl Sunday.

I cracked the door an inch, and when my head didn't fill up with more lead than a dental hygienist's bib, I slipped out into the florescent lighted 13th floor hallway.

At least I didn't have to waste an hour trying to figure out why this particular floor of the telephone company building was so familiar.

I'd told Gwendolyn Johnson -- she with the impressive rack and low-rent cheating husband (which at that point was starting to look like my P.I. dream job) -- that I'd dated a dame who worked for the local Ma Bell franchise.

If I'd had friends, they would have told me to steer clear of her. She was a hot-tempered Latin number by the name of Senorita Tamale, and she was gainfully employed as the worst telephone operator in town. Her overriding qualification for the job of screaming at customers who'd made the grave mistake of dropping in a dime and punching "0" was the fact that she barely spoke the language, and by union proclamation there can never be enough incomprehensible accents tying the American phone system into knots. By day she wore a headset and jammed plugs in and out of a switchboard; by night she wore a red rose behind her ear and jammed a metaphorical stiletto in and out of my heart. Also, an actual stiletto in and out of the tires of the city bus on which I'd attempted to flee after our horrifying first date. She was a feisty firecracker who was so bad for business a Joe would be nuts not to hang a "closed for lunch" sign in the front window and sneak out the back door with his ass intact while she smashed the display cases, looted the cash register and burned the joint to the ground.

It had been a few years since I last saw her assaulting a teenaged greenskeeper at the miniature golf course, but not so long that I didn't remember that Senorita Tamale and her fellow phone operators slogged through their days of drudgery on the 13th floor of the Telecommunications International & Telephone Service Building.

The chorus of voices I'd heard from the stairwell were evidently those of the "number puh-lee-az" brigade. I stole as quickly up the hall as blind terror and a pair of sensible legs that were trying for all they were worth to get me to run in the opposite direction would permit. The door to the warehouse-sized room that housed a thousand banks of switchboards was open, and I stuck my head in with the usual concern that I might not be able to fit my fedora on properly any longer if my head were to be inconveniently shot out from under it.

The big room looked largely as I remembered it from my infrequent visits to pick up Senorita Tamale at the end of her shift.

Row after row of switchboards stretched back to infinity, or at least to the gray, primordial mists of the back wall near the mini-fridge and a tray of half-eaten Danish one of the gals had thoughtfully brought in that morning.

Sitting before every switchboard was a dame in outfits that were only slight variations of the same prim blue or black skirt and schoolmarm blouse buttoned up to the neck. The Joan Crawford hairdos circa 1957 completed the spinster librarian look.

The only real difference about the joint that I could detect at a glance was the crazed supervillain screaming at the masses from the front of the room.

"Yes! Yes!" Dr. Cohen cried, the redundant affirmation being a necessary feature of egomaniacal assholes the world over. (I figured that at that precise moment the odds were better than even that some maniac in a personal jetpack was screaming "Oui! Oui!" outside the Louvre as his henchmen loaded fancy-ass Renaissance art, including Whiskers Mona Lisa, onto his Vespa.)

There was a plain wooden stage about two feet high that ran along Cohen's end of the room. There were a couple of portable chalkboards that could be rolled around for operator training purposes, it being as complicated as aortic valve replacement surgery to stick a plug in a socket and connect somebody at 16 Sycamore to the Peoria Wal-Mart. It was my dumb luck that the boards were arranged in such a way as to nearly completely block my view of the ringmaster SOB of this particular traveling circus who was to blame for me being loaded into a cannon with a sizzling fuse.

I saw a couple of raised hands. Something glinted on an unidentified finger on his left hand. It might have been a wedding ring, a class ring, or one of those pinkie rings so beloved by assholes the world over. From a distance I couldn't even see if it might have been the tab off a beer can, so I sure as hell couldn't identify the make and model.

"Keep going!" Dr. Cohen yelled. "Don't stop. More calls! More! More!"

The dames at the switchboards were nothing if not accommodating. They continued to yank out plugs rapid-fire. They didn't even pause to adjust their headsets, check a run in their nylons, or to put somebody on hold for an hour of "Muskrat Love" torture. As quick as they were through with one call they snatched up another plug and jammed it into yet another socket, and they were off and yammering again.

Most of what was being said was the indiscernible hum of hundreds of combined voices, but I did manage to catch a couple lines of the nearest droning dames.

"I'm calling on behalf of the Scalawag Association of America. Are you aware that scurvy is the leading cause of death among pirates age fourteen to…"

"Hello. Do you want to lower your monthly credit card rate? If you're not stupid, please stay on the line…"

"This is an important message from the committee to reelect Congressman Ralph Fink. As your congressman, Congressman Fink has worked tirelessly these past 90 years to guarantee that Congressman Fink will remain your congressman. There is no greater cause for Congressman Fink than Congressman Fink. Also education and infrastructure."

"Banyon! Psst! Hey, Banyon!"

That last one hadn't been blabbed in a nasal whine into one of the headset mouthpieces, but had been hissed, sotto voce, at yours truly. I located a desperately bouncing black mane of hair and a pair of raven's eyes peering out from within it.

Senorita Tamale made a show of plugging in and out of her switchboard, but unlike the other dames in her row she wasn't speaking into her mouthpiece. As her hands went through the motions of working her board, she was glaring frantically at me.

"Tres," she hissed. She held up three fingers.

I don't generally engage in life-and-death charades with semi-bilingual ditzes, especially when their primary lingual isn't mine and even more especially when the death is. Those three slender fingers might have been some sort of Latina Boy Scout salute and "tres" could have meant trespass, trestle or the number of hot meals I still owed her.

She jerked her head so hard to the right that she nearly flipped her headset off. She held up two fingers, indicating (I now understood) two goons that I couldn't see.

She made the same motion in the opposite direction and held up one finger, indicating a single goon I couldn't see.

She recognized the cowardly look that presaged retreat on my face, the same look that had overtaken me when she'd assaulted the restaurant's cigarette girl on our third date for the dual crimes of being nearly as sexy and not carrying Junior Mints. I knew from the furious crease in her brow and the threatening fist that she was suddenly waving in my direction that, assuming she managed to get out of there alive, I'd be in traction for a month if I abandoned her to whatever sinister scheme Dr. Cohen had shanghaied her and the rest of the telephone company dames into.

I very carefully stuck my head further into the room to try to get a view of the henchmen who were still invisible to me, and suddenly Senorita Tamale's eyes were spinning like pinwheels and she was unsubtly waving both arms over her head and pointing to my right where a very large figure was standing close enough to be my long-lost Siamese twin, assuming it was biologically possible outside the Omni Consumer Products summer catalog for two humans to be joined by either end of a machine gun.

In most fight or flight situations, I find the latter to be the infinitely more sensible choice. Why risk busting your knuckles when you can run away to the nearest saloon and put your intact digits to far better use caressing multiple shot glasses of whatever gets you loaded fast enough to forget about the spinelessness that brought you there?

When, however, there's a gun at your ear with the momentarily surprised face of the goon you've just inadvertently stepped in front of on the far end of it, you've got only a moment to react and, unfortunately, running away at that point just isn't in the cards.

Before Dr. Cohen's henchman could react to my sudden, shocking presence, I grabbed the barrel of his machine gun with my left hand and redirected it at the stage, simultaneously sending my right elbow back hard into the goon's face. The pleasant crunch of bone -- which, happily, was not one of my own -- was completely overwhelmed by the explosion of gunfire that erupted from the collapsing moose's gun barrel.

"Are ju, crazy! Ju going to gets us all killeded!" Senorita Tamale shouted, giving the double past tense to show how absolutely killed she imagined my heroics would render she and her automaton workmates.

She needn't have worried about the telephone operators. The single burst of screaming lead ripped apart one of the chalk boards on the stage and took out several dozen ceiling tiles. The last stray bullets sent a few shattering florescent lights scattering delicate shards across the room but, other than Senorita Tamale, the gunfire failed to disturb any of the switchboard dames. I saw nothing but row upon row of blank eyes as they continued to plug in and out of their switchboards.

I wished the rest of the room had reacted to my astonishing arrival and dazzling feat of derring-do with the same blasé acceptance. Rather than permit me to slink off and hide out in a broom cupboard like the magnificent hero upstairs, the universe suddenly dumped four simultaneous crises in my lap, each uniquely horrible.

First, Senorita Tamale knocked her stool over backwards and came charging at me like she was a bull and I was decked out red union underwear.

Second, an unseen bastard somewhere far to my right responded to the short burst of initial gunfire by shooting up his corner of the room like a maniac in, I imagined, an attempt to teach the furniture that was piled there who was boss.

That asshole was not to be outdone by…

Third, the son of a bitch to my left who started blasting apart every ceiling tile within close enough proximity to my precious ass to make me momentarily the least worried of all about: four, the shout (which under other circumstances would be most shocking of all) that rose up from within Dr. Cohen's concealing chalkboards.

"*Banyon!*" shouted the city's newly minted physician archvillain who, as far as I knew, I'd never seen before and, thanks to the strategically-placed barriers, still hadn't.

I dealt with all four goddamn catastrophes pretty much as they were thrown at me: concurrently, but with a soupcon of my trademark finesse.

The retreating and beautiful Senorita Tamale plowed straight into me. I grabbed her by the wrist and spun her out the door into the hallway in the one and only tango we'd ever danced, allowing her falling momentum to drag me out right along with her.

We dropped on the floor outside the room just as the bastard to my left drew a bead on my position. Chunks of the doorframe in which I'd been standing exploded into the hall. Ricochets zinged off one of the hinges, and bullets punched through the wall to offer a dotted-line glimpse of the SOB on the right who'd ceased executing a stack of old chairs at point blank range in his little corner of the room and had come running for the chance to aerate a living (for the time being), breathing (until he was through with me) human (the jury was still out on that, according to my ex-wife) being.

"Stop shootin', I'll get him!" the second goon bellowed. Lucky for goon two, the first goon obligingly didn't cut his moron pal to ribbons as the idiot darted straight into the line of fire.

I didn't give the second mook a chance to reach the shredded remains of the door. I got a bead on him through the newly minted holes, and when he passed the largest collection of punctures his buddy had blasted into the wall, I let loose with a blast from the ray gun I had wisely kept clutched in my hand since running down from the roof.

The ensuing pulse blew out a section of wall the size of an easy chair. Apparently the guns packed a hell of a lot more of a wallop for mere mortals than they did superheroes. Through the hole I saw arms and legs flapping like windsocks as the skunk flew backwards through the air over row after row of telephone operators.

"*No!*" I heard Dr. Cohen command. "We retreat."

From his tone, it was clear the second, unseen goon had been ready to charge. I gave another wild blast of ray gun rays further up the wall at roughly the spot from where the remaining henchman had let loose his barrage. The beam blew out a second section of wall and gave me a back view of a white-headed jerk fleeing in the distance, accompanied by his last remaining henchman, through a door at the rear of the stage.

"That caped closet case upstairs is right," I mused as I scrambled to my feet. "This guy's harder to spot than Waldo."

(Waldo Ray Lynch was the second most notorious serial killer in U.S. history after Fred "The PBS Tote Bag

Strangler" Rogers. Waldo Ray was famous for selecting victims in vast open spaces or large indoor areas where people were packed together like sardines. Beaches, open-air concerts, circuses, airports terminals, the Grand Canyon, you name it. Only after the crowds thinned were the victims' bodies discovered just barely sticking out from behind tents, walls, trash cans, shrubs, sandwich boards, umbrellas, hot dog stands, benches, wishing wells…pretty much anywhere a body could be semi-concealed. It took an FBI profiler with a keen eye and a black felt-tipped pen to find and circle Waldo Ray's mug in all the security photos the Bureau had collected over the years. They should have found him sooner, considering he always wore the same red-striped shirt and hat, but the sick bastard had a knack for hiding right out there where everybody could see him. They found him easy enough at the end: on the floor of the gas chamber.)

I started back into the room, but the dame hopped to her size-four Carmen Miranda's and grabbed me by the arm.

"Ju be crazzy to are going after heem!" Senorita Tamale shouted in disbelief.

That accent was responsible for 6,788 ½ official complaints, nearly putting Senorita Tamale in the record book of top thousand all-time worst telephone operators. I could see why her over-the-top, Speedy Gonzalez pronunciation might be problematic for some poor slob with a dying cell phone battery stuck in a blizzard who was trying to get through to a local tow truck company, but I'd had enough experience with her garbled syntax that my delicate ear heard, "You're not crazy enough to go after him."

"No, I am not quite insane enough," I admitted. "However, the alcohol more than compensates."

Jim Beam and I dashed back into room.

The dames at the switchboards kept right on plugging in and out and regurgitating their spiels as if the world wasn't coming to the end, and I heard Senorita Tamale clomping along behind me like a Clydesdale on her wooden ultra-platform clogs.

It had only been seconds since Dr. Cohen and his trigger-happy lackey had vanished through the exit behind the stage, and he was not so far away that I didn't hear his voice clear as a bell shouting back through the open door.

"Kill the man in the coat and hat!" he thoughtfully screeched.

If mine were the only ears his crudely bellicose words fell on, there wouldn't have been much of a problem. For years I'd already been very slowly following that command every night from my boozy perch at O'Hale's. But there were a couple hundred other sets of ears in that room, and the instant the command was given every telephone operator obediently dropped her plugs and jumped efficiently to her heels. The whole herd of dames charged en masse for the front of the room.

Senorita Tamale and I had made it to the stage, and I put my survival instinct on hold just long enough to yank her keister up alongside mine. She clop-clopped across the wooden platform like a tap-dancing mule as we made a mad dash for the rear door.

I snatched the door and waved her through. "Hurry up, Senor Ed," I snapped.

The stampeding dames had reached the stage. Any P.I. worth his salt has outrun a zombie horde, but real zombies are a hell of a lot easier to manage. A few rounds of lead to the face, maybe cut off a head, a little fire, then dump the re-dead corpses out a 13th floor window just to be on the safe side. But despite the slack jaws and grasping claws, these weren't actual zombies. These were living dames, somehow hexed by Dr. Cohen.

The telephone broads were dead-eyed as they clamored up onto the wooden platform and stampeded for the narrow door.

I managed to stuff Senorita Tamale through and hauled the door shut. The instant before it closed completely, an arm wrapped in a blue sleeve shoved through the narrow gap. Lucky for me Senorita Tamale lacked my natural chivalry, and with a furious howl she leapt into the fray and sank her perfect white choppers into her coworker's forearm.

The arm vanished back through the opening and I managed to slam the door shut with an echoing clang.

I heard the army of telephone operators smack into the door like a swarm of fat bugs against a windshield. Hundreds of delicate hands began pounding like mallets until it felt like the whole T.I.T.S. building would come down around my ears like the walls of Jericho. The door jerked open an inch, and a dozen manicured hands lunged for the sliver of space, but I managed to yank it shut before they could get a grip on the coat on which Dr. Cohen had screamed for them to focus their subliminal, mind-controlled dingbat rage.

"It appears to me, Senorita Tamale," I said to the dame who was standing five feet away and chewing the end of a thumbnail as the door bounced at my back, "as if you are hanging around over there waiting for a bus. Seeing as this is the 13th floor, it's unlikely even the most stewed transit authority unionized bus driver will be able to get a regulation-size bus up in the elevator. So it'd be just incredibly goddamn delightful if instead of waiting for me to get flattened under this door, you'd pitch in and sashay your perfect ass over and get me one of those goddamn chairs."

There was a stack of folding chairs leaning against the wall. While I kept the stampede of telephone operators from filing through the breach and murdering us to death, she darted forward to grab a chair. Unfortunately, the vibrations from the pounding fists had already been rattling them where they stood, and before she could nab the top one, the stack finally gave up the ghost. First the top one slipped away, then all the others followed suit, sliding one-by-one and rapid-fire to the floor, scattering all around her stumbling feet. Between her absurd footwear and her blind panic, Senorita Tamale was unfocused. She tripped and staggered an inappropriately-timed recreation of most of our drunken dates through the fallen stack before she managed to snatch up one chair. She immediately dropped it, picked it up, dropped it again, dropped it a third time, then managed to half-carry, half-kick it over to nowhere near where I was.

"It is becoming clearer to me, Senorita Tamale," I called from twelve feet away from the spot where she was dropping the chair for a fourth time, "why you selected such an undemanding career. You are clearly spectacularly awful at anything more complicated than sitting on your ass and stranding callers on indefinite hold."

I'd missed my calling as a motivational speaker, probably mostly because I wasn't a soulless, boldfaced crook and that I wouldn't have enjoyed the long hours bouncing from hotel ballroom to local civic center to PBS swindling people out of their hard-earned cash just for telling them to get off their own asses and wipe their own goddamn noses.

Not only did my pep talk finally inspire her to grab the chair up off the floor, she nearly beat me to death with it.

I wrestled the folding chair from her enraged hands and got the legs jammed up under the handle of the door and wedged against the frame. When I released the handle, the door bucked like mad as the dames outside yanked and shoved at and on the handle, respectively, but it remained shut.

"Only a momentary Band-Aid," I said. "It, like the eternal flame of our undying love, won't last two minutes. Come on."

The dame was busy holding onto the ancient grudge from the crack I'd made about her near total worthlessness as a human being an entire thirty seconds before.

"I should help them kill ju, Crag Banyon," she snarled, arms crossed angrily beneath her amazing rack.

"You're absolutely welcome to join the mob," I said. "In fact, if I know my jerry-rigged door locks, that chair now has significantly less than two minutes of life left in it before they're pouring in here. Of course, they seem pretty single-minded, and once they do break through they might just stampede you to a high-heeled puddle on the way to their ultimate, pulchritudinous target, which, as you may or may not recall, is some guy in a hat and coat. Your choice. Either way, I'm going to do my best to not get killed."

I raced down the backstage hallway. An instant later I heard following me the angry *clomp-clomping* of her absurd Seabiscuit footwear.

"This is not their faultses," she shouted as we ran. "He make them all take some kind of pill. He say it prescription diet pill, so all the girls loving it. I no take it."

"Here's something you're unlikely to have heard unironically in your entire life," I hollered over my shoulder as we ran, "so don't let the shock knock you off those ridiculous, three-foot wooden stilts with which you're violently assaulting your feet: smart goddamn move, Senorita Tamale."

We ran around a corner, through a door and out into the main 13th floor hallway. The instant we poked our groundhog heads into the sunlight we nearly got cut in two by a brilliant burst of machine gun fire.

Bullets tore the fiberboard and shattered a couple of floor-to-ceiling windows that offered a spectacular and suddenly incredibly windy view of the decrepit city.

I slammed on my Florsheim brakes and launched back into Senorita Tamale, and the two of us collapsed back through the doorway from which we'd just fled.

I liberated my gat from its holster and slapped it into her delicate hands.

"Here," I snapped. "The capitan of the local junta must've taught you how to use one of these. Cover me."

As I bravely ran back into the open and into the awaiting arms of pretty damn certain death, she screamed, "I am from Bangor, Banyon!"

I'd abandoned my piece to the Maine freedom fighter, but I'd kept the big gun for myself. At my reemergence, the bastard with the machine gun nearly opened fire once again, but balked with momentary terror when he saw the ray gun in my hand.

It turns out his instant of trepidation was a positive boon to me, since the goddamn supergun selected that precise moment to shit the bed.

I pulled the trigger twenty times in ten feet like some desperately losing *Jeopardy!* contestant who thinks jamming his thumb on the button like it's a detonator switch will blow up his two opponents and give him a clear shot at the category: "I Suck at Jeopardy." All I got for my trouble was a sore finger and a manic, victorious grin on the bastard who was about to give my torso that delicate dash of lead it desperately lacked.

The instant before the SOB murderer in front of me squeezed his trigger, the Srta. moron behind me finally guessed where the corresponding piece of hardware was on my gat.

Senorita Tamale fired a half-dozen wild slugs up the hallway, and it was only serendipity that didn't plant one in my spine.

The cowering bastard with the machine gun was thrown off his game long enough for me to chew up the distance between us and plant a knuckle kiss on his wide-open chin. His tommy gun flew from his hand and he tumbled backwards.

As was the norm for my short-lived, uncelebrated victories, the Lord barely gaveth before he tooketh massively away, and even before the henchman hit the floor in a glass-jawed heap I felt the rumble of about a million stampeding high heels heading up the narrow hallway from which I'd just escaped.

"*They through! They through!*" Senorita Tamale yelled in a blind panic as she clomped out into the main 13th floor hall, waving my empty piece over her colossal and miraculously immobile hairdo.

Dr. Cohen's order had been to kill the poor slob in the coat and hat. I quite sensibly stuffed the napping goon on the floor in my hat and coat and ran like the coward I always knew I was down the hall in the company of the lovely Senorita Tamale.

The army of telephone operators exploded into the wide open space behind us and with dead-eyed purpose descended on the catnapping henchman.

As the methodical vivisection was taking place on one end of the 13th floor hall of the T.I.T.S Building, it turned out Dr. Cohen was effecting his escape on the other.

The villainous doctor had constructed one of those stainless steel personal escape pods that Ronco used to sell on late night TV back in the Seventies. The thing was planted in one of the elevators, and he was already seated inside the plastic dome, a pair of oversized goggles and a World War I scarf obscuring most of his face. As I ran like mad to stop him, he punched the launch button and the teardrop-shaped pod exploded in a brilliant font of fire from the floor of the elevator and blasted straight up through the roof of the car.

Senorita Tamale and I were tossed back by a fist of wind and flame, and I heard the echo of the escape pod bouncing off the walls of the elevator shaft on its rapid ascent to the roof. A moment later there came a distant crash followed by a shower of bricks.

The elevator car promptly detached from its cable and the whole mess slipped from sight and presumably plummeted all fourteen floors to the basement, failing utterly to stop along the way at ladies lingerie, pet supplies, men's galoshes, kitchen appliances, and alternative career opportunities for moron P.I.'s too stupid to realize that there might be other ways to make a living that don't involve winding up a bruised, burned, beaten and bloodied middle-aged corpse flying backwards into sudden, dark, violent oblivion.

7

I deduced that I'd cracked the back of my head on the floor, since I came to somewhere out in the open air with a throbbing pain in my skull and with what I at first mistakenly concluded was the worst paramedic in the history of the human race trying to rouse me from unconsciousness by smacking me repeatedly across my tender mug.

"Ju wake up. Ju gots to be faking by now. Ju not really asleep."

Each disturbingly anti-Semitic-sounding statement was accompanied by a revivifying smack to the kisser.

I opened my eyes and found myself staring into the concerned open palm of nurse Senorita Tamale.

Despite the fact that the hot-tempered dame couldn't have missed that my eyes were now wide open, she gave one last, hard slap for good measure. I figured the last wallop, and probably another eighty while I was out like a light, most likely had less to do with waking me up so that I could take some well-earned bows for my performance this particular day (which by any fair measure of above-and-beyond the call of duty was as heroic as all hell) and more to do with me ditching her on a ferry to Nova Scotia five years before after claiming I was going to the john when in reality I snuck off the boat, swiped her car from the lot, and enjoyed a week of peace and quiet at the ostrich races in sunny Orlando.

"Thanks, Senorita Tamale," I said as I hauled myself to a sitting position. "Next time try using a closed fist. I could use a cheap, relaxing vacation, and a prolonged coma is in my meager price range."

I was on the sidewalk in front of the telephone company building. There were ambulances and fire trucks mixed in with the many police cars I'd seen from the roof. Genuine paramedics were dealing with those in need of medical attention that didn't involve getting punched in the face. Of those being treated, there were some security guards as well as administrative and executive staff, but mostly it was the platoon of telephone operators who'd tried to pound me to applesauce who were being dealt with by the small EMT army that had assembled on the sidewalk. The dames were quieter now than last I saw them, their bloodlust having been exhausted on the smear of hench-man who would be hell for the janitorial staff to mop up on the 13th floor. The gals had been formed into dazed lines and were receiving treatment for their prolonged waking trance.

City paramedics have the standard Red Cross anti-hypnotism training, and I saw a whole bunch of them were dangling emergency silver pocket watches in front of the worst cases. Down the various lines, some of the women were already coming out of it on their own while others were flapping their arms and clucking like chickens.

Seeing that gaggle of whacked-out dames produced a sudden onset of intense mourning over the loss of my hat and coat, which must have been mutilated beyond rec-ognition in the brilliantly orchestrated defensive bullshit I'd arranged to transpire on the evil ass of the machine gun-wielding bastard who'd tried to pockmark a replica of Edward James Olmos' driver's license photo in my chest.

I was experiencing the phantom pain of a lost limb in the fedora department, but when I reached up to absolutely demonstrate its loss to my subconscious, my conscious was elated to feel the familiar brim, band, and beat-up felt of my trusty chapeau.

"I know how important jour chit is to ju," Senorita Tamale said, tossing me my wadded-up trench coat which had apparently been pulling double duty as a pillow under my head while she was beating me senseless on the sidewalk.

"You are still an enchanting study in contradictions," I informed her as I shrugged on my intact coat. "Say, Senorita Sweetheart, as long as we're momentarily not attempting to kill one another or one of us -- I'm not saying who -- isn't abandoning the other on a ferry to a godforsaken Canuckistani province, I've got a favor to ask."

I didn't have the chance for her to refuse and, possibly, machete me.

"Well, well, well," chimed in an intensely disagreeable voice at my back. "If it isn't the sleaziest P.I. in town, finally awake from his beauty sleep. It didn't work, Banyon, you're still as ugly as ever."

I turned to find Detective Daniel Jenkins of the local cops loitering behind me, a Styrofoam cup of coffee in his hand and a superior smirk twisting his razor-thin lips.

"Beauty is only skin deep, Detective Jenkins," I informed him. "Flay me with your cutting remarks and I'll merely be the Visible Man version of the matinee idol you see standing before you. Likewise, you are you from surface to core. Given the choice, I'd rather be skinned alive yet still be me rather than the intact asshole that is you any day of the week. That goes double for whatever day it happens to be today."

I'd had a personal bet going for years that one of these days I could make Jenkins draw his gun so hastily in anger that he'd shoot off one of his own toes. This day all the moron flatfoot did was squeeze his coffee cup until the plastic lid popped off like the top of Popeye's spinach can, causing boiling mud to launch out onto his hand.

Jenkins dropped the cup and whipped out his bracelets. "You know, Banyon, I think we're going to take a little ride downtown. You were caught up in the middle of all this for some reason, and I'm really looking forward to hearing all about it. But first I think I'm going to accidentally forget that I've got you locked up in a cell for a few days."

He took a step toward me with the handcuffs.

I was weighing the pros and cons of assaulting an officer against the sheer, goddamn fun of it, when Jenkins' teeth were saved by a sudden gust of hurricane-force wind that erupted somewhere above all our heads and nearly blew us all off our feet. The coffee cup Jenkins had dropped turned cowardly and bounced down the road, propelled by the wind, and disappeared under a hook-and-ladder truck. Discarded fast food wrappers swirled all around us and when I pulled off the Arby's wrapper that momentarily slapped across my eyes I found that towering in our mere mortal midst was a lummox wearing yellow tights and an expression of lantern-jawed solemnity.

"Officer Jenkins, Mr. Banyon, ma'am."

Minus gave each of us a nod in turn, and he boomed out each name like a cannon firing from the deck of the frigate, HMS *Asshole*. I didn't see the jerk's charm, but I noted that when he nodded in her direction, Senorita Tamale's knees looked for an instant like they were about as sturdy as a couple of strands of boiled spaghetti. She grabbed onto me for support, but if a court order couldn't get me to do it for alimony what chance did she have? I propped her up on her own two damn feet.

Beside us, Jenkins' face soured. His cuffs still dangled from the tip of his index finger. I could tell it was killing him they weren't already encircling my innocent wrists.

"Oh, hello, Minus," droned the flatfoot. "Don't tell me you know this joker?" He deigned to aim his chin in my direction.

"Mr. Banyon is helping me in a capacity that I really can't discuss, Detective Jenkins," Minus assured him. "I will say that his assistance has been invaluable. Not that I would or ever could minimize the contribution to our shared mission provided by our great metropolitan police force."

"Yes," I agreed, wading knee-deep into the rising tide of horse shit. "For one thing, we'd all drown in a sea of uneaten doughnuts. And what rational man doesn't dread the thought of a vast army of criminals wandering our streets not knowing what to do with all that excess graft? Not to mention that I'd have nobody to sue for wrongful arrest. So, yes, I agree wholeheartedly with the Savior of the City. We need our thin blue line between civilization and anarchy, even if most of that thin line can't squeeze into a fifty-six inch blue waist."

I had to hand it to Jenkins. Not only did the gun not come out, he managed to put away his handcuffs instead of trying to horsewhip me with them.

"I didn't know Mr. Banyon was working with you, Minus," the worst cop in the world said, through teeth so tightly clenched he was one ill-timed sneeze away from launching a couple of grinding molars out the top of his head.

"A recent development," Minus assured the flatfoot. "You can't be faulted for not knowing. In fact, it's my fault for not telling you." The big, yellow gorilla turned to me. "Officer Jenkins has been named liaison officer between me and the department."

"Do you hear that?" I asked, cocking an ear to the breeze. "It's the sound of an entire city being flushed down the can."

"I will have jour babies," volunteered swooning and fertile Senorita Tamale.

"Store those castanets back in your hope chest, seester," I told her. "You're making a Latin spectacle of yourself."

Minus seemed more embarrassed than he should have at Miss Senorita Tamale's indelicate suggestion, although having dames toss themselves at his purple boots was probably still a pretty new development for a dope like him. His cheeks flushed, and he covered for his weirdly out-of-place bashfulness by turning his purple mask to Jenkins. Jenkins, in a case of ironic juxtaposition, wasn't capable of embarrassment, even though he was the one individual present who should have been because, among other professional shortcomings, he was so spectacularly bad at his chosen profession that police training manuals around the country included an entire chapter largely devoted to his on-the-job exploits entitled, "For the Love of God, Don't...Just Don't."

"I'm afraid Mr. Banyon and I were briefly separated," Minus said. "Would you mind filling me in on everything that happened here, officer?"

Jenkins fished out a notebook and flipped it open in the same bored, efficient manner as all the real-live actors he'd seen playing cops on TV. (What a jerkass.)

"Approximately one hour ago an unidentified supervillain entered the telephone company building in the company of a dozen henchman," Jenkins droned. "The supervillain in question disabled the video surveillance system, so we have no record of his face. He entered the 13th floor room where the telephone operators work and informed them that he was with the company health plan and offered them what he claimed were sure-fire diet pills. We don't know what those pills actually were."

"Yes, we do," I said. "They were obviously hypno-pills. Mad doctors are always prescribing them left and right. How the hell those things got FDA approval, I have no idea."

"You're jumping to conclusions, Banyon," Jenkins sneered. "I work with facts."

"You work with a thousand cops who somehow manage to trudge through every workday without pushing you out a very high window," I replied. "Open your eyes, Jenkins. Even you had to hear about that mad doctor on the Miami city council last year who slipped a page from his prescription pad into a park beautification bill and got a ton of hypno-pills dumped into the water supply. The water department dutifully mixed them in with the usual fluoride-chlorine cocktail. An hour after the hypno-pills kicked in, he took over the city with trained alligators, made himself Lord Mayor, and started ruling from his impregnable castle fortress in the Telemundo headquarters building."

"He *has* improved the quality of programming," Senorita Tamale offered. "Eet is always now the twenty-four hours every day of heem ranting about taking over the world with an army of spiders. Much better than those estupido soap operas."

"I agree, Senorita Tamale, that the ravings of a madman are more engrossing than high-definition close-ups of

Mexican nose pores. Also, kudos to Lord Mayor Blood-fist's 'Executing the Stars,' the number one rated cross-over mainstream juggernaut. Although, after he spent an hour, minus commercials, hunting Burt Reynolds in the Everglades last week and mounted his bloody toupee on a pike in the final act, there's probably nowhere to go in the Nielsens but down. However, you missed my point which, while disappointing, isn't unsurprising, since you've got that sucking, black hole, vacuum, whirlpool, 'no thinking allowed,' vacant lot where a human brain would ordinarily go."

She came at me with tooth and talon, it apparently being a capital offense in her baffling culture to observe the obvious.

Minus plucked her from the sidewalk before she could tear out my throat, and the dame instantly melted in his hands like a parboiled Popsicle. She was sighing contentedly in the afterglow as he placed her back in the spot she'd vacated, all thoughts of murdering me completely banished from the untenanted void between her perfect ears.

"My point," I said, picking up where I'd left off, "is that Dr. Cohen has obviously drugged the city's legion of telephone operators with hypno-pills. To what nefarious end I am in this one instance like you are at all times, Detective Jenkins: clueless."

Jenkins' grunt of unadulterated hatred was more subdued but no less effective than Senorita Tamale's earlier, impressive outburst.

"So, Minus told you about Dr. Cohen," Jenkins said. "You really shouldn't share any information about ongoing investigations with civilians, Minus."

"Not that it matters," I chimed in, "but this particular civilian outranked you when I was a cop, Jenkins. And it might further interest you all to know that if it wasn't for me, your city's great new flying savior would be a partially vaporized pile of sludge on the phone company roof right now. There *might* be enough of him left to Swiffer into a body bag, assuming that is some kind of mop. Is it?" I asked Senorita Tamale.

She nodded. "But I think it is for the dusting," she replied.

"I defer to your genetically preprogrammed house-cleaning expertise. But you'd almost certainly be using some kind of sponge or shop vac to clean up the remains. And as I was just nearly killed indirectly rescuing every last one of those dames who are over against that wall being dehypnotized by emergency medical personnel even as we speak, and since I'm the hero they tried to tear limb from limb while I courageously chased bastard maniac Dr. Cohen out of the telephone company building, maybe a little less snot and a hell of a lot more bootlicking might be in order, Jenkins."

Minus looked sheepish, the timid jerk from his two visits to my office briefly resurfacing. "Mr. Banyon *was*... rather...helpful."

"Yes, you heard that right, Jenkins," I said. "It doesn't get more effusive than a lukewarm 'rather helpful.' I only wish I had a pair of sunglasses to protect me from the UV rays emanating from that glowing defense from the superhero whose ass I just saved. Is that the best you can goddamn do?" I asked Minus.

The masked moron shrugged his purple cape. "*Very* helpful?" he said, clearing his throat. "Mr. Banyon was *very* helpful in this matter."

Confronted with the reality that the city owed me a debt of gratitude for which I would have accepted as reward an insincere thanks and a bottle of cheap Maker's whiskey, Jenkins merely ignored us, flipped another page in his notebook and began speaking as if we hadn't opened our yaps.

"It has yet to be determined if it was Dr. Cohen," the flatfoot muttered.

"That is who he said he was," Senorita Tamale volunteered.

Jenkins gave a prolonged sigh that was directed squarely at me, and noted in pencil her contribution to the investigation he was certain to eventually screw up.

"Once the telephone operators were under his control, he used them to tie up the city's entire phone system," Jenkins said. "No one could make an outgoing call. People were getting calls that have been described by those who received them as 'nuisances,' since they came at supper-time or when people were in the bathroom, on ladders, out in the yard, helping kids with their homework, or otherwise occupied. According to eye witnesses, people all over the city were racing to their phones thinking it was a loved one, a friend, or something possibly work related, only to be offered a discount coupon on a chimney sweeping, one free storm window with every five purchased, or membership in the AARP." He flipped his notebook shut. "This Dr. Cohen is one sick bastard."

Rarely did I agree with Detective Daniel Jenkins, but if what he was saying was true Dr. Cohen had plumbed depths of indecency so unfathomable that he'd need to spend the next month in a hyperbaric chamber to decompress.

"My God," Minus said.

"Mi dios," Senorita Tamale said.

"My fee," I said. "It just went up," I added.

I figured that as usual it would fall to me to save my client, who was tied inextricably to this Dr. Cohen lunatic, a creature so lacking in soul that he'd orchestrated the takeover of the telephone company and its slew of operators merely to irritate everyone in town with nuisance calls. Exactly how inextricably Minus was tied to Dr. Cohen I would now have to find out, since my ass was now on the line. Thanks to my aforementioned shithead client, I was now a fat blip on the mad doctor's radar rather than an anonymous blob teetering on an O'Hale's barstool where I rightly belonged.

There wasn't much more that Jenkins knew, which was a Hiroshima-level understatement. The flatfoot finished briefing Minus, who stood there like the mountain of stupid that he was, nodding somberly as if he actually knew what the hell he was doing and didn't need to run out and hire private detectives to do half his superhero day's work.

Jackasses with cameras were starting to show up, and I backed away a couple of feet behind the obscuring comfort of a SWAT van, since getting splashed all over the front page of the *Gazette* looking like a dwarf next to that gigantic asswipe would be the perfect end to a goddamn perfect day.

Once Jenkins was through with his worthless briefing, he gave a manly handshake to the idiot in the cape, during which he made sure he was facing the local news cameras. Jenkins made a point of utterly ignoring me as he, his notebook and his pencil wandered off to misidentify that half of the multitude of telephone operators who'd been brought out of their medication-induced hypnotic states.

Minus turned to where I was hiding in the company of Senorita Tamale behind the SWAT van and nodded deeply.

"Dr. Cohen needs to be stopped," he insisted, continuing to nod so firmly I thought his head might drop off. "Did you get a look at him, Mr. Banyon?"

"As you indicated in your first visit to my office, the bastard clearly doesn't want to be seen," I replied. "Security cameras off, absurd goggles obscuring his face. Mostly his lower face, which is probably significant, but it beats me how at the moment." I turned to Senorita Tamale. "As the only dame in that building he didn't dose, did you get a look at so much as a scar, a dimple or a mole?"

She shook her head. "He wore the scarfses over his mouthses."

"Adorable mangled English notwithstanding, I'm still at square one," I said.

Minus thrust out his heroic chin so far you could have set the grocery bags down on it while you put away the butter and eggs.

"I have faith in the local police to track down this villain," he insisted loudly. (A couple of reporters on the other side of the police sawhorses scratched down his thunderous sucking-up in their notebooks. TV cameras whirled, dutifully recording his embarrassingly asinine pronouncement.)

"First off, do you have goddamn parking tickets you're trying to get out of?" I asked. "Second, you can't have much faith in them or you wouldn't have hired me. Third, you weren't wrong to do so since you can't spell incompetent without 'cop.' Here's a fun, germane and, depending on your perspective, possibly absolutely terrifying fact: Jenkins actually tried to do precisely that one time back when he was a rookie playing Scrabble at the station. No one but he knew what 'inmetent,' meant. He still managed to get fifty points for it because the three cops he was playing with couldn't be bothered to investigate a dictionary, and the ones who were watching said the disputed word was a civil matter and didn't want to get involved."

"I'm sure they'll do fine, as I'm sure you will, too, Mr. Banyon. I'll be in touch. Call me if you need me. Off into the wild blue yonder!" he cried.

The burst of displaced air shook the SWAT van at my shoulder, and I had to grab Senorita Tamale's arm to keep her from falling out into the road.

The spandex creep cracked the cement square of sidewalk from which he launched spectacularly into the air. His cape became a shrinking purple streak and he was gone in a flash over the rooftops of the city.

"Well, there goes my goddamn ride," I said.

I turned to Senorita Tamale, who was staring at the vacant air which Minus had only briefly occupied, part of which was now being employed by one of the T.I.T.S Building's resident pigeons as a midair toilet.

"He's just like every other penniless street performer," I informed her. "He jams himself into those tights one massive calf muscle at a time. Come on, you're doing me a favor as a reward for me being the actual guy who actually saved your actual ass."

"Do ju know who he *really* is, Banyon?" she asked. A thought suddenly occurred to her and she tore her eyes away from the smog-clogged heavens. "*Banyon*," she repeated, as if I was one of her dingbat coworkers who'd forgotten my own name. "Dr. Cohen knew jour name. Ju did not tell the policia that."

"I have placed the gendarmerie on a need to know basis," I explained. "Since they don't actually *want* to know anything and are incapable of learning even if they did, the system I've set up works out swell for everybody involved. Let's go. You're going to help me crack a different worthless case."

I took her by her sexy, hot-blooded elbow and led her away from the cops, the press and the army of half-hypnotized babes back through the gleaming glass front doors of the telephone company building.

8

It was just after dark when I finally turned the corner onto the grubby street which ten years before I'd chosen as the home of Banyon Investigations because of its convenient proximity to downtown bus routes, schools, hospitals, churches, libraries, supermarkets, and, primarily, the only distillery in town..

Night is the best time of day in the city, and early evening especially so. The bars are all open and the package stores have not yet closed, so intemperate drunks can stop in for a paper bag of liquid sunshine on their way to get seriously loaded.

The putrid stench of a city heaped with rotting garbage and decomposing dreams is less pungent in the cool of the evening. Whores do their best work at night, but process servers don't usually venture out after the sun has dipped below the horizon. Evening is a magical world where junkies and muggers frolic like happy meadow bunnies in the rancid damp that coats streets, rusted-out cars and cardboard refrigerator box palaces and which might be, but almost certainly isn't, dew.

As usual I didn't have a whole hell of a lot of good news, so I was running the above pathetic inventory through my head as I approached the headquarters of Banyon

Investigations, Inc. It's not like I didn't know that I was mixing up a batch of metaphorical lemonade, and that I was doing so purely to boost my miserable spirits, which were miserable in part from a lack of the kind of spirit-boosting spirits dispensed by my friendly local barkeep who, if I didn't make a grand entrance at O'Hale's soon, would be up panicking on the roof, launching emergency flares and setting fire to half the neighborhood, an act which the fire department might frown upon but which could justifiably be spun as the first, necessary step in genuine urban renewal.

I got a tiny little bit of positive news in the form of a dead bike messenger lying on the sidewalk out in front of my building.

Two figures stood with the body, one eternally undead, annoyed and wearing a black cloak and cowl; the other sporting an organ grinder's comical mustache and a fat gut wrapped in an apron so filthy that in a rare case of governmental competence, the health department had ordered it condemned.

Vincetti, proprietor of the For the Halibut Fish Market, which occupied the majority of the first floor of my building, was an irate Italian cliché.

"You ain't a-gonna jussa leave him there!" the old fishmonger demanded. "He block-a alla my business."

"Not my problem," replied the Grim Reaper. "Call a cop. Besides, business looks like it ain't all that hot right now."

Vincetti let loose a string of vicious Italian along with a series of convulsive hand, arm and full-body gestures, then grabbed up a broom and attempted to sweep the 130 pound corpse away from his door and into the gutter.

The late bike messenger was in his twenties. A scrawny college graduate hipster with the requisite tattoos and pathetic tufts of scraggly facial hair. I never knew him in life, but I knew with utter certainty that I would have hated him if he'd crossed my path before that of the car that had run him over, if the twisted frame of his bike was any indication. Vincetti had already swept the dead kid's busted-up Schwinn back out into the nearer lane of traffic where a car swerved around it about five minutes too late.

Death nodded his skull at me as I stepped over the body on my way across the sidewalk to the building's side door.

"Hey, Banyon." The Grim Reaper indicated the corpse on the ground. "Hit and run. Cab. Nearly finished him with the traumatic brain injury, but I got the fatal hematoma. Hey, you going to O'Hale's later ? Save me a stool, will you?"

"I absolutely will do precisely that," I said, erasing the vow from my hard drive the instant the words met air.

I left Death, Vincetti, and the recently deceased bike messenger on the sidewalk and headed inside for the elevator.

Upstairs, Mannix was in the process of pulling the cover over Doris' typewriter as I entered the room. All evidence of the repair job he'd done in my inner office was gone with the exception of the faint stink of latex paint, and the chill from an open window, so at least the dump was mostly back to the normal bleak perfection I demanded.

The elf gave me his usual enthusiastic smile. "Hello, Mr. Crag. I saw your elbow on the news. Were you able to help Mr. Minus?"

"I saved him and half the city, Mannix," I replied. "If you consider that being helpful -- and I could mount a persuasive case for the opposition -- then helpful I was. I only thank God that you only saw my elbow. I'm already swamped with two dead-end cases. The last thing I need is a third client dumped in my lap because somebody out there saw me hanging around with that halfwit shank. Messages? No? Good." I didn't give him time to answer as I marched past him into my office.

"Actually, there were a few," Mannix said, not getting the hint.

He dogged me into the room, where I was already stripping off my coat and hat and dumping them onto my crummy sofa. After their near-death experience earlier in the day, I didn't dare leave the kids hanging around out of sight in the next room.

I noted that my office was back in pretty much perfect slob shape but for the addition of the brand-new framed photograph of Johnny Johnson toiling away at his desk at the Panhandler Federal Ameribank. Mannix had given the photo a prominent position over the corner water cooler, and at first glance I decided it wasn't a terrible addition to the decor. I couldn't miss the picture when I looked up from my desk, and the constant reminder of a life more miserable than my own might be the perfect distraction from the depressing private eye license hanging on the opposite wall.

"Miss Doris' mother called," Mannix said, looking at a yellow Post-It note in his little hand. "She wanted to know if Miss Doris was here. I told her she hadn't come to work today. Her poor mother seemed very upset."

"Yes, I imagine that being a desiccated, postmenopausal hag with enough testosterone in her system to grow a Yosemite Sam mustache would be quite upsetting."

"She thinks Miss Doris ran away because of her troubles with the IRS."

"That sounds like the beginnings of a third case,

Mannix," I warned. "We are definitely *not* taking on a third case. Give it here." The elf reluctantly gave me the Post-It note, and I crumpled it up and successfully missed landing it in the trash barrel by two feet. "Doris will find her way home when she misses her mother's cooking. No one can open a can of SpaghettiOs like that harridan in the handlebar mustache."

A second yellow Post-It appeared in Mannix's hand. "Miss Gwendolyn called. She wants an update on her naughty husband."

"If that check she gave me didn't clear, her husband can get as naughty as local indecency laws will permit with every skank he may or may not be managing to sneak in and out of that rat-infested motel."

Mannix nodded. "I brought it to the bank this afternoon. It was real."

"Excellent," I said. "I'll be certain to inform our paying client tomorrow that further investigation has revealed that her semi-mysterious, mind-numbingly dull husband continues to be as superficially boring as the list of charges IRS prosecutors will be reading out in court in the People versus Doris Staurburton."

"Oh, you don't have to wait," Mannix reported happily. "I told her she could stop by the office this evening. I thought you'd be back after I saw your elbow on the news and I realized that everything was sorted out thanks to you and Mr. Minus." He was beaming with pride one second, then abruptly nodding somberly the next. "It's too bad that the bad man got away."

"Yes, well, my elbow can't be everywhere at once," I informed him. "If you need it for autographs, in about twenty minutes it will be tipping at O'Hale's in the company of a lovely senorita whose moron parents encumbered her with the regrettable given name 'Senorita.' So technically she's Senorita Senorita Tamale, but don't call her that or her blistering Latin blood will kick in and we'll both wind up in intensive care sucking candy canes through a straw. My candy cane will technically be vodka, but you get the point. I only hope she remembers to bring her purse. My liver is starving."

Mannix glanced at the wall clock and did the necessary mental arithmetic to account for its chronic inaccuracy.

"Don't sweat it, Mannix," I said. "If Gwendolyn Johnson is late, send her along to O'Hale's. That dame has seen the inside of a sleazy dive more than once in her life. Probably even more than ten times. Possibly less than a million, but I wouldn't bet my rotten reputation on it. Besides, she might not be thrilled to see that we've made her husband's surveillance photos part of our office decor."

In gratitude to me for saving her Mexican bacon, Senorita Tamale had done me the illegal favor of sifting through Johnny Johnson's phone records. I'd felt bad anew for Gwendolyn Johnson's boring bank manager husband.

"She should be here soon," the elf said, with more hope than conviction. He pocketed the Client #1 Post-It and produced a stack of others. "You also got a call from a nice lady offering to enroll you in the AARP. I don't know what that is, but it sounds like a wonderful opportunity. Another nice lady called to offer you a deal on storm windows. Another nice lady phoned to give you the opportunity to lower your monthly credit card interest rate. I didn't have the heart to tell her that you don't have one..."

He had a stack of about eight more rare, exclusive-to-me Post-It opportunities which various hypnotized nice ladies called to pester me and half the city about, which Mannix apparently dutifully sat and listened to without hanging up in all their ears.

I let him ramble on and pretended to listen while I fished around in my desk drawer making a point not to listen. I found one item I was looking for, but after slamming through every drawer I managed to not find any trace of the other.

Mannix was winding down his stack of Post-Its with news of an incredibly rare opportunity to shovel money into the dirty slush fund of some corrupt local mayoral candidate who would have gotten my vote only if a.) I was registered and b.) he signed in blood in triplicate an ironclad vow to immolate himself on the day of his inauguration.

"Finished?" I asked when the last of the Post-Its was shifted to the back of the pile. The elf glanced up with an expectant expression that asked how in the world I was going to decide which terrific prospect I was going to avail myself of first.

Mannix nodded.

"Good. Toss those Post-Its out the window. Vincetti, our ptomaine-peddling fishmonger neighbor, hasn't enjoyed a really good tickertape parade since he and the rest of Mussolini's forces bravely routed the unarmed employees at that Esso station in Milan. Plus it will give him something else besides a dead bike messenger to shake an impotent fist at and vainly attempt to sweep out into the gutter. Then get me a Glad bag and a FedEx envelope, stat."

The elf dutifully tossed the little scraps of yellow paper out the open window. One Post-It didn't clear the fire escape and flutter to the street with the rest. It fell on the landing just outside my window and caused the whole metal structure to groan under its massive .00000000001 ounce weight. After a harrowing couple of seconds, the protesting fire escape grew silent.

"That'll end well," I said. To no one, apparently, since Mannix had already hustled out into the outer office

The elf returned momentarily with the two items I'd requested. I very carefully dropped the one of the things I'd found in my desk into the Glad bag, which was the second item I thought I had in my desk but didn't. I sealed the bag and dropped it into the FedEx envelope, a supply of which I knew Mannix kept on hand at all times. I dashed off a quick note with my stub of a pencil and stuffed it inside to accompany the contents of the Glad bag on its long journey.

"Send that off to Jack Wolff," I said. "His contact information is in my files, assuming Doris didn't use that particular paperwork to mop up one of her Exxon Valdez nail polish spills."

"Yes, sir, Mr. Crag," Mannix said. "There was one other thing. A bike messenger delivered this a little while ago."

Before hustling from the room, the elf handed over a white business envelope that I was lucky had made it upstairs before the hipster bike messenger's final encounters with a runaway taxi, the pavement, Death and Vincetti's broom, respectively.

I'm suspicious of any sealed envelope that doesn't have anything written on it. The unmarked envelope might have contained anthrax or a bill. I was rooting for the former as I tore it open and pulled out the single, crisp sheet contained within.

I was right. I would have been better off with anthrax.

At the very top of the page was embossed the legend "From the Desk of Dr. Cohen." The O in Cohen was particularly stylized, and was darker than the rest of the letters. The interior was lined with a couple dozen rounded bumps, which resembled an inside-out Reese's Peanut Butter Cup.

Other than the distinctive "O," the paper could have come from any of the million Cohens, M.D. in the yellow pages.

There was a handwritten note halfway down and smack dab in the middle of the page which read, in its entirety:

Watch it, Banyon.

"Mannix, did that bike messenger say where he picked this thing up?" I hollered out into the next room.

The little face poked back around the door. "No, Mr. Crag. He was listening to music and didn't say anything. He just sort of grunted and handed over the envelope, then left. Do you want me to try to track him down for you?"

He obviously didn't know the messenger was stinking up the sidewalk downstairs.

"No," I replied. "I don't have the dough to hire a necromancer, and nine out of ten psychics are frauds and the tenth one is nuts."

Mannix bowed backwards from the room, happily oblivious, and a minute later I heard him leave Doris' office and close the door to the hallway behind him, presumably taking off to drop off my vitally important FedEx package to Jack Wolff.

I pondered Dr. Cohen's cryptic note, holding it up to the light. I hate P.I. stereotypes, but as long as I was alone I dragged out my magnifying glass and carefully went over the scrap of paper. No watermarks, and the only prints I saw were my own.

There were about a million bike messenger services in a town this size, and the spotty employment histories of the lowlifes they hired revolved largely around whether or not they had enough cash for dope stuffed in the pockets of their moldy khakis or if some venue in the tri-state area was hosting a Phish concert. The decomposing kid downstairs could probably go missing for weeks without anybody but his medical marijuana supplier noticing he'd taken the big powder.

I leaned back in my seat to take a look out the window. Neither the cops nor an ambulance had yet arrived. The city's entire force of full-time emergency responders was probably still busy doing nothing across town at the telephone company.

I took great solace in the fact that I worked in the opposite of an upscale neighborhood. A better neighborhood could expect a cruiser and paramedics on the scene in under ten minutes, and I figured Vincetti or some passerby had called about the dead bike messenger twice as long ago as that. On my fancy-ass block, the arrival of local emergency personnel was coordinated with the advancing and retreating leading glacial sheets of the most relevant, bracketing ice ages.

Examining a dead body before the cops get their mitts on it is fraught with danger, mostly in the area of getting a murder rap pinned to your chest like a corsage. Cops are eager to embrace the easiest way out, and the fact that the guy had obviously been pummeled by a speeding car and polished off by Death wouldn't matter if they drove around the corner and found me elbow deep in the punk's pockets.

It would have been quicker to use the fire escape. Unfortunately, that would be doubly true if it tore loose from the wall under the weight of my middle-aged ass, fatally combined with the massive bulk of the errant yellow Post-It note that was still stuck to the rusted metal and flapping in the breeze outside my window.

American impatience took a prudent back seat to

self-preservation, and I grabbed up my hat and coat from my busted, old office couch and hustled from the office, riding the elevator down to the ground floor.

The first thing I nearly tripped over was an elf with a FedEx envelope tucked up under his arm running back and forth on the sidewalk.

"What the hell are you doing, Mannix?" I demanded.

"Collecting the notes I threw out the window," the elf replied. "It was a fun game, Mr. Crag, but littering is naughty." He said it as if it was the most obvious thing in the world, and as if I was in on the joke and gave two shits if the Post-It notes blew into the reservoir, in some jerk's moped engine, or down some sleeping wino's throat.

The Grim Reaper had fled the scene. Vincetti had successfully swept the dead bike messenger into the gutter and escaped to the safety of his customer-deficient fish market. Mannix and I were the only two souls out front, but I could see the nosy old fishmonger peering through the pair of faded cartoon eyes of the pathetic lobster that was painted on the inside of his filthy store's filthy front window.

"I've found all but one," Mannix announced worriedly, taking inventory of the stack of Post-Its in his little hand. A gentle breeze delivered the final note directly in front of his nose, and he failed to take note of the groaning fire escape above his head as he happily plucked the once-in-a-lifetime storm window opportunity from the air.

"I'm taking you to Atlantic City," I vowed. "In the meantime, and before you FedEx that package, I need you to go into Vincetti's deathtrap and pretend to shop around. He knows you work for me, but you'll be the first thing in months with less than a hundred legs to scurry through the front door, so he can't afford to ignore you."

Mannix was tucking away the Post-Its. "But if I go

into a store and I don't intend to buy anything, it's kind of like lying."

I fished in my pocket and handed him one thin dime. "Buy one clam. But unless you've got a craving for intestinal parasites and the inevitable accompanying colostomy, you'll avoid eating it like the plague. Which, no kidding, it probably also carries."

Mannix ducked inside the For the Halibut Fish Market and, as expected, Vincetti's eyes instantly disappeared from within their cartoon lobster frames.

I squatted quickly down next to the dead bike messenger.

The dead punk wasn't wearing anything that identified him with any particular messenger service. The only stickers on his bike were hemp-related. I fished around in his pockets and came up with a roach clip; twenty-two cents in change; a brand-new, folded-up flier advertising Vincetti's For the Halibut Fish Market (that old guinea bastard was without shame); and three combs. That last collection of matching items was particularly laughable since the kid's lunatic hair made him look like a stray collie that had spent the past decade living in a sewer pipe.

The only thing of note about the college pothead puke was something I nearly missed thanks to the way Vincetti had dumped the body in the gutter.

The corpse was wearing short pants, and I noticed a large purple bruise on the outside of his left thigh. It was obviously a result of the accident, but what caught my eye was that it was a perfect O with rounded bumps along the interior that exactly matched the stylized O in "Cohen" on the cheerfully threatening note the dead kid had delivered to my office in the final minutes of his worthless life.

That bruise had come from the impact, which meant

that the *O* in question was prominently displayed some-where on the front of the car that hit the hipster. Which meant that the sinister Dr. Cohen was the only M.D. in town who still made house calls. At some point in the previous forty-five minutes, Dr. Cohen had flagged the messenger down, paid him to deliver the note, then ran him down and -- since there was no folding cash on him -- took his money back. It was such a cheap bastard move that I was, frankly, surprised that he hadn't tried to hire me at one point like all the rest of the shameless deadbeats in town.

A cab was pulling to the curb as I stuffed the dead punk's pocket garbage back inside his baggy, khaki shorts. A very long right leg exited the taxi's rear door accom-panied a moment later by a mirror image left gam, both ending in a pair of high-heel clogs that I imagined were similar in podiatric comfort to strapping a couple of copies of *The Complete Works of William Shakespeare* to one's feet.

"Ju are not stealing from the drunks to pay for my dinner," Senorita Tamale insisted, horrified, as she teetered on her towering footwear.

"No, on several points. One, this jerk with the worthless, four hundred grand sociology degree is dead, not drunk. Two, he has nothing in his pockets worth stealing, unless there's resale value for Kinko's aquamarine fish market fliers that have been stuffed into corpse pockets postmor-tem by entrepreneurial dagos. Three, I am not paying for dinner, you are. Four, we're not having dinner."

Showoffs in tights steal all the hero thunder in every town they decide to make home, but the true hero of that moment was Senorita Tamale's cab driver.

The Arab cabbie was completely uninterested in involving himself in any way whatsoever with the dead body in the road. He made a point of not looking at the corpse under the accepted taxi driver rule that if a hack doesn't see something, it does not exist. This worked great for traffic signals, stop signs, other cabs, every other car and truck, pedestrians in crosswalks, dames pushing baby carriages, mailboxes, sidewalk cafes, and P.I.'s seemingly mugging corpses in the gutters of crummy neighborhoods. He accepted Senorita Tamale's dough, groused the absolute minimum amount of union-dictated time over the tip, then sped off around the nearest corner posthaste.

Senorita Tamale was nudging the corpse with the cautious toe of an enormous platform shoe to confirm my diagnosis of terminal death as I glanced around.

The sidewalks were as dead as the corpse rolling away from the senorita's foot.

I was living in a world obsessed with shinnying up every light post to hang a security camera, yet I was standing in a neighborhood which that particular privacy-invading technology had passed by. The only outfit that might have had a camera was the check cashing joint across the street but, thanks to Minus, the window behind the steel security fence had been blown out by an exploding bolt from my fire escape a couple hours earlier. There was a fresh sheet of plywood covering the window.

If anyone had seen the accident, nobody had stuck around to give an account to the cops. It would be no use questioning Vincetti. The old guinea justifiably hated my guts. Even if he'd seen anything, he'd clam up like one of his months-old mollusks. Not that he'd say anything to the cops, whose sirens I'd just begun to hear in the distance. He believed firmly in the principle of *omerta* when it came to dealing with government representatives, a code that had kicked in right around the time Il Duce was getting strung up by his fascist heels, and which as a lifelong policy had extended decades thereafter and across the Atlantic to apply to meddlesome local health inspectors.

I led Senorita Tamale back toward the downstairs corner door that led to the elevator, intercepting Mannix en route as he exited the fish market. Vincetti's beady eyes were back inside their lobster goggles as I plucked the clam from Mannix's tiny hand and rolled it like a grenade back through the old fascist bastard's front door.

"Oh, didn't you want that one, Mr. Crag?" the elf asked. "I can go back and exchange it for a different one."

The resultant Italian invective that issued from somewhere along the cartoon lobster's faded orange carapace made a return trip inside Vincetti's fish market by Mannix an unjustifiable risk.

"I think I'll forgo food poisoning for the evening and concentrate on alcohol poisoning," I said. "Why don't you hurry up and get that in the mail."

Mannix dutifully trotted off down the sidewalk, the FedEx envelope tucked firmly up under his little arm.

The sirens were on the far side of the building and closing in around the block. Fortunately, a second cab pulled to the curb before their arrival on the scene, and I spied annoying client Mrs. Gwendolyn Johnson emerging from the back seat.

I hustled a confused Senorita Tamale back across the sidewalk.

"Mr. Banyon--" began Gwendolyn Johnson, the dame with the possibly cheating, definitely boring husband.

"I'm afraid you've arrived after office hours," I interrupted before my annoying client could drone out a fifth, irritating syllable. "But you're fortunate to have timed your arrival to coincide with my need to beat a hasty retreat ahead of the imminent arrival of the inquisitive, moron local constabulary. So, as recompense for your exquisite timing, I'll tell you everything about your case that I've collected since our last meeting once we arrive at our destination which, forewarned is forearmed, is an utter dump. You're paying for the cab. Your carriage awaits, Senorita Tamale."

Gwendolyn Johnson's eyes hesitated just a split-second longer than the rest of her flawless feminine carcass. As a client, my autonomic response was to be irritated by her, but I found myself momentarily admiring her for her quick decision and a rapid response time that put the local cops to shame. She dumped herself back into the rear of the taxi and permitted the two of us to pile in beside her as she slid to the far side of the seat.

"You'd better not disappoint me, Mr. Banyon," she warned.

"You're a dame. I invariably will."

"Ju said a mouse-full," Senorita Tamale interjected.

The last time I was flanked by a pair of hostile dames in the backseat of a car it was my ex-wife and former mother-in-law on my wedding day. Unless this night ended with me dumped on a desolate stretch of rabid raccoon-infested highway covered in melted Carvel wedding cake with a bleeding gut wound (the result of a busted ceramic groom shiv attack), I figured it'd end far better than had that other blissful evening.

I settled back in the rear of the grubby cab as it sped off in the direction opposite the approaching patrol car and the accompanying superfluous ambulance.

9

O'Hale's Bar was so dead that even the lazy dust mites weren't motivated to get up off their asses for the swinging front door.

The booths and barstools were empty. No one was splashing around in the can, which had been declared a toxic Superfund site by the federal government the previous month. Even though Jaublowski kept cutting through the yellow hazard tape to make the john more inviting to desperate souls who had abandoned all hope of reaching the alley out back in time, I could see through the open door that it was empty.

An old dame in tattered B-girl threads snoozed on a pillow made from a folded-up apron on the end of the bar near the cigarette machine. The smoldering stub of the butt that dangled from her cracked lips was being slowly extinguished by the puddle of drool that oozed from her open mouth. Chardonnay, the sometimes-waitress at O'Hale's, would die in that post, assuming she hadn't already snuffed it. I didn't bother to check if she was still breathing. I'd dealt with enough corpses already for one day.

The only sign of a pulse in the joint was Ed Jaublowski, who was standing lonely sentry duty behind the bar and came to life when he saw the biggest crowd in O'Hale's history piling through the door, then collapsed back to sullen reality when he saw it was I leading my female entourage into his booze-drenched crypt.

Neither Mrs. Gwendolyn Johnson nor Senorita Tamale seemed particularly overjoyed at the pigsty rum parlor into which I had gallantly escorted them, so I turned up my gentlemanly charm as I dumped their attractive asses at a sticky table.

"I know that it looks like the kind of joint where serial killers do their shopping, but according to a pal in the FBI that has only been the case sixty or seventy documented times. And, contrary to that scurrilous report in the *Gazette*, it is not technically the suicide capital of the state, it just happens to be where many of the most successful and flamboyant ones stop off first. O'Hale's is more a suicide suburb."

"We *not* staying here," Senorita Tamale insisted.

"Give it a chance. I know it doesn't look like much right now, but just wait until the cabaret atmosphere kicks in. The mice don't even start can-canning across the bar until after midnight."

Gwendolyn Johnson touched a manicured fingertip to the tabletop and seemed a hell of a lot less horrified than you'd imagine a dame who was trying to pass herself off as classy would be when she removed it and left her epidermal layer behind.

"We are supposed to be discussing my case, Mr. Banyon," the bleeding Johnson dame droned.

She didn't even attempt to retrieve her index fingerprint from where it had fastened like a remora to the surface of the table. Good thing she wasn't too attached to the flap of skin, since the only ice in O'Hale's was in the toilets, where the freezing started in late autumn and the thaw didn't kick in until April. This being February, the crappers in the ladies room would be frozen so solid it'd take an hour with an ice pick to chip loose enough to pack up her fingerprint for the ride to the hospital for delicate reattachment surgery. Still, even though it was so small a chunk of skin it probably couldn't be stitched back on, the emotional detachment with which she accepted her digital detachment was unsettling enough that I needed to settle it by getting loaded.

Gwendolyn Johnson left her sloughed-off skin as would any cold-blooded reptile and removed a handkerchief from her purse to wrap up the bloody fingertip.

"We will discuss your case momentarily," I told the ice queen, "although I warn you there isn't much to discuss. But first, excuse me for just one minute, ladies. I'm in demand more than usual this week, and I have yet another case to discuss with that disturbing-looking gentleman with the hairy ear-holes lurking behind the bar. Don't be alarmed by his gruesome expression. He's leering at your pocketbooks, not your racks."

I stepped over to the bar, pleased for a change of pace that I didn't have to crawl over a dead bike messenger to get someplace I wanted to be. Jaublowski was already pouring me a glass of something that I'm pretty sure the Navy could have used to strip rust off aircraft carriers.

"The Reaper been in here tonight, Ed?" I asked, downing my belt and immediately tapping a finger on the rim for a refill, which the barkeep obligingly supplied.

Jaublowski's face soured, which was a pretty mean feat considering it already looked like he peeled it off every night like a *Mission Impossible* Third World dictator disguise and soaked it in a corroded bucket of battery acid.

"I hope I seen the last of that joik," the barkeep said. "You got any idea how long I had to deal with the headache of gettin' that dead bike bum outta here? Wasted half a day dealing with cops, some asshole from the health department, that buddy of yours…what's his name? That old son of bitch? Runs the morgue?"

"Doc Minto," I supplied. "The only civil servant in this worthless burg who actually earns his million dollar retirement package."

"Yeah, him," Jaublowski grunted. "He couldn't send out somebody younger who could actually move their ass. No, he's gotta comes out personal. Old buzzard did half the autopsy right where youse standin'. Chardonnay found half a kidney under the cigarette machine after he left." (The moribund waitress at the end of the bar stirred at the mention of her name, obviating the need for a return trip by the multitude that had descended on O'Hale's to deal with the dead bike messenger.) "I'm lucky she dropped her lighter or that thing would of stunk up the joint for months before nobody found it."

I wasn't as sure as Jaublowski that the addition of rotting internal organs wouldn't be an improvement on, or at least offer a welcome olfactory distraction from, the usual pungent O'Hale's bouquet. I didn't share this observation since I needed to ask the Reaper a couple of life-and-death questions, and I didn't need an even more irate than usual Ed Jaublowski chasing the hooded bastard out of the joint before I could do so.

"Grim Reaper son of a bitch screwed up my whole day, Jinx," Jaublowski groused, winding down. "Couldn't finish off that bike jerk someplace else…no, he's gotta dump a dead body in *my* joint in the middle of the afternoon rush. I should tack an extra fee for all the aggravation on the end of *your* tab. It was *your* fault that bike bastard was even in here. What was so important you needed it right that minute anyways?"

"You see the young lady with the bleeding finger who is about to fire me and is contemplating suing you for personal injury because you won't shut up? She's a client, it was for her case. More than that I can't say, since client confidentiality is as important to my business as the thumbs you use to crush peanut-dwelling millipedes is to yours."

"Right," Jaublowski muttered, topping off my glass. "More pals of yours adding to my misery. That's all I need. You know that Death buddy of yours left here today owing me seven cents? Screw that bike messenger corpse, I should of called the cops on *his* bony ass."

I fished in my pocket and dropped a dime on the bar.

At first, Jaublowski didn't know how to react, so long had it been since he'd seen legal tender emerge from the depths of my trousers.

"Are you dying, Jinx?" he asked, worried like an actual human being for only approximately two seconds before flashing angry. "If you *are* buying the farm, I hope that elf is gonna settle your goddamn tab."

"Your concern for my continued well-being has so touched my heart that I only wish that was a defibrillator in your hand instead of a grubby bar rag," I informed him. "Let Death know when he comes in that I generously settled his bill for him, Ed. And do me a favor and try to act like a human being around him. You've seen enough real people stagger through this dump to fake it for five minutes. I need to talk to him. In the meantime, give me my change and some drinks for the ladies. Senorita Tamale is partial to tequila, which is a reprehensible stereotype but you try telling her what she should and shouldn't get loaded on. The other dame isn't staying but, as I said, she *is* a client, so pull out all the stops and give her something cheap with fruit and an umbrella in it."

The only umbrella Jaublowski had was a black number in the lost and found that some limey bastard had left behind on a rainy day six years before, and the only fruit came in on Wednesdays every couple of weeks to croon karaoke to the ancient jukebox. He had a good set of pipes, but that fact didn't do me any good with Mrs. Gwendolyn Johnson's fashionable drink order.

I returned to the table with a couple of glasses of tequila for the skirts, my own glass of booze, and a bowl of stale pretzels.

"Dinner is served," I informed Senorita Tamale. Before she could rip my head off and dump the contents of the cracked plastic bowl directly down my esophagus, I gave her a tip of the head as I addressed Client #1. "It's lucky that Senorita Tamale has graced us with her presence, as she was of invaluable, illegal, unremunerated assistance to me with your case this afternoon."

"You mentioned in the cab that you worked for the telephone company," said Mrs. Johnny Johnson, whose husband was nuts if he *was* cheating, given the pornographic manner in which the blonde bombshell filled out a black cocktail dress.

I'd had to silence the two dames on the ride to O'Hale's. What with the cryptic note I'd just received from Dr. Cohen, the maniac supervillain who had spent the later afternoon hours wreaking havoc on the city via the local phone system, I didn't think it the most genius move to share too much telephonic insight with the anonymous hack with the hairy neck slouching behind the steering wheel and listening in on our every word.

"Senorita Tamale checked the phone records of every room your husband has stayed in at the Happy Hobo Motel since I began following him," I said. "In those four days he placed only five calls from the motel. One was to his mother in New Schenectady and two were to the bank where he works. You know, that bank where the two of you share a joint account containing a whopping $11.37.

I'm figuring the calls were work-related, and that he didn't drive across town to a crummy hotel just to call back to the bank he just left to drain an account that wouldn't buy him one new shirt."

"And the remaining two phone calls?" she asked.

It was just my pain in the ass luck that the dame could do complicated arithmetic.

"Those two calls were made to the local police," I informed her. "They went to the switchboard, so we have no idea who exactly he called there or why."

"Can't you find out?" She directed her question to Senorita Tamale.

"The policia might have the records," the helpful hot-blooded Latin dame replied as she nibbled around the edge of her tequila glass. "Banyon has the times the calls were made, but ju would have to find out from their switchboard where they was directed."

Mrs. Johnson nodded firmly. "Do that then."

"You see, the complication there is that the policia pretty much hate my guts, and in fairness to the corrupt, incompetent boys in blue it's not entirely without cause."

"You must have an in with the police department," Client #1 insisted. "A friend on the force who helps you look up license plate numbers, that sort of thing."

"That's a TV sort of thing," I replied. "The real life sort of thing I deal with is open hostility and closed jail cell doors with me on the wrong side."

She tapped the sharp, careful end of a blood-red fingernail on the table next to the curling remains of her detached fingerprint. "I want you to check into that lead, Mr. Banyon," the dame insisted. "That's why I'm paying you." She checked her watch and abruptly stood up, leaving her glass untouched. "He must be back at that dirty little motel right now. I assume since you're here that an associate from your office is staking out the location."

"Since we're assuming things that have no basis in fact, I'm going to take my turn and assume that you want me to lie and say yes."

I ascertained from the dame's icy glare that I had clearly misread her cue.

"There isn't much point in me sitting out there every night any longer," I explained to her frigid baby blues. "The chance of actually learning something of value from staking out the joint would be low, while the potential of getting driven into the ground liked a tomato stake by a rampaging ogre chambermaid would be quite high. I'm going to have to come at this from a different angle, which angle will be easier to sneak up on once I've limbered up by getting really, really pounded."

"Ole," interjected Senorita Tamale, who was lapping the last of her tequila from her glass and was clearly already outpacing me around the aforementioned sharp right angle.

"Those calls to the police," Mrs. Johnson insisted. "Find out who in the police department my husband is calling. If it's some cheap little meter maid, I'll serve the divorce papers down his throat."

Decree issued, she said not another word. She grabbed up her purse, pulled her magnificent caboose out of the station and sashayed on a straight line of track right on out the grimy front door.

As the door was swinging shut, I was reaching for her glass but found that it was already in the slender fingers of Senorita Tamale, who downed the tequila in one swig.

"I see ju still have only the bestest clients," she commented.

"They pay the bills," I replied. "Or, rather, the seven percent who aren't deadbeats do. Apparently, even when they don't get full reports."

Gwendolyn Johnson had failed completely to ask about her husband's cell phone, the number to which I'd requested during our first conference and records of which Senorita Tamale had very kindly supplied to me in the wake of my great heroics at the telephone company that afternoon. Nearly all the calls from Johnny Johnson's cell had been to his wife, with the few remaining going to the bank where he worked.

I figured her husband's cell phone records would be important to her as well, and so I watched the door for the next ten minutes as Senorita Tamale groused about life, work, family, hypnotized coworkers, O'Hale's, and me. (Mostly me, which was a subject she particularly warmed to after a multiyear break in the action.)

Throughout the increasingly slurred, semi-Spanish monologue, I assumed that Gwendolyn Johnson would suddenly remember the cell phone and reverse course back to O'Hale's, but the dame persisted in remaining gone.

Life inside O'Hale's returned to what passed for normal in the seediest speakeasy in the tri-state area. Jaublowski sullenly fed us watered-down drinks and at one point took out a .22 to shoot at something bigger than a rat but smaller than a breadbox scurrying down near the mildewed baseboard behind the bar.

Chardonnay, the B-girl barmaid, snored once deeply enough to choke on her soggy cigarette butt, swallowed it, then fell back into blissful slumber with her belly full with what was probably her first solid meal in a week.

Something sinister gurgled in the depths of the men's room that at first sounded like pipes justifiably rebelling against humanity, but after a single loud splash and grunt the noise settled into a pathetic, slimy shuffling, so it was probably just the toxic waste monster that periodically emerged from the john to look for any dropped change Jaublowski might have missed on his daily inspection.

A half-hour after I'd given up my boyish daydreaming about Client #1 returning, the front door of O'Hale's burst open. I glanced up from the beautiful, nagging Senorita Tamale hoping to glimpse Death's skull face, since it might have become vitally important to my future existence to question the reaping grim bastard.

Instead of a figure in black wearily schlepping around an oversized scythe, there entered a streak of yellow that had the appalling gall to brighten up the dingy dump.

A swirling maelstrom of various street garbage (including but not limited to a couple Styrofoam plates, a Subway bag, several copies of the *Gazette*, two Budweiser cans, and a couple goddamn For the Halibut Fish Market fliers) circled the table that I was sharing with the lovely, slightly pounded Senorita Senorita. The wind stopped, the garbage tornado dumped itself out on the floor, and in the flotsam's midst towered a yellow-suited asshole with a purple cape and an apologetic smirk.

"I'm *so* sorry to bother you, Mr. Banyon," intoned Minus, a hero so unheroic he'd had to rely on uber-unheroic me to save his pathetic hide.

"Of course it's you," I said. "What the hell else could ruin my night off in so spectacular a fashion other than the Savior of the City, with the exception of maybe a massive natural disaster or possibly an all-out thermonuclear war?"

(It was only for rhetorical flourish that I added that bullshit about nuclear bombs. I sure as hell didn't realize that out there somewhere at that very moment one of them was counting down to zero, probably with the large-scale plan to level the city and slaughter everyone and everything wretched enough to attempt to scrape out a daily existence there, but possibly with a playful eye on the small-scale amusement of utterly screwing up my goddamn Friday night.)

10

"Your assistant told me I might find you here," Minus said, even as the junk pile that had swept into O'Hale's in his wake continued to settle around his purple boots. He nudged away a beer can that settled on his toe, misjudged his own strength, and accidentally sent it soaring through the open men's room door from which emanated a very loud thump accompanied by a grunt which was immediately followed by a fat splat.

"Oh, great," Jaublowski called over from the bar, an eye trained on the bathroom. "Toxic Shit Monster is gonna sue *my* ass for getting knocked unconscious in here."

"Sorry," Minus said. "I'll pay any damages."

"Right," Jaublowski grunted. "Hey, Jinx, you plan on pickin' up all that crap your buddy just dragged in here? I already had to clean up one of your messes today."

"Can't you see I'm in conference with a client?" I hollered back.

The barkeep was muttering something about charging me extra for using his joint as a conference room, which would have been fine with me so long as he tacked the fee onto the end of my massive bar tab which I had no intention of paying in this or any future life I might have to suffer through. Fortunately, something furry and orange chose that moment to leap up from the floor and race along the shelf at the back of the bar, jangling the line of half-empty bottles as it attempted to pour itself a freebie without the assistance of a necessary pair of good opposable thumbs. Jaublowski went after his latest deadbeat customer with his .22 peashooter and forgot all about the out-cold creature from the dank latrine as well as the fresh mess that Minus had dumped onto his filthy floor.

Over at my table, Senorita Tamale greeted the arrival of the jerk in yellow tights with a mixture of one part joy and three parts tequila.

"Hello there, Meester Handsome," she said, wiggling her inebriated fingers suggestively an inch from Minus' face.

Once again, the big yellow dope didn't seem to know what to do with the special attention his newly acquired celebrity status garnered him. He was as uncomfortable as he'd been that first day in my office which, according to my calculations, had to be a million years ago because no one human being could possibly have been so great a pain in my ass as the Shithead in Spandex had been in less than ten hours.

"I know it appears as if I'm merely sitting here getting loaded in the company of the lovely senorita, who actually *is* merely sitting here getting loaded, but in point of fact I'm working on your case," I informed Minus. "I've got a potential lead on Dr. Cohen from a guy who might even have eyewitnessed Cohen driving over a bike messenger. The grim lead in question indicated he might be stopping in here tonight."

"A bike messenger?" Minus asked. "I don't understand."

"They're adult hophead nuisances who peddle around city streets like demented circus clowns, weaving in and out of traffic as if they're the only creatures on the face of the planet, adding immensely to the general air of daily urban misery. Since you spend the majority of your time in the air these days menacing birds and small aircraft, you may have forgotten how much everybody down here hates them."

I wasn't just being a jerk, which was merely an added bonus. I was trying to gauge the reaction, if any, on the big dope's face.

Minus seemed legitimately puzzled, but that didn't necessarily mean anything. Even a bad actor can sometimes turn in a great improv performance.

I'd had my doubts about the flying SOB ever since that afternoon when he conveniently remained MIA the entire time I had to deal with Dr. Cohen. Minus didn't show back up again until after the good doctor had fled the telephone company building in his silver escape pod. I wasn't quite ready to out Minus and his archnemesis as one in the same person, but in my business it's prudent to mistrust everybody, which went double -- and occasionally triple and quadruple -- for clients.

If Minus did know something about the dead doper and his late, lamented Schwinn outside my building, it didn't show on his lantern-jawed mug.

"Oh, no, no, no. You misunderstand, Mr. Banyon. I know what bike messengers are. I meant I don't understand what one has to do with Dr. Cohen."

I fished in my jacket pocket where I'd stuffed the note before leaving my office, and slapped it down for dramatic effect on the table. I immediately realized that my grand theatricality -- while a tour de force worthy of whatever the goddamn swish Oscar-equivalent award is for stage plays -- was a mistake of *Chevy Chase Show* magnitude.

The paper instantly stuck to the gluey surface of the table, and when I tried to peel it off most of it wound up sticking as if the tabletop had been recently varnished with a hundred years of spilled booze and every bodily fluid known to man.

I managed to tear off the two relevant portions of the sheet of paper, and when I tried to hold the ripped sections up for Minus to peruse them I had to work around Senorita Tamale, who was subtly trying to violently sexually assault him.

"Ju so beeg and strong," she slurred.

She groped, he weaved, I held the scraps of paper in between the floor show.

Minus frowned as he scanned the "From the Desk of Dr. Cohen" header to the even more sinister "Watch it, Banyon" content.

"How does he know your name?" the yellow bastard asked.

"I don't know," I replied honestly, as I studied those parts of his face that weren't obscured by his mask or by the drunken telephone operator who was attempting to slobber all over it. "The cops know me. Jenkins might have mentioned me in his report, although being an asshole he would not mention that I'm the one who actually saved the day. If Dr. Cohen has an in with the cops, he could have found out who I was that way. As a mad genius, he could have hacked their computer or read my mind or, if he's a more down-to-earth lunatic, followed me back to my office. On the other hand, he could have found out a completely other way. You have any steroid-fueled thoughts?"

The jerk looked legitimately baffled. Could have been an act or the real deal; there was no way to know. My neck was in a noose either way.

"What about that 'O,'" I asked, tapping the first vowel

of the name in the good mad doctor's letterhead. "You ever see an O like that anywhere in your travels in either your public or secret identities?"

Minus seemed to examine each rounded bump along the interior of the O in "Cohen," but his baffled expression never wavered.

"I'm sorry, I don't think so. Is it important? Do you think it's a clue?"

"I think it's not worth whatever you're paying me to find Cohen," I said, sticking the fragments of paper into my trench coat pocket.

"Oh, but he's why I'm here," Minus announced abruptly, suddenly remembering his swirling trash-dervish entrance from a minute before. "The police called me. Which is to say, the chief of police yelled for me from the roof of the main precinct. It's Dr. Cohen. He's back. I need you to come with me again, Mr. Banyon. You were very…well, let's face it, *helpful* last time. And I still need a set of eyes to see him which, darn it, no one including me has yet. And once you see him, you can track him down. I mean, I *hope* you can. It's what you do, after all."

The cogent argument he'd made earlier that day for me to accompany him to the telephone company still stood, but it was balanced now by the fact that I'd almost gotten my ass blown out from under me on that job. And now Dr. Cohen knew who I was, while I still had no real idea and only one long shot guess who he was, which meant that the threat of certain death from a madman out to trash the town had shot up like mercury in a thermometer on the first, freakishly hot day in early spring.

In the end, I reached the only prudent destination at which a truly rational man could arrive.

"Make sure you inform me via Western Union how it all works out," I said, raising a glass to toast his departure.

"Unless he succeeds in killing you this time, in which case you don't have to bother. Don't let the door hit you in the purple Speedos on the way out. That's sound medical advice. There have been several cases of gangrene."

"Ju a coward, Banyon!" Senorita Tamale snarled.

"If this is already the part of the evening where we drunkenly state the obvious, you're going to have to give me a little time to catch up," I informed her. "Let me get fifteen minutes-worth more hammered and I'll start in on your shoes and how your out-of-proportion ego and intense feelings of inferiority are both up there teetering right alongside your daddy issues on those ludicrous orange crates."

She apparently still had the adorable quirk of planting a furniture exclamation point at the end of her furious squeals. The dame staggered back then lunged for the back of her chair, giving me a momentary twinge of memory of an ancient bruise in the shape of a piano stool in my lower back. My internal as well as other, more vital organs were spared a Mexican clobbering thanks to Minus, who leapt between us in a single bound.

"It's a *nuclear bomb* this time, Mr. Banyon," he blurted.

Senorita Tamale very calmly dragged her bloodshot eyes from me to Minus. She then equally calmly parked her chair back under the table and, spinning on her ridiculous high heels, clip-clopped briskly and wordlessly to the nearest exit. Before the door swung shut she was already screaming at the top of her Latina lungs for a taxi.

"She can't get away in time," Minus insisted. "It's set to go off at midnight, and Dr. Cohen said the blast radius will wipe out the entire city."

And, just like that, my personal inner teeter-totter flipped back in the other direction. My impulse to not help was superceded by my intense desire to not become a P.I.-shaped cloud of radioactive ash.

"I assume," I said, "that our city's genius fathers aren't planning on doing the only sensible thing and giving him *double* whatever it is he wants. It only makes sense to save money on postage and prepay now for the next time he holds the city hostage."

Minus merely shook his head.

Everybody else seems to catch a break sometimes, but life has a terrifically consistent habit of only offering me the shit end of the stick. If I ever lucked out and picked the opposite end, it would also have shit on it, just slightly less. Then life would take it back and beat the hell out of me with it for not picking the shittier end.

There were no other options available. I downed the last of my drink in one gulp; downed the rest of Senorita Tamale's tequila bottle (which her light fingers had somehow liberated from under Jaublowski's hairy nose); took one final, bleary look around my home away from home; determined that I was wise to choose O'Hale's as my main watering hole since I didn't give a damn if the dump was ground zero and my regular stool was the plunger Dr. Cohen used to set off the nuke that turned the whole town to one big cinder; and marched bravely for the door.

"If Death comes in, hold him here until I get a chance to talk to him," were my final shouted words to Jaublowski. I hoped like hell they wouldn't turn out to be my final words ever to Jaublowski or to any other human being, of which, all outward features notwithstanding, Ed Jaublowski was technically one.

"What are Cohen's demands?" I demanded of Minus as we hustled outside.

"He wants five hundred million dollars in unmarked

bills, his student loans forgiven, and his own parking spot at the opera house, along with season tickets."

There was a cab parked at the curb with no driver behind the wheel. Minus flung open the rear door and waved me into the back.

"You didn't seem very comfortable during the flight downtown today, so I borrowed this," he explained as I piled past him and he slammed the door.

I wasn't alone in the back of the hack.

"*Finally*," the dozing dame who was already parked in the rear of the taxi exclaimed, a tequila-contaminated cloud exploding from between her furious lips. "No monkey business. Ju get up in frontses now and drive me the hells away from here."

Senorita Tamale offered me a quizzical look of hazy memory before the reality of whose mug she was staring into abruptly settled in. At the same instant, she suddenly recalled why she had stumbled out the front door of O'Hale's in the first place, and for the second time in under five minutes a wave of tenuous sobriety washed over her.

"Get out of my cab, Banyon!" she gently screamed. "I got to gets out of this city. If ju is smart ju will come with me, but if ju do ju pay half the fare. Not like when ju made me pay for both of us then left me on that Canadio ferry, ju cheap son of a beetch."

For dramatic effect and to prove she meant business, she flung open the door and nearly fell thirty stories to a fairly certain, definitely sloppy and assuredly spectacular death.

Unseen and unfelt during her tirade, Minus had lifted the cab off the ground, slipped smoothly underneath and raised us high above the tenements and old office building rooftops of the seedy neighborhood in which O'Hale's

Bar lurked.

Few professionally trained human voices could have held a note as long and as piercing as the sustained scream that challenged Senorita Tamale's already habitually over-taxed larynx. Dogs howled in the streets far below, windows rattled in sympathetic disharmony. The Doppler shriek woke babies, frightened the elderly, shattered flowerpots in rooftop gardens, and caused at least one pigeon that I saw to commit accidental suicide by flying in a panicked flurry of feathers straight into the saw blades of a roof fan to get away from the horrifying blast of noise.

The pigeon made the easy way out look inviting, and for a moment my eardrums and I were tempted to take a long leap out the open door to flee the reverberating horror show. I reconsidered the moment the thought occurred to me. Any afterlife that would accept me would almost certainly be worse than the miserable excuse for a corporeal existence I was presently stumbling my way through. Instead of giving in to temptation and taking a dramatic swan dive for 115th Street, I leaned across the yelling dame, copped a quick feel, and slammed the cab door shut.

She couldn't keep screaming like that forever, but she gave it the old community college dropout try. After a minute, she wrapped up the impressive Jamie Lee Curtis act in an anticlimactic gurgle that sounded like the last of the bathwater finally running down a clogged Tijuana drain. She frantically sought to buckle her seatbelt, but since our ride was up to usual strict city taxicab standards, the buckle ends came off in her hands.

"Mios dio," she exhaled. She knotted the remains of the belt around her waist.

"You know, I never took Spanish in my life and even I know that pretty much all of it that comes out of your mouth is gibberish."

"Is something wrong in there?" a mighty voice intoned from somewhere beneath the gum-ravaged floor mats.

I checked out the window to confirm that we were still half a mile above the city in an airborne taxicab.

"Everything," I shouted at my shoelaces.

The distant lights of the city were a cheery lie in the ugly night. Up close, faces appeared surrounded by haloed yellow squares as we soared past apartment and office windows. Up ahead, one particular set of lights caught my eye.

January 1st was old by a month and a half, and the next one wouldn't come around for nearly a whole year in the other direction, yet high above the city, at the very peak of the Sonny Bono Building, the digital clock that marked the six-hour countdown to midnight on New Year's Eve was blinking its ominous way down to zero.

The clock was never switched on but for those few hours on the night of December 31st, and the fact that it was telling me I had 37 minutes and 12 seconds until blastoff suggested that I'd either enjoyed the bender of a lifetime and missed out entirely on spring, summer, autumn and half of winter, or somebody had screwed around with it.

I banged my foot on the floor. "Take us for a tour around the New Year's clock," I called between my Florsheims.

Minus had clearly not even noticed the lone digital timer blinking high over every rooftop in the doomed city, since he'd been flying straight past it at a hundred miles an hour. The flying cab abruptly banked left, my stomach did a somersault, Senorita Tamale squeaked in fear, and we were suddenly zooming up to and then circling around one of the top three highest rooftops in the greater metropolitan area.

Minus circled around the roof for three full, fast laps. The cab was suddenly the airborne NASCAR version of that contraption they use to test G-forces on astronauts, and I wondered if that was Buzz Aldrin's puke I'd been smelling on the floor mats.

"Thees ees crazzy!" Senorita Tamale yelled as the whip-sharp turn around the south end corner of the Sonny Bono Building dumped her hard against me.

"If you mean your accent, I agree that it's crazzy like a zorro. Otherwise, this is pretty much as hazardous to my health as a normal day at the office."

I kept my eyes peeled all the way around as we completed three tours of the building and saw no sign of any kind of bomb -- nuclear, conventional or recent Jim Carrey DVD -- at the base of the twin poles that held the countdown clock aloft. I didn't see any goons on the roof, but I hadn't seen any on the telephone company roof either, and that adventure several hours ago had ended spectacularly shittily.

"We better land," I hollered. "Park us up tight against the roof door."

The cab dropped, the roof flew up to meet us, and we were suddenly in the highest parking space in town and jammed up snugly against the roof's metal access door.

Minus appeared next to Senorita Tamale's door, opened it, and gallantly escorted the lovely, blotto dame out onto the roof while the sad sack private eye who'd been enlisted to save his ass yet again had to climb across the reeking seat in order to deplane.

At least I didn't hear anybody pounding on the roof door, and thanks to the fact that we were on top of the highest building in the area, nobody tried to vaporize us from adjoining rooftops as we crossed over to the countdown clock.

"Do you think the clock being activated like this means something, Mr. Banyon?" Minus asked.

"It means a couple of things," I said. "It means that you are at least as bad at this as the local police, since clearly none of them noticed from the parking lot of Dunkin Donuts that a clock that isn't supposed to be switched on for another ten-plus months has mysteriously turned on at the precise instant a flamboyant maniac has announced that he's holding the city nuclear hostage. It also means that that is how much time we have left to live, assuming Dr. Cohen, bastard, M.D., follows through on his threat."

The gravel roof crunched underfoot, particularly under Senorita Tamale's feet which, positioned as they were atop tree stump heels, sounded like a cattle stampede through a bag of Uncle Ben's Perverted Rice.

"I do not know what it is I am looking on," she announced at the base of the twin poles that supported the clock.

"Go dangle that preposition off the edge of the roof," I said. "I'm working."

High above, the New Year's clock continued to tick down the seconds and minutes, and stood now with only an unsettling 33:42 remaining. The traffic noise from the street was a dull roar of engines and honking horns, and was far enough away that I could hear the seconds clicking down to doomsday over my head.

The clock had been a permanent fixture on the building for decades. It made sense that it would have been operated from one of the floors below us, with the major plumbing running up one or both of the hollow posts.

"It is more than a little unsettling," I said to my oblivious companions, who never would have gotten through one semester at P.I. University, "that I'm clearly the only one here who sees that the symbol of our great city's joyous countdown to another inevitably rotten year has quite obviously been hotwired by a maniac bastard."

A square hole had been freshly cut in one of the wide steel poles. The missing piece of metal hadn't even fled the scene. The curved square along with a pile of silver metal shavings sat on the roof at the base of the pole.

Two wires, one blue and one red, snaked from the hole in the pole and slipped over the north side of the building.

I followed the wires to the roof ledge and leaned over to get the full, bird's eye view of the shell-domed roof of the Luciano Mankowitz Opera House.

The opera house consisted of four visible stories, with two more stories of parking garage buried beneath it. The huge conch shell that jutted out of the roof, under which was the main stage, was lit up in rotating blues, greens, reds and yellows.

The building was a million stories below us, and in the dark I quickly lost clear view of the pair of skinny blue and red wires that ran from the New Year's clock and over the side of the Sonny Bono Building. Every time the yellow spotlight flicked on and brightly lit the dome of the opera house, I caught faint sight of a pair of slim black cobwebs snaking through the night sky to the adjacent building.

"If we were smart, which I am assuming based on recent experience that only I am, we'd all pile back in that cab and you'd fly us as fast away from this exact spot as is superhumanly possible, stopping only to pick up my office assistant elf who is the only living soul in this rathole worth saving, present company -- including me -- included."

Minus didn't want to let on that he didn't know what the hell I was talking about, so he furrowed his brow so seriously I was afraid his eyes would pop under the pressure and he nodded so somberly it was as if he were already practicing for the endless funeral procession for the entire victim population of the city he was about to fail to save because he was evidently incapable of anything remotely approaching thought.

"I'd push you off this roof if I thought you'd forget you can fly," I said. "Which probably has a better than fifty percent chance of being the case."

He stopped all the fruitless furrowing and pointless nodding and threw up his gloved hands in surrender. "I'm sorry, Mr. Banyon," he said, shrugging confusion. "I'm just not…well, let's face it. This is *not* my wheel house."

"Yes, I can see why this would be complicated. After all, one of Cohen's demands was only a parking space at the opera." I pointed at the opera house. "That's the opera." I stabbed a thumb over my shoulder. "That's the clock counting down to Dr. Cohen's threatened nuclear blast with wires running out of it that lead down to the opera house. I know I'm goddamn stumped."

Senorita Tamale's face had been scrunched up in deep concentration as I spoke, but suddenly blossomed with understanding.

"The bomb!" she cried to Minus. "Eet is een the opera house!"

The big dummy's own face brightened and the pair of morons shared an exultant moment of deductive triumph which left me wondering if I'd come down on the right side vis-à-vis saving a goddamn city wherein dwelled clods of such exquisite caliber.

Lucky for the two clapping idiots, my ass dwelled there as well and, as I had grown attached to it over the years and vice versa, I piled it back into the rear of the rooftop taxicab along with moron #1 while moron #2 hefted us back up onto his mighty shoulders and flew us down to the street in front of the Luciano Mankowitz Opera House.

There were no legal parking spaces, and it was hell persuading Minus as we hovered eight feet over the street to double-park next to a silver Porsche. The asshole was actually writing a note of apology to leave for the cops under the cab's windshield wiper as Senorita Tamale and I floored it up the marble steps to the main entrance.

It was a stroke of rare luck that the manager had seen us swoop down out of the sky with the Savior of the City(goddamn TM), and any reluctance the effete jerk might have had about letting us in without our having shelled out three hundred bucks for tickets evaporated in the withering burst of part-Spanish, part-Teamster invective that issued from the pouting lips of my screeching Latina companion.

"Oh, dear, a bomb?" the manager asked, dogging the pair of us through the gleaming black lobby. "Oh, dear, are you *certain*? Tsk-tsk. First that messy bike messenger, and now a nuclear bomb leveling the city? Oh, dear, this is *not* my night."

"This is just a wild guess," I said as we ran, "but did the Grim Reaper stick you with a dead bike messenger?"

"Oh, yes," the manager said. "He just touched that bike boy on the shoulder and the lobby chandelier came loose and fell on the young fellow's head. Just like that. And the moment it was over, Death left, free as you please. I'm just lucky I got the mess cleaned up by intermission. It took two whole rolls of Bounty, and that's the *quicker picker upper*, for goodness sake. Icky mess. We've got him tucked away in the wine fridge until after the show. This is simply *not* my night. *Sigh*."

We were running and I was winded. Add to that the fact that I was busy saving a city that I hated, so I broke

my cardinal rule of punching any asshole in the mouth
who spoke aloud one-word descriptions of things they
could just goddamn do.

The manager swished us up a hall and unlocked an
unmarked door.

"Tell that caped idiot to meet me on the roof," I hollered as I bravely charged through the door and up the
stairs beyond.

The manager spun and flounced back down the hall
to the main lobby.

Senorita Tamale made a game effort to keep up on her
clomping Romper Stomper shoes, but I lost her by the
second floor. I could hear her huffing and swearing down
the stairwell as I broke through the door to the roof.

I was assaulted by the twin blasts of cold night air and
rotten kraut screaming.

The playbills and posters I'd seen as I ran through
the lobby were advertising the latest German operatic
import, *Die Hoppy Nazi*, by Fred Goebbels. Downstairs,
the noise of the audience being bellowed at in full-blast
German had been muffled, but it was a whole different
story out on the roof. The giant dome ahead of me was
vibrating so much from all the operatic screaming it was
at risk of shattering and collapsing on the audience tucked
unsafely away somewhere unseen beneath it.

Before I'd taken two running steps I was joined by
Minus who flew up from the street out front. I took only
a second to note once more the flapping purple cape and
pair of matching boots that would have embarrassed Elton
John in a duck costume, circa 1977. Far above our heads,
barely visible at the edge of the Sonny Bono Building,
the New Year's clock continued its relentless countdown
to the vaporization of my beloved posterior.

"Find out where those wires coming from the clock

go," I ordered the hovering jerk in yellow, who didn't seem to have a clue what specific superheroics to engage in without somebody screaming orders at him.

He whooshed off into the darkness, where he became a shadow occasionally illuminated by stabs of alternating blue, green, red and yellow floodlights. In those flashes when I could see him clearly, I watched him follow the wires from the clock (which I could no longer see counting down to my imminent vaporization) down from the side of the Sonny Bony Building to the dome of the opera house.

Both Minus and I reached the edge of the dome at the same time but were on different sides. Behind me, Senorita Tamale clomped breathless onto the roof, spied the two of us over at the dome, and hustled over on absurd footwear to join us.

"Over here!" Minus called, waving to me and the senorita. We ran to join the great dimwit around the back of the dome.

The multicolored floodlights only illuminated the front of the dome, and the rear was a battle between shadow and ambient city light. It was bright enough that it was now impossible to miss the pair of wires that ran down from the skyscraper. Up close, the wires were red and blue once more and they led into a closed trapdoor beside the dome.

Rather than mightily tear apart the locked trapdoor, Minus hesitated.

"This is destroying private property," he ventured, biting his lip. "I know these are maybe special circumstances, but could we...*I* get in trouble for breaking it?"

"Yes, I think it is vitally important that we sit down on this roof right now and ponder all the possible legal ramifications." I looked up at the roof of the adjacent building, and found that from this fresh angle I could see the New Year clock once more. "Of course, we'll have to hurry, as we only have twenty-five minutes to contact my bloated, crooked attorneys at Shyster, Pilfer and Fraud before the radioactive remains of Senorita Tamale and I will need to be sifted into a business envelope and mailed for booking to the nearest police station that, unlike all the ones in this city, won't be a smoking, radioactive crater in less than a half-hour. Or, hell, for a change of pace we could do something the *opposite* of stupid and see how that works out."

I pulled out my gat, blasted a couple of holes around the lock, and flipped the trapdoor wide open. It slapped back hard onto the roof.

My method of forced entry had an unintended, additional benefit, which was that it had managed to shoot the hell out of one of mad Dr. Cohen's machine gun-toting henchmen who had been stinking up the alcove beneath the trapdoor.

I'd clipped the bastard in the shoulder. The big baby was lying in the corner, clutching at his bleeding shoulder and asking for his parole officer as Senorita Tamale and I climbed down into the tunnel and hustled past him. Minus floated down on angel's wings, apologizing to our would-be murderer and vowed to call an ambulance if the need for one wasn't obviated by the fact of us all being dead in twenty-four minutes.

The pair of shifty red and blue wires snaked down through the narrow hallway, which led to a catwalk above the stage.

Far below, a bunch of fatsos in Viking helmets were waddling around the stage screaming at one another in German. I hoped they all had the choreography down pat. A lot of them were carrying spears, and if one of the starring lard-asses tripped and harpooned a Zeppelin in the chorus, the ensuing explosion of pretzels and knockwurst would be a hell of a lot worse than some sissy atomic blast.

I don't speak German, never having lived in goddamn Paris, but it wasn't hard to get the gist of what was going on in *Die Hoppy Nazi*. The facades of a bunch of hollow V-2 rockets were arranged along the rear of the stage, and the fattest dame of all was gooey-eyed as she screamed her heart out, as well as about a gallon of phlegm, at a picture of Wernher von Braun.

The wires from the countdown clock ran down the catwalk and into the back of the second phony V-2, in which was secreted a silver casing covered in blinking lights.

"Ees that the nucleus bums?" Senorita Tamale whispered.

"That would most definitely be the nucleus bums," I replied, not whispering since nothing short of a nucleus blast would be audible to the rest of the hall as long as the fat kraut dame in the bull's horns helmet on stage continued to shriek bloody murder from her extraordinarily vast and terrifying mouth hole.

"I'll go down and get it," Minus volunteered, trying to sound heroic.

I grabbed the moron's bicep before he could hop the railing, fly down, and get everybody killed, with the exception of his own super, presumably nuke-resistant ass.

"You're one hundred percent sure there is absolutely no way that the city is going to give this Dr. Cohen everything he asked for?"

"The five hundred million isn't so much of a problem," Minus said, "but the chief of police told me that it's up to the opera board who gets spaces out front, and that they're really snooty, and that when the mayor called them their chairman told him that the board only takes up new business on every second Tuesday of the month."

I shifted my fedora back on my forehead and sighed. "Okay, then we have only one option. *Two* options, if you count the one where we take the nuke and stuff it up the tailpipe of the opera board chairman's goddamn Rolls Royce."

I was the only proponent of plan B, and I was consequently voted down two to one by the raised hands of my parochial companions.

Plan A was less satisfying, but did have the possible outcome of me not dying along with the opera board director, Senorita Tamale and the rest of the city.

And so three minutes later, with plan A the lousy but democratically unavoidable strategy of the day, Senorita Tamale and I stepped down from the last of the long network of ladders which we'd climbed down to reach the backstage area like a pair of wheezing, aging zoo chimps who were this close to being given up for lion food.

The stage crew wore earmuffs to muffle the racket out front. The fat dame was bending the creaking boards at center stage as she continued to emit a heartfelt blast of what sounded to my Visigoth's ears like a mouthful of garbage truck tipping over.

Clearly culture was thriving in our great metropolis. The Luciano Mankowitz Opera House seated five thousand. It had been paid for with mounds of tax dollars and was maintained with big bucks tax breaks from a succession of administrations. *Die Hoppy Nazi* had done a gangbusters job on attendance compared to most cultural events in town by managing to pack in just under two dozen opera victims. The attendees were scattered around the large auditorium wearing either plastered smiles or looks of intense fascination, lest some member of the opera board happen to look over and catch them tearing their playbill into strips and stuffing the wadded-up pieces in their aching ears.

"Do ju see heem?" Senorita Tamale asked.

I had my eye up to a sliver in the curtain and was peering out at the audience. There were a couple of white heads in the theater, but I didn't see the shock of snowy hair I'd glimpsed at the telephone company on the elusive, batshit-loonball Dr. Cohen.

"I assume he's either temporarily or permanently left town," I replied, shaking my head. "Temporarily if he gets what he wants and can return in triumph with a new parking space and his student loans paid off. We'll know it's permanent if that morbidly obese frauline's final bellowing shriek of the evening is followed by an armload of flowers, a large sausage pizza and a mushroom cloud."

In truth, there was no way of knowing specifically what class of maniac Dr. Cohen belonged to. He might have been the kind who would leave town to await the city's decisions on his demands, or he might have been the other kind who'd sit in the audience with a detonator in his hand ready to cut loose with a hydrogen hissy-fit. My words of comfort were for Senorita Tamale, who was stuck with the first stage of plan A.

I had to hand it to her, the dame didn't shrink from blind terror like a sensible person. She left my side, ducked down a nearby staircase, and a moment later emerged through a side door and began walking across the front of the hall and up the center aisle.

Even if he was not at the opera house, Dr. Cohen was most likely monitoring the events in town from his lair away from home. An opera buff would have more than likely placed cameras out front to watch what was potentially the final show of this or any season, especially with his real-live bomb planted up on stage amongst the phonies.

Given the fact that he'd messengered me a note to back off, the diabolical doctor evidently knew me. If my mug had appeared in the audience at the opera, it might have been curtains for the entire city. He'd seen Senorita Tamale as well, but she'd mostly been one of a vast army of telephone operators to whom he'd prescribed hypnopills, so one of those faces, even one as flawless as hers, would be lost in the crowd.

I took as a positive sign the fact that we weren't all vaporized the instant Senorita Tamale made her debut in the opera hall.

She reached the midpoint of the center aisle, which was dead center in the hall, at what I guesstimated to be the fifteen minute point before the bomb was due to go off.

The telefono operator stopped in her tracks, tipped her head back, and let out a scream of rapid-fire words so loud and piercing that she even startled the fatso dame up onstage. The opera singer was so surprised that she made the mistake of jumping. The last anybody saw of her, she was doing a vanishing act through the massive hole her portly hooves had smashed through the stage. A cloud of displaced dust launched up from, I assumed, either the center of the Earth or China.

Senorita Tamale, who was still screaming like a lunatic, became the main opera attraction by default, and all eyes turned to her. Unfortunately, between the panic and enthusiasm, she'd neglected to flip the LP in her brain over to English, and so all the stuff about nuclear holocaust she was supposed to be hollering at the crowd was coming out as full-throated, rapid-fire and completely nonsensical Spanish-lite.

An opera fan tried to get her to autograph his playbill

and she stuffed it in his mouth, which got a smattering of applause.

I could tell by the look of incomprehension on her face that Senorita Tamale was utterly baffled that no one seemed to care about her apocalyptic screaming. What she failed to realize was that these were opera fans, and therefore were accustomed to women screeching unintelligible horrors at them in a foreign language.

When I felt a sudden gust of wind at my back I knew that it didn't matter.

I spotted a streak of yellow tearing over the heads of the performers who were still arranged around the massive hole at center stage, the curtains on either side of the stage shook loose clouds of fine dust, and I heard a faint whoosh that was barely audible over the clanging orchestra and the screaming madwoman flapping her arms in the main aisle.

At the rear of the stage, the second prop V-2 rocket wobbled very slightly back and forth, seemingly of its own volition, as if somebody had left a door open on a draft.

I didn't even see the yellow streak disappear back up into the rafters. I was only aware that the blur had reversed course when the blue and red wires that had run down to the stage were suddenly no longer hanging down from the catwalk.

I counted down our prearranged ten seconds in my head.

I added another minute, because Senorita Tamale was on the screeching roll of a lifetime, and I didn't want to ruin her chances of a Spanish Golden Globe Award.

I added another dozen seconds for the hell of it.

I added one more second to think about my ex-wife, at which point I didn't much care if the whole damn world was incinerated.

I took a loving, last swig from my hip flask, one deep breath, and then ran out onto the stage like the loony bin's answer to Helen Hayes.

"The management regrets the nuclear bomb that's about to blow everybody sky high," I hollered. "Everyone who doesn't want to spend the rest of the opera season as a radioactive puddle should haul his or her fat ass down to the parking garage!"

To punctuate the importance of my announcement, I hopped dramatically down into the orchestra pit and nearly busted my leg on a timpanist.

No one enjoyed screaming at strangers more than Senorita Tamale. (Nor, for that matter, at friends, close relatives, telephone company customers, chipmunks, water fountains, malfunctioning appliances, tardy city buses, and at every noun one can shake an irate Spanish fist at.) However, the instant she heard me yell, the lovely senorita clammed up, spun around, kicked off her insane shoes, inadvertently knocked some guy in the first row out cold with a cannon-launched ludicrous right heel, and ran on fleet, bare feet back over to the door next to the stage.

The rest of the hall might not have paid attention to my hollered command if not for my hilarious, neck-breaking pratfall into the orchestra pit. In the moment immediately after I plummeted off the stage, the musicians ceased abusing their instruments. In the ensuing, abrupt silence that enveloped the opera house, there came a sudden, faraway boom. There was no dismissing the sound as a car backfiring. Atomic explosions have their own unique, terrifying noise; a fact I would have happily staggered to my premature grave never knowing. It was a sound I felt in my hair and in the soles of my shoes.

I wasn't sure if my appearance had triggered the bomb, if Minus grabbing it and fleeing the building with it had set it off, or if the New Year's clock had finally counted down to zero. At that point why no longer mattered.

"*Door, door, door, door, goddamn door!*" I yelled at Senorita Tamale as I clambered up out of the orchestra pit. I was already sprinting like mad, and I barely paused to shake a piccolo out of my pant leg and kick an autoharp from around my ankle as I booked it for stage right in the company of the lovely senorita.

The panicked orchestra dropped their instruments, achieving their sweetest racket of the evening, and fled the pit like termites escaping a tented condominium.

The seated opera patrons who'd refused to budge mere moments before were suddenly stampeding over one another, joined by the fat flood of obese singers who were thundering down from the stage in a reckless, jiggling dash for the stage door exit.

I'd sprinted past Senorita Tamale, and so I was first to the door. I got her safely through and immediately surrendered my doorman gig to the rampaging mob.

Two hundred men and women in tuxedoes and Viking helmets swarmed in behind us and raced in our wake to the stairs marked "parking garage," a sign I'd spotted from the catwalk above the stage while I was hatching this moronic scheme.

Although, even I had to admit that as moronic schemes went, we seemed to be pulling this one off. Senorita Tamale had offered a distraction, reverting as expected to her native quasi-Spanish so nobody would know what the hell she was ranting about. If Dr. Cohen was watching, the dame had bought the time Minus had needed to supersonic down, snatch the bomb and zoom it out the roof trapdoor. That we weren't clouds of glowing dust in the bombed-out ruins of a taxpayer boondoggle opera house meant that Minus had made it far enough away to spare us the worst of the initial blast.

"Eef the bums has gone off and we are not dead, why is we running?" Senorita Tamale panted as we continued to do just that, down a flight of stairs, through a subterranean tunnel and to a door marked "Parking Level 1."

The deafening sound of hundreds of stomping, trailing feet echoed down the stairs and through the narrow concrete corridor at our backs.

"Radiation can do amazing things," I replied as casually as was possible with my overtaxed heart getting ready to explode in my chest while my burning lungs rebelled against the whole impromptu workout by trying to flee up my throat. "However, for the creation of every single super-powered rocket man or justifiably vengeful fifty-foot woman, there are about a million more individuals who merely get very sick and then drop permanently dead. We are statistically far more likely to fall into the latter category."

I found the stairwell inside the parking garage, and I led the charge to the second level down. There were no cars, since most of the city was more sensible than I gave it credit for and consequently there were scarcely any opera patrons. Everybody who'd used the on-site facilities had parked on the upper level of the parking garage or in the reserved spaces in the street out front which were so coveted by the opera board.

Once the last pair of Viking horns was through the steel door, I slammed it shut.

All told, it had taken about thirty seconds for me and Senorita Tamale to reach what was hopefully the safety of the buried parking garage two stories beneath the city. The last stragglers from the woodwind section and the fattest dainty German maidens had managed to waddle through the door a respectable three minutes later.

The evacuation had gone smoothly, the opera house hadn't been leveled, only three fat slob opera screamers appeared to be in the process of enjoying cardiac arrests, and I was pretty sure mine and Senorita Tamale's heroics had saved everybody from the risk of sprouting flippers and twelve eyes from contact with nuclear fallout.

I took approximately two whole seconds to catch my breath and pat myself on the back for a job well done.

And then there was a roar like an incoming mortar blast, the center of the parking garage ceiling collapsed, the foundation of the Earth shook beneath our feet, and cement and twisted rebar dropped through the hole along with an Audi and two BMWs.

Through the middle of all the rest of the junk which exploded through the newly-blasted opening shot an unconscious mound of glowing yellow Spandex, which slammed like a cannon-launched bowling ball into the blacktop twenty yards away from my merry band of fatso evacuees and, presumably, because it would be just my crummy luck, immediately went to work nullifying my previous few minutes of unparalleled bravery by irradiating the hell out of -- which would eventually kill, because why stop the fun there? -- us all.

11

An hour later I was sitting on the bumper of a SWAT truck and refusing a steaming Styrofoam cup of crummy coffee from some do-gooder Red Cross dame wearing the phony concerned smile of a cold sore model on an anti-herpes billboard. Her shallow smile vanished and she gave me a look like I'd just dug something out of my ear and asked for a knife and fork when, in fact, all I'd done was unearth my hip flask from my pocket.

"I don't figure we've ever met, since I doubt I'd forget such a transparently insincere smirk, so you're unaware of my lifelong reputation, established in kindergarten with Frankie Spaulding's bloody nose over a playtime fire truck, of steadfastly refusing to share what I got," I told her as she hovered in front of me resolutely clinging to both her cup of unwanted java and a newly minted, heartfelt disapproving glare. I held out the flask to her nose so that she could see her own appalled reaction in the gleaming silver, then drew it away. "Get loaded on your own dime, Pollyanna."

"Well, I never," she said, proving that some dames still said "well, I never."

She rolled her little cart of coffee cups away, and I bid her a fond adieu by toasting her retreating ass with a hearty hit from my flask.

"I forgot how ju *always* go out of jour way to offend people, Banyon," said Senorita Tamale. She was leaning her rear end on the lucky bumper next to me, wrapped in a police-issued blanket and looking lovely, disheveled, alluring and annoying.

"I don't *need* to go out of my way, sister. More than enough offensive people seem to know my zip code by heart."

For the first time in the million years I'd known her, the dame didn't flex her throat and launch into a three-alarm argument. The night we'd just been through had wrung the fight out of her like slimy water from a moldy dishrag.

It was closing in on midnight. The New Year's clock on the Sonny Bono Building was no longer up there keeping inaccurate time. After grabbing the nuke, Minus had flown straight up past the clock, grabbed the digital countdown to Armageddon under his free arm, and taken both bomb and timer high up into the atmosphere.

From what I'd been told, the explosion had been mediocre. Too far away to impress like Fourth of July fireworks, not close enough to make anybody jump in their easy chairs like they would for a firecracker in the mailbox.

The blast hadn't even been low enough in the atmosphere to screw around with electronics, so most people were informed about it a half-hour later on their TVs. By the time they wandered outside to stare up into the night sky, all that was left was the moon, a wash of ambient city light that wiped away any trace of the stars, and a little low-level radiation that was no worse than thawing a frozen bagel in the microwave.

That hadn't stopped city and state officials from descending on the area around the opera house with more Geiger counters than Hans Geiger himself could have counted in a month of radioactive Sundays. When they found nothing interesting that was going to murder everybody in the air, they concentrated their beeping firepower on Minus.

The Savior of the City had gotten the full force of the atomic blast somewhere up in the ionosphere. The explosion had knocked him out cold and sent him on a rocket ride straight back to the loving embrace of the opera house.

If I stood on my toes I could just see the sticking-up conch shell dome and the ragged hole the falling bastard had punched through it. It was a clean break, straight through the roof, the stage and two levels of parking garage.

When the paramedics fished him out of the hole, Minus had been babbling something about "animal yields" and apologizing for not wiping his feet.

It took a couple of minutes for the dazed clod to come around. The government bigwigs had been worried that he was emitting a ton of radiation, since he was throwing off more heat than Michelle Pfeiffer and was glowing brighter than a Crest smile. But the Geiger counters remained silent as they passed the devices around him. Eventually, the glow faded and a faint smell of lilacs permeated the air.

It turned out that amongst his superpowers was the previously unknown ability to absorb a massive amount of radiation and convert it to a delicate floral scent, which was a gift that would come in handy in a Japanese men's room. When he'd tossed the bomb into outer space, he'd also inadvertently managed to blow up an invading Moon Man saucer. Homeland Security was fishing little green bastard bodies out of the ocean a mile offshore. There was apparently nothing that Minus touched that didn't turn to good press, which in and of itself was reason enough to hate the son of a bitch.

The Savior of the Goddamn City was off being interviewed in front of a bunch of TV cameras in front of his borrowed, double-parked cab that had already gathered a couple of parking tickets under the windshield wiper. He was far enough away that I didn't have to hear the fawning of the press, but I could see him holding up the palms of his purple gloves as he modestly deflected some suck-up comment.

"Have you noticed that when it comes time to passing around the credit, he doesn't seem quite as generous as his carefully cultivated media persona?" I said.

"Ju told him if he mentioned ju to the presses, ju were going to stuff Kryptonite down his Froosts of the Loomses," Senorita Tamale replied.

"Not a hollow threat," I said, nodding. "Although I don't think he would have asked us to the prom even if we hadn't already told him we were staying home to wash our unmentionables. Still, I wouldn't bet he won't screw up and try to drag us in front of the cameras, despite what we told him. He's an idiot, after all. I recommend we sneak out of here and get to work on those unmentionables I mentioned."

A familiar voice chimed in behind me, since fate hadn't already shafted me with a perfect enough shit-tastic night.

"Not so fast, Banyon."

Detective Daniel Jenkins was a lousy cop but would have made a great jungle cat, what with his unerring ability to sneak up behind prey. On the other hand, PETA would have had his scalp for irritating a gazelle as frequently and thoroughly as he did me. Jenkins was holding his notebook and pen as, for the second time in less than twenty-four hours, he nabbed me and Senorita Tamale hiding out behind a SWAT truck.

"I just want to clear up a few things in your witness statement," the flatfoot said.

"If you want it clear, soak it in Visine, detective. I'm off the clock."

Senorita Tamale jabbed me in the ribs with such uncharacteristic gentleness that she probably only cracked two. "Banyon," she warned.

The dame was dog tired, and so was I. It was now just after midnight, today had abruptly become tomorrow, and we both just wanted to get the hell out of there.

"I don't have the energy to go through everything that's confusing you, Jenkins. Can you just pick the biggest thing and get back to me tomorrow with the rest?"

I had been very careful to avoid including my fingerprints on any of the property damage that had gone on that night.

Minus was the one who had carted the bomb and New Year's countdown clock into the heavens, and he was the one who'd crashed through the roof of the opera house. The only thing they might have had me on was the busted trapdoor I'd shot out to get inside, as well as the thug with the slug in his shoulder, but for a change I'd lucked out with both. The roof door had been smashed beyond recognition and flung halfway across town when Minus had blasted up through the trapdoor exit with the nuke. When it came flipping down end-over-end, it bisected a tree, a parked Prius, and a poodle over on Walnut Avenue. As for Dr. Cohen's henchman, the guy with the slug in his arm had vanished. So, provided Minus kept his yap shut, I was golden on both fronts.

Jenkins pressed us for ten minutes, but neither I nor, to her credit, Senorita Tamale cracked. We'd both just been spectators, dragged along for the ride in a flying taxicab, who'd done the good citizen act and pitched in at the risk of our own hides only at the very end to selflessly save everybody in the auditorium.

"At this very moment, somebody over in Iceland is writing a saga to our great bravery, Detective Jenkins," I said, once the cop was through grilling us. "If they turn it into an opera, I'll score you some tickets. As of tonight I've got about fifty tons worth of banshees who owe me a big, fat favor."

Jenkins was the opposite of thrilled as he angrily stowed away his notebook and pen in the breast pocket of his cheap suit. "Don't leave town, Banyon," he ordered.

"Ju esta estupido," Senorita Tamale snapped, in her peculiar, non-Spanish Spanish dialect. The dame shoved her rear end off the bumper of the SWAT truck so fiercely that it rocked on its shocks. "I do not feel well. I will be over at the ambulance."

The senorita dropped her police blanket and clomped away from Jenkins on the huge high heels which she'd gotten the fire department to rescue from the ruins of the opera house after screaming for five minutes that they'd cost her three week's salary and two cashed-in savings bonds from her *quinceañera*.

"Well, her Spanish is technically nothing but strung-together nonsense," I told Jenkins, "but I do agree with the fiery passion with which her gibberish was delivered. Before you go and as long as you're here harassing innocent, upstanding citizens, you might as well fill me in on Dr. Cohen. Has anybody heard from him since all this?" I waved a finger in the air in the vague direction of the nuclear fallout.

I probably could have found out most everything on the TV at O'Hale's or in tomorrow's *Gazette*, and it was clear the flatfoot didn't like the chummy relationship Minus had forced him into with me. Jenkins glanced over at Minus, who was wrapping up his impromptu press conference, and decided the fight wasn't worth the headache.

"He issued a statement on the Internet," the cop grunted, shrugging his shoulders and adjusting the cuffs of his rain-coat. "Said he's not happy that we didn't keep our appointment to die and that he was going to reschedule."

"Far be it from me to tell you how to do your job," I said, "but somebody ought to before the whole town is forcibly relocated to Neptune. One of Cohen's demands was a primo parking space at the opera, which probably means he's a patron. I intend to follow up on that angle, but given the unlimited taxpayer-funded resources at your disposal (including three police helicopters, twelve police catamarans, and your new giraffe mascot, Mr. Spot), I don't mind bringing you in, even if it means running the risk of slipping on a puddle of doughnut jelly and busting my hip."

"We've already *been* searching the opera's attendance records, ticket purchases, and interviewing eyewitnesses from the manager down to the ticket booth attendants."

Jenkins stopped, leaving a smug silence to stink up the lilac-scented air.

"So did you find a match?" he forced me to ask.

"Yeah, Banyon, your face and my ass." The flatfoot flashed a smirk of parental pride at the birth of his third-grade putdown.

"I suppose it's at least nice to know that the Almighty awarded you a handsome posterior after the curse of that ugly mug he shafted you with," I replied.

He was suddenly a teapot that was sending out steam from every orifice, but if this was to be the time that Jenkins finally removed his revolver and put a hot lead period on my piercing wit, we'd never know.

Minus selected that nick-of-time moment to whoosh over and land in a flurry of purple cape instead of just walking over like a goddamn normal person.

"Hello, Detective Jenkins," the loudmouth boomed. "Were your men able to find Dr. Cohen through the opera house records?"

Jenkins paled. He turned red. He paled again. He turned a shade of purple not too far off from Minus' disco-era boots.

I smiled, which managed to shove the needle from purple to maroon.

"Yes, Detective Jenkins. Were your men able to find out what my pal here just asked? Or -- wait? -- were they even able to find the opera house? It's that big building right there with the hole in the roof and the poster out front of the obese Valkyrie in the steel Texas Longhorn bonnet screaming at a spear. Turn right at that gum wrapper. You can't miss it."

"We found nothing, *Minus*," Jenkins replied, once he realized that the super jackass was looking for more of an answer than dumb silence broken up by the squeaking of grinding molars. "There are Dr. Cohens who are season ticket holders, but none match the description. Although we don't have much to go on. Just the white hair, which a lot of these opera watchers have. None of the employees were helpful."

"I can't, Jenkins, assume that I'm stating the obvious (since, after all, you're a moron), but *all* the Cohens who are ticket holders should be checked out, not just the M.D.'s."

The flatfoot didn't even look at me. He answered me directly at Minus. "We're doing that right now."

"I'm sure the dedicated men and women of our local

police force will make every effort to track down this fiend," Minus said, hitching his thumbs in the band of his purple underwear and shoving his chin heroically skyward.

"God, you never switch it off, do you?" I said. "Hey, as long as we're all pals here -- notwithstanding the fact that one of us can't stand the other two -- I've got a favor I'd like you, Minus, to ask our dedicated buddy Detective Jenkins. I'd ask him myself, but I think if it came from you there would be less of a chance that the answer would be me getting deloused and tossed in the drunk tank for a week."

"Of course," Minus said. "I'm sure Detective Jenkins will give you all the assistance you need in this case, isn't that right, detective?"

The super-powered Cub Scout wasn't applying pressure and it definitely wasn't a threat. He sincerely meant every word. In fact, he asked the question with such utter goddamn sincerity that before I left the scene I intended to stop for a bottle of Maalox at the ambulance behind which Senorita Tamale was at that very moment standing as an EMT ran a beeping Geiger counter around her Latin curves like a Formula One racecar.

"The department's stated policy is to aid the superhero Minus in every way possible, and as liaison officer it is my responsibility to see to it that he has the necessary departmental cooperation and tools to succeed in his noble mission to make our city a better and safer place."

It was easier for Jenkins to give a monotone recital of the pledge his bosses must have hollered at him not to screw up than it was to just say yes.

The cop had a glazed look in his eyes and was staring off at nothing in particular as he rattled off the hollow words.

Minus and Jenkins more than likely thought my favor involved nuclear terrorist and all-around bad egg Dr. Cohen. I didn't have the heart to tell them it was for a lousy little cheating spouse case but, hey, Mrs. Johnny Johnson had paid her bill upfront, too, and since a bomb had unfortunately not leveled the city and wiped out the loving Johnson family, I was still stuck working that other case.

"I need you to check a couple of phone calls for me," I said. "You'll have to be at work for this one, Jenkins. I'll call you tomorrow with the details."

"I would be happy to help," Jenkins said. "I'll talk to you soon, Minus."

The flatfoot turned as if he had too much starch in the pants of his cheap suit and walked woodenly off, but when he got about ten feet away a great shudder overcame him. His shoulders sank, and he took a few shallow puffs of air as if recovering from a punch to the solar plexus, before his back stiffened once more and he marched off to be completely incompetent in some other corner of the opera house complex.

The departure of Detective Jenkins marked the return of Senorita Tamale, who had just walked over from the open back of the ambulance.

"You okay?" I asked, proving once and for all in two of the most caring words she'd ever heard plummet from my mouth that I was a spectacular date and not the callous bastard she'd claimed I was when she clobbered me with that piano stool.

"I am fine," she said, angrily snatching up the blanket she'd dropped on the sidewalk before she'd stormed over to the ambulance, and flinging it furiously at (and nearly smothering in the process) the startled Red Cross dame who'd made the mistake of choosing that moment to walk back by us. As soon as she'd tossed away the blanket, she started visibly shivering. Her face flashed to anger and she immediately decided against surrendering her blanket. She snatched it back, spinning the Red Cross dame around like a top and sending a dozen paper cups of cold coffee splattering across the sidewalk and blacktop. The entire crazy act took a grand total of five seconds.

The dizzy Red Cross worker staggered off as Senorita Tamale shrugged the blanket back around her shoulders as if her behavior was perfectly normal and justifiable and not that of a violent schizophrenic, which was pretty much the definition of a schizophrenic. But, in her defense, she really did have an amazing rack.

"Are ju going to take us home?"

She posed the snarling question to Minus, but he didn't hear a word she said since he was already talking over her.

"Oh, dear. Oh, no. I've got to go. I'll be in touch, Mr. Banyon."

He was already airborne before he'd finished his panicked babbling. The truck at our backs rocked like a boat on rough seas, and a network of fine cracks appeared in the sidewalk where he'd been standing. He was quickly a bright yellow dot that zipped through the illuminated canyon between the tallest downtown skyscrapers.

Minus cleared the buildings, and the yellow dot became a bright streak that vanished like a reverse-falling star across the night sky.

"He going to just dumps us here?" Senorita Tamale demanded.

"I believe he has somewhere else he needs to be," I replied.

I'd kept a beady eye on Minus, and the last thing he'd been looking at before he'd taken off was the clock on the front of a real estate office across the street. I figured the dope hadn't realized the fallout from his heroics had dragged past midnight. There was likely something pressing on the private side of his duel identity.

"Lucky for you, there is a 12:30 carriage that stops within strolling distance," I said, looping my arm gallantly around the senorita's. "And by carriage I, of course, mean a reeking, wino-infested city bus. I hope you have enough exact change for both of us."

We were walking off arm-in-arm into the romantic, radioactive fog when a voice so phony and fragile that it could have been constructed from matrimonial lies chimed in from the open door of the nearby ambulance.

"Excuse me! Excuse me. Woo!"

The manager of what was now the ruins of the Luciano Mankowitz Opera House came scrambling down out of the back of the ambulance and hustled over in the tatters of his Christian Dior tuxedo.

"I am *so* glad I spotted you," he said, taking my free elbow and leading me and Senorita Tamale away from an apparently invisible horde of eavesdroppers. "That little matter we discussed before all this unpleasantness? The--" He dropped his voice to a barely audible sibilant whisper. "--*bike messenger*? We're saying that happened as a result of all this. Insurance purposes. There were chandeliers falling all over the lobby when Minus crash-landed, and who's to say it didn't come down on that poor young fellow's head then? It's just, well, Death is so elusive, and he never shows up when you expect him to and *soooo* often seems to do so when you don't. It's tidier this way."

"I think I speak for the senorita when I say we don't give a shit," I said. "Plus I happen to hate both bike messengers and insurance companies, so defraud away."

The little twerp's face brightened so much it was clear

we'd made his night which, in his defense, must have been crummier than even a normal night at the opera.

He released my elbow, but it was my turn to grab his before he could trot back to the ambulance to scrounge up some free samples of amyl nitrite.

"Hey, before you mince off, did Death happen to say he was heading to O'Hale's Bar after he finished up here?"

"Oh, no, he didn't say where he was off to. But, then, he's always so mysterious, isn't he?" He stared into the ruins of his opera house and exhaled, clearly longing for Death's icy embrace. "He's been here many times in the past. We have so many elderly patrons, you see, and once you've passed one hundred it gets harder for the old dears to withstand the full impact of a twelve hour Austrian opera with no bathroom breaks. Of course, the lovely young bike messenger was only choking on a Granola bar…that is, before Death got all grand and artistically expressive with that chandelier."

The nuclear excitement portion of the evening had nudged the growing pile of deceased bike messengers off of my personal front page.

The neo-beatnik bastards were always turning up dead. Racing out in front of laundry trucks and tractor trailers perched atop a pair of desperately pumping hula hoops is as safe for an asshole human as it is for a running squirrel, with the major difference being that the squirrel's brain, not being pot-addled, at least tries to keep itself from getting squashed. But three dead bike messengers, all of them connected even tangentially to me, was probably a one-day city record.

"If he was only choking to start with, did anybody standing around to try to save him?" I asked. "I mean, taking into account that, yes, the birds sing more sweetly in the trees and an angel gets his wings every time a bike messenger snuffs it."

"Well, there simply wasn't the time, my dear," the opera house manager insisted. "Death was suddenly in our midst." He fluttered his fingers mysteriously in front of his face, as if the Grim Reaper had materialized out of the ether. "The girl at the booth let him in," he explained, ceasing all fluttering. "I asked him if he was at least going to try the Heimlich maneuver, but he told me not to tell him how to do his job. A bit rude, I thought, but that's celebrity for you. Actually, the first time I saw him... that was *years* ago when he stopped in to collect Mrs. Brazzo, a frail old dear and *terribly* wealthy supporter of the opera who suffocated between a pair of Carmens at a backstage cocktail benefit. Well, when I saw him way back then all dressed in that sexy black hood of his I thought he was *in* the show, didn't I? Ooh, but wouldn't it be a coup to get *the* Grim Reaper to trod our humble boards? The box office would simply go M-A-D *mad*. But I don't know if the dear can sing. I can't have a repeat of that disaster of epic proportions from last season. Nicolas Cage in *Rigoletto. Cringe*."

"Let's go, Banyon," Senorita Tamale insisted. "I am freezing."

She was wrapped up tight in her blanket and, although she was visibly shivering, her face was covered in a sheen of sweat.

I held up a staying finger which, uncharacteristically, she didn't try to snap off.

"One final thing," I said. "Who was the messenger delivering a note to?"

In all the merry calamity the manager had evidently forgotten all about the bike messenger's message. He reached in his pocket and pulled out an envelope.

"Nobody I know," he said, shrugging as he handed

over the message. "Certainly not one of our patrons. Keep it as a memento, my dear. Whoever he is, he's not picking his mail up here. We're closed for business."

He abandoned us and headed up the broad steps of the opera house, slipping through the shattered remains of the front doors.

Senorita Tamale stood beside me, wrapped in her horse blanket and tapping one gigantic hoof as if she was counting to one hundred by twos.

"The autobus will be here in un poquito momento," she insisted, completely ruining actual Spanish for the rest of us. "If ju wants to stay, stay. *I* am going."

She didn't give me a chance to argue, which had been her lifetime M.O. ever since that first day when she out-screamed all her maternity ward nurses. She left me curbside and marched down the sidewalk in the direction of the bus stop.

I flipped the envelope over in my hand to read the name printed neatly on the front. When I read it, I gave the envelope another 360 degree flip just in case the name that had revealed itself wanted to change into something that made more sense.

No dice. Same name as the first time.

Johnny J. Johnson

I tore open the envelope and slipped out the note. It read, in its entirety:

Watch it, Johnson.

Way up at the top of the single sheet of paper was the letterhead with which I was already intimately familiar. *From the Desk of Dr. Cohen*. The same oddly designed *O* in "Cohen" with the peculiar bumps arranged within it strummed once more some tripwire of memory in the back of my brain, but I couldn't place it for all the tea in China. I figured I'd have a better chance accessing the mysterious subconscious memory if I utilized a more palatable tonic than limey lemonade.

"And if all the bourbon in O'Hale's doesn't jar it loose," I informed a nearby interested fire hydrant, "at the very least I will forget everything else about all this, the goddamn worst day of my life."

I slipped into my pocket the second threatening note from Dr. Cohen to enter my sphere that day; this one, for some baffling reason, intended for the boring, possibly philandering banker husband of hot-to-trot Client #1, and I trotted lukewarmly down the sidewalk to my awaiting sizzling senorita and the arrival of a smoke-belching city bus.

12

Dawn didn't break so much as shatter across the cold cityscape. Shards of unwelcome daylight scattered first across rooftops, then managed a molasses-slow crawl down the sides of stoic buildings which hadn't asked for an end to the tranquil slumber of a peaceful urban night but which, like the rest of us, were stuck with crossing out yet another worthless date on the same worn-out calendar the whole lousy world shared.

The light descended further as the city shook off the cloak of darkness for one last, game go of it before the full weekend at last kicked in and the baying universe could be locked outside for at least one miserable day.

The horror of rejuvenating daylight finally clawed its way deep enough into the crevices of the city to unearth me hiding out in the back of a grimy cab parked across and down the street from the Johnson residence.

After leaving the opera house the night before and the ensuing bus ride to nowhere, Senorita Tamale had begged off my usually infallible charms with a hearty slap to the mush, and so it was that I'd stumbled in through and, eventually, out of the door of O'Hale's solo, the latter after the dump had closed for the night.

I'd managed to find a hack desperate enough for the

cash he didn't know I didn't have in my wallet that he was willing to pick me up in the crummy neighborhood where O'Hale's was sloughing off its most faithful inebriates and ferry me over to the even crummier West Side.

At least there weren't any gangs of roaming punks dancing and singing in the dying hours of night before just before dawn. I'd read in the arts section of the *Gazette* (which some wino at the bus station had been using as a blanket) that the toughest gang members always got home to their lofts by two most nights in order to soak their feet and wrap their throats in hot towels to prepare for the next night's teenaged urban warfare.

The only gang activity I'd encountered as I slumped in the backseat of my cab was a lone punk singing his heart out about some dame while doing a little modified, modern ballet down a double yellow line. The cops had swarmed out of nowhere with nightsticks and beat him into the back of a paddy wagon. Kid would probably never dance again, so at least there was that little bit of good news in an otherwise rotten night.

The Grim Reaper had come and gone at O'Hale's before I'd returned after midnight, unencumbered in the post-opera house hour by Senorita Tamale. Jaublowski swore up and down that he'd informed the skull-headed bastard I wanted to talk to him, but who knew if he'd truly gotten around to it? Most of the time while I'd been there the barkeep had been so distracted from his booze-peddling duties that I'd had to fire stale peanuts at the back of his head just to get him to top off my glass.

Turned out the animal Ed had pegged with his .22 earlier in the evening was a Lorax. The homely little flea-bags sometimes wander in from the suburbs looking for a condemned tree to chain themselves to. They claim it's the environment, but the only thing they really care about is the free press and the dimwit college dames that come along with it. Furry, tree-hugger bastards can't keep their pelts zipped. This one had made the mistake of hauling his hippie, "no such thing as personal property" bullshit into O'Hale's and had learned the fatal way that Ed Jaublowski guarded my booze as if it was his own, and as if he had the receipts to prove it.

Jaublowski had worked a con on one of my fellow frequent O'Hale's patrons, Marvin Sturpin, an elderly basket case who owned Dead to the World, the ramshackle taxidermy shop on the corner. The barkeep had convinced Marvin to stuff and mount the Lorax in exchange for a few nights of free intoxication, to which Marvin, who was a raging alcoholic and whose rundown shop hadn't seen a customer since the mummified Hobbit craze died down a decade ago, had eagerly agreed.

The pair of them had spent most of my time overnight at O'Hale's arguing over a bowl of Lorax entrails at the end of the bar. On a scale of 1 to 10, it rated about a 3 as one of the worst nights I'd ever spent at O'Hale's. (Nothing would ever beat that 10 night five years back when Jaublowski accidentally flipped the TV over from a hockey game to the Demon Graveyard Channel and a young, black-and-white Shirley Temple escaped from an old movie and started tap dancing on the bar and tearing out the throats of a bunch of visiting Shriners by the cigarette machine. I hate tap dancing.)

Despite the fact that the first warming rays of sun had finally reached over the shadow of the building under which my cab was parked, the cold had started seeping back into my extremities. Up in the front of my cab, the driver felt it as well. He wordlessly turned the engine back on to reheat the interior, as well as to warm up some stale breakfast baklava which he began arranging on the dashboard vents.

He'd been switching the taxi on and off ever since we'd parked down from the townhouse that banker Johnny J. Johnson shared with suspicious, independently wealthy knockout wife, Client #1, Gwendolyn Ice Princess Johnson.

I didn't know for sure what to make out of the note Dr. Cohen had sent to Johnson at the opera house via bike messenger the previous evening. I had a nascent suspicion that was shuffling toward becoming a hunch, but at the moment it was too clichéd to invest too much of my fatigued brainpower in it.

At that moment, it was the stationary on which the note had been printed that had me the most goddamn vexed.

I slipped the envelope addressed to Johnson from my pocket, slipped the letter from the envelope, and stared at it for the millionth time since midnight.

I was now absolutely convinced that I'd seen that stylized O in Cohen's name before. It was the only nonstandard letter in the entire embossed letterhead. The bumps were arranged around the interior of the O like the rounded nubs on a Stegosaurus.

In the wee hours I even had a crazy thought that he might be a doctor over in Dinosaur Town, but the parts I'd seen of Dr. Cohen were definitely human, and dinos are notorious about trusting only their own for medical treatment, even after most of them had been wiped out by the flu sixty-five million years ago. (The dinosaur kingdoms of Old Earth had topnotch medical care according to all the detailed prehistoric records, but their doctors were mostly Tyrannosaurus Rexes. When the outbreak hit, their stubby little arms couldn't keep up with the injections and complicated cotton swabbing.)

I shoved the opera house note intended for Johnson back in my pocket and waited for the blinds to go up on the front windows of the townhouse.

The upstairs bedroom was first. I caught sight of the wife in a negligee. Client #1 gave the neighborhood a good little peepshow for a minute as she examined the street. I was sure she spotted my cab three houses down before she drew away from the window.

I didn't see Johnny J. Johnson for another half-hour. The tired schlub appeared on the front steps at quarter past eight and hustled down to his old Dodge minivan.

"Follow that shit-heap," I instructed.

My cabbie turned the engine on yet again and we trailed Johnson across town to the downtown headquarters of the Panhandler Federal Ameribank.

The drab, gray bastard looked more drab and gray than usual as I snapped a couple of shots of him climbing out of his rusty crap-pile in the employee parking lot and trudging over to the main entrance.

It was a banker's half-day on Saturday, so according to the wife Johnson wouldn't be back home from work until twelve-thirty at the earliest. I made sure through the plate glass window that he was stranded behind his pathetic little desk before I instructed the cabbie to haul me back across town to the West Side.

We got stuck at an intersection thanks to some society dame who was taking her sweet time scooping up the scat her pet emu had deposited in the crosswalk, and when I checked my watch I realized there was a bird that wasn't on a diamond-studded leash that I could kill and not wind up with a hatpin in the throat.

"Pull over here," I ordered.

The hack drew up next to a sidewalk pay phone outside an upscale consignment store that specialized in used jodhpurs. I was lucky my driver took his time parked by the curb to flip the sausages he was cooking on the vents, and so did not see me scrounging around deep in my pockets to scrape up my last handful of change.

"Welcome to the Metro Police Department phone service," intoned the automated irritant on the other end of the line that made me long for the insulting pidgin English of real-live Senorita Tamale. "Your phone call is important to us. If you know your party's extension, please press one. If you do not know your party's extension, please press two. If this is an emergency, which includes but is not limited to life-threatening events such as illness, shock, pratfalls gone awry, purple nurples, evisceration and decapitation, please hang up and dial 911. If your hands have been bitten off, sawed, ripped, or otherwise removed or if your call has to do with general police business, press one or remain on the line and the next available dispatcher will ignore you for twenty minutes that will seem like two hours because of the music."

The answering machine played "Stop In the Name of Love" and "Every Breath You Take" in rotation for the next twelve hundred seconds while I fought the impulse to take out my piece and blow several large holes in the pay phone. Instead, I fed into it my last remaining change as well as, eventually, a button that was a perfect quarter shape which I excavated from the lining of my coat.

When a police operator finally wandered lazily onto the line, I quickly asked for Detective Daniel Jenkins at the Main Police Headquarters, Precinct #1 before the minutes on my button ran out.

As usual, the flatfoot was thrilled to hear my voice. I already had out the scrap of paper on which I'd jotted down the times of the two phone calls to the cops Johnny Johnson had placed from the Happy Hobo Motel, and I passed them on to my cop pal.

"I'm only doing this because the department expects us to cooperate with Minus, and *Minus* wants me to do this," Jenkins droned.

"I love you, too," I said.

Jenkins put me on hold with an angry grunt and a sterile click. He was gone too long for so simple a task, even for a moron like Dan Jenkins, and I was worried that the last few seconds of my button would bleed away to a dial tone when he finally came back on the line.

"I suppose you think you're a real laugh riot, Banyon," Jenkins said.

"It only seems that way because you provide such a rich vein of comic material, Detective Jenkins," I replied.

"Yeah. Hah-hah. There's a law against wasting police time."

There actually wasn't, but I wasn't able to inform him that he was as lousy at quoting local statutes as he was at all other aspects of police work because the rat bastard flatfoot hung up the goddamn phone in my ear.

I fished in the change return slot for my button but only found a wet wad of gum which wasn't mine so I left it there for its rightful owner.

When I dropped back into the rear of my cab I was puzzled, which wears about as well on me as chartreuse leg warmers, and I don't even know what the hell color chartreuse is. Maroon, maybe. The driver was basting a small roast pig over the dashboard vents, and I took him away from his culinary endeavors to get him to drive me back over to the Johnson place.

The wife opened the door before I could even knock.

"Good morning, Mr. Banyon."

Gwendolyn Johnson wasn't surprised in the least to

find me standing on her step. She was wearing a prim, calf-length gray skirt that hugged her keister like a koala wrapped around a eucalyptus trunk. A long-sleeved white blouse with only the top button unbuttoned, and hair drawn into an imperious bun completed the naughty librarian look.

The dame turned and marched away from the door, leaving me to shut it behind me before I followed her into the living room. She was already holding down the couch, legs crossed sharply, arms spread across the back of the cushions, ample bazooms pointed in my direction like a couple of libido-seeking missiles.

"I saw you follow my husband," she said. "You're not *always* so unsubtle, are you?"

"I'm sorry, I didn't hear you. I'm terrified that your impressive rack, which you've just obviously aimed at me to throw me off my guard, will pop a couple of zip gun buttons at my forehead. You were saying something about subtlety?"

She retracted her arms as well as her superior smirk.

"What did you learn about those telephone calls to the police, Mr. Banyon? Is my husband seeing a cheap little meter maid on the side?"

I noted that she had used exactly the same meter maid phrase, word for word, the night before at O'Hale's.

"There were some crossed wires with the cops where the calls are concerned," I said. "I'll have to check up on those later. For now, I'm wondering if you can help me out with a little something."

I fished in my pocket and pulled out the pair of envelopes that had been delivered by two of the three dead bike messengers who'd fallen into my gravitational field the previous day. I removed the notes from their respective envelopes and laid them out on the coffee table, side by side. Mine was a little difficult to assemble, since it was in large, jigsaw puzzle shapes after I'd accidentally torn it up on the table at O'Hale's the previous night, but both of the important sections were still there.

The dame leaned forward. Not so much as a single eyelash quivered as she scanned the pair of notes. When she was finished perusing my little show and tell, she gave me a chilly glance with her baby blues.

"Are these supposed to mean something to me?" she asked.

"I'd at least think you'd be curious why your husband would be getting private correspondence from the super-villain who tied the entire local phone system in knots yesterday afternoon and then tried to blow up the city with a nuclear bomb last night."

She leaned in again and drew close to her the note that had been sent to her husband, as if she'd failed to read the letterhead the first time around. Maybe she had. Maybe not. The dame was as cold as a Popsicle suppository and as unreadable as *Moby Dick*.

"Is this *that* Dr. Cohen?" she asked. "My God, what is Johnny mixed up in?"

I got the sense that she was trying to force a couple of drops out of her tear ducts, and I buttoned up my trench coat just in case a little freezing rain started firing out.

"I'm still not entirely sure," I said.

Spring came early that year. The veneer of ice abruptly thawed as the pent-up magma below the surface instantly cracked the glacier and burned off the rime.

"Isn't that what I'm *paying* you for, Mr. Banyon?" she demanded. She shoved her husband's Dr. Cohen note across the coffee table. "What do these even mean? Why do you and my husband both have one? I could very well ask you what *you're* mixed up in."

"I'm mixed up in a couple of cases that both look simple on the surface but which have more stumbles and twists than a drunk Slinky taking its pants off in the dark. Is your husband an opera fan, Mrs. Johnson?"

She shrugged the padded shoulders of her spotless white blouse. "We've been to the opera a few times. *Only* when there were free tickets available through Johnny's bank. Just last month we saw *Dueling Aidas* with Kirstie Alley and Roseanne Barr. *I* believe in expanding our cultural horizons."

"When you were hanging out at the lobby juice bar you didn't happen to rub elbows with a mad doctor by the name of Cohen?"

"*No*, Mr. Banyon," she insisted, "we most certainly did not. And, frankly, I don't know what this is all about. I'm paying you to follow my husband, not stand in my living room grilling me. Do you even have any idea where he is right now?"

I gathered up the notes and slipped them back in their respective envelopes. "He is safely, deeply mired in a tedious life which at this moment has him slouched behind a dull desk at a boring financial institution."

"Not *so* tedious," she insisted. She was on her feet and ushering me to the living room door. "There's still the matter of what he is up to at that motel. You still haven't found that out, and you've had a whole week. And now instead of that, you bring me something about this Dr. Cohen who has everybody so frightened in town. I'll bet it's money. A supervillain needs cash to work his schemes, doesn't he?"

"As a general rule," I admitted as I was propelled by evil looks and angry gestures out into the front hall. "Henchmen don't work free and death rays cost."

"Well, there you go. It's money. My husband is

somehow funneling cash through the bank for Dr. Cohen and getting some kind of kickback. He's some kind of lackey or stooge or something, and he's using his ill-gotten money to hire floozies at that rundown hotel. I want you to follow up on that lead, Mr. Banyon."

"Technically, wild conjecture isn't what we in the business generally call a 'lead,'" I informed her. "The preferred term, if you want to get really precise, is 'time-wasting bullshit.'"

"It's a *lead*," she stated firmly, yanking open the front door. "Follow it up. Find out whatever it is my husband is up to with this Dr. Cohen."

The kitchen was opposite the front door at the other end of the hall, and the side of the expensive stainless steel fridge and beyond it the matching stove were prominently positioned so that visitors could see that Gwendolyn Johnson owned matching expensive stainless steel kitchen appliances. Something caught my eye that I hadn't noticed on previous visits, probably because it was brand new.

"Back there," I urgently announced from the front door.

I pointed at the living room door which we'd just exited, and when Mrs. Johnson glanced over her shoulder, I slipped out my camera and coughed loudly as I snapped a quick photo of the kitchen. My camera as well as my insanely clever fake cough were safely stowed away before Client #1 turned back around.

"What?" she asked.

"My hat," I said.

"It's on your head," she replied.

I checked with both hands. "So it is. I thought I'd left it on your lovely credenza. That's not an anatomical crack, I meant that fancy-ass slab of living room furniture."

I got the look of disapproval shared by dames of all

nations the world over, no matter their political or socio-
economic differences, when it comes to hatred of me.
As she shooed me onto the front stoop, she wrinkled her
nose in disgust.

"You stink like stale booze."

"Oh, don't worry about that," I assured her. "I'll stink
of fresh booze as soon as humanly possible."

I knew she was studying my back as I trotted down the
stairs, since I didn't hear the front door of the townhouse
click shut until I tumbled into the back of my cab. My
driver was lounging behind the wheel picking pork from
his teeth with his keys.

"It's refreshing to find a Third World Neanderthal who
understands the importance of dental hygiene," I said.
"Once you're finished chipping away all that recalcitrant
tartar, take me to the world headquarters of Banyon Investigations, Incorporated."

The nagging thought that had been trying to form in the
back of my brain was suddenly strumming all my remaining five synapses at once, and I quickly pulled from my
pocket the pair of envelopes that Dr. Cohen had sent to
both me and Gwendolyn Johnson's husband. I yanked out
the uppermost fragment of the note he'd sent to me and
took my million-and-first good, hard look at the letterhead.
I was so engrossed in my stroke of genius that I failed to
hear the driver the first, second or third times around.

"What did you say?" I said, coming out of a haze that
for once had nothing to do with alcohol poisoning.

"I said," he said, much more loudly than the three previous attempts, "where the hell is this Banyon Investigations
Corpro-whatzit place youse want me to take youse to?"

I gave him the address, he wiped the worst of the accu-
mulation of flicked dental residue from the windshield,
and we were soon speeding out of the West Side and back

into what passed for civilization in an only marginally civilized metropolis.

Through it all, I kept the chunk of note Dr. Cohen had sent me clutched in my hand while sporting the kind of smug bastard expression which, if I was my driver and I saw it in the rearview mirror, would have sent me speeding straight into the nearest bridge abutment just to wipe the shit-eating grin off an undertipping asshole fare's face.

13

My taxi driver didn't try to Travis Bickle me, but he no longer trusted that I'd return to the mobile scene of his recent gastronomic crimes. When I told him that I didn't have the cash on hand to compensate him for the past few hours of sitting on his ass and that I'd have to collect it from an elf in my office, the suspicious bastard insisted on traveling up with me in the elevator, which was far worse than being locked in a cab with him for five hours since there wasn't a window I could roll down and vomit out of.

Mannix was sitting in the corner under the front, frosted hallway window at a little desk he'd been building for himself and, apparently, had finally finished. The room smelled of fresh stain and I could see through my open inner office door that my window was open yet again to carry fumes out into the cold February air.

When the hall door opened, the elf glanced up from the newspaper in which he'd been circling items with a new pen which bore the logo of my insurance company. A can of breakfast orange Crush and a plate of Oreos sat at his elbow. How elves didn't lose all their pointed teeth before they were out of diapers, the ADA and I had no idea.

"Several things, Mannix," I announced as I marched

into the middle of the room as if I owned the joint, accompanied by my unshaven coachman companion. "First, pay off this untrusting and slovenly cabbie. Do it fast, as I don't want to have to steam clean the stench of roast pork and Brut out of my delicate draperies. Get a receipt and tack it on Gwendolyn Johnson's bill. Second, get this developed pronto." I tossed him my most recent roll of film. "I know it's not full. We're going to live like Rockefellers today. I'm particularly interested in the fridge picture. Get me blowups of everything on the side of that refrigerator. Third, have you heard from Doris?"

The elf was already scampering to his feet. "No, Mr. Crag."

"Damn. I know that's the opposite of the usual cartwheels I do down the corridor when I discover that Doris is MIA, but we are living in extraordinary times, Mannix." I glanced at Doris' desk, but opted against foraging around amongst the gross of empty Miss Clairol bottles inside to look for something that might not even exist. "We do this the hard way. Is that list of Dr. Cohens still on my desk?"

"Yes, sir, Mr. Crag. There's also an envelope from Mr. Jack...*from the FBI.*"

He announced the last three words with hushed reverence, as if privileged to be associated with somebody who breathed the rarified air shared by one of the fifty-billion overpaid members of the bloated, wheezing federal bureaucracy.

"I would be deeply concerned about keeping you in this unhealthy environment, Mannix, if I thought the fact that you are so easily impressed meant for one second that you are impressionable." I tipped my head to the cab driver. "Take care of that stuff I mentioned, starting with paying this heating vent gourmand to stop stinking up my offices. If you want to, feel free to tip him down the elevator shaft, but that's it."

I set my sights on my inner office, leaving Mannix to take care of paying the cab driver and developing the roll of film.

There was an overnight envelope sitting in the middle of my desk. I barely noted the Quantico, Virginia return address as I tore it open.

FBI Special Agent Jack Wolff owed me. I'd worked a case a few years back involving a trio of anthropomorphic pig siblings. Real sickos. Wore little vests and sailor hats, but refused to wear pants. Insisted it was a cultural thing. Real nice. They'd been arrested by local cops a whole bunch of times for indecent pigsposure. I'd been hired to track down the oldest brother by his ex-girlfriend, whom he'd swined and dined and left with a litter of piglets. Turns out he had a history of living high on the hog for a time with some dame and then making off with all her bacon.

I had no idea while I was working my case that the Feds were looking for my pig and his brothers for an entirely different reason. Apparently the three little perverts were deep into selling pignography across state lines. The FBI had raided two of their houses, and they'd left little more than a pile of straw at one location and a pile of twigs at the other, but they'd come up with nothing but ham and egg on their faces.

Jack Wolff was the agent in charge of the case, and after two failed raids there wasn't a judge who'd grant him a search warrant for the house of the third pig, a big brick number over on Orwell Avenue near the old animal farm. Wolff did a little huffing and puffing at the door, but without a warrant he couldn't get past the threshold.

The G-man was lucky I was under no such restrictions.

In the process of settling the paternity case for my client, I delivered the three pig brothers to Jack Wolff on a silver platter. As a bonus, I also got him a collar on three blind mice who were selling internet kitty porn from the pigs' basement. Wolff got a commendation and a promotion out of the deal, and as a result was one of the few chits in government I could call in.

I sat down at my desk as I shook out the contents of the overnight envelope.

The Glad bag I'd mailed dropped out along with the single item I'd stuck inside it. There was some accompanying official FBI documents, which included analysis and some computer printouts, along with a brief, handwritten note from Wolff:

Consider us even, Banyon. Don't write to me again.

"It's nice to see that you're such a enormous fan of gratitude, Assistant Director Wolff," I muttered.

I set the ingrate bastard's note aside and picked up the official documents.

I only had to scan the top sheet to confirm what had already been a growing suspicion. Then it was simply a matter of pawing through my desk drawer to find a matchbook that still had a match left in it. I found three empty books before I located one from a liquor store with a single match still clinging to life inside.

I slid all the FBI information from Jack Wolff into a pile, tapped it neatly together, and set it ablaze, dumping it into my wastebasket.

When Mannix came charging into the room carrying a fire extinguisher a few seconds later, I was nudging at the trash can with the toes of my Florsheims to make sure the last curling bits of paper burned completely away to ash while wishing more than usual that I had chosen another line of work.

Mannix relaxed and set down the extinguisher once he realized I hadn't deliberately set ablaze a dump with a half-busted fire escape and with no actual smoke alarms, since the building's owner had realized it was cheaper to hire a starving art student to paint simulations of alarms on all the ceilings rather than purchase the real things.

"I *could* quit, Mannix," I informed the elf. "Thanks to your expert office management skills, I've finally got some FU money. That dough would pay for at least one semester at Florist University, and my brother-in-law has offered on numerous occasions to take me on at his flower shop. Although I don't see me cheering on their football team, the Screaming Pansies, so I suppose I'm stuck with the life I've got."

"Is something wrong, Mr. Crag?" my little pal asked with genuine concern, even as he hustled over to tend the dying embers of my fire.

"Only that I should have identified the cliché from a mile away," I replied. "On the other hand, it does explain a lot. But on the *other* other hand, it makes everything more dicey. How fast can you get that film developed?"

"I can have the roll finished in less than twenty minutes," Mannix said. "The one photo you asked me to blow up will take a little longer."

I drummed my fingers on my desk. I hated thinking on a sober stomach.

"Fine. Quick as you can, Mannix."

He took slightly more time than that, since he first hustled over to the water cooler to get a mug of H2O to dump on the embers in my trash barrel lest I accidentally set fire to myself in his absence. Afterwards, he trotted over and snatched up the fire extinguisher to haul it from the room.

"That thing probably doesn't work," I informed him.

"It hasn't been inspected in the decade I've been here, and it came with the office."

The elf flashed an enthusiastic smile. "Oh, I have it checked every six months, Mr. Crag," he informed me, just before he ducked out the door.

I momentarily pondered, as I often did, how the world wouldn't be the horrible dump it is if everybody was less like me (a supreme asshole) and more like Mannix (who isn't). Also, the dentists would make a fortune.

It was this latter thought that nudged my wistful daydream of a perfect goddamn world into the crapper and returned me to the reality of the shit-hole I was stuck with.

I hauled out the yellow pages, a pair of scissors, and the list of Doctors Cohen Mannix had compiled for me. At least I could now narrow my focus down from the seventeen white pages listings of Cohens, concentrating on a subset of specialists in the yellows.

Forty-five minutes of trimming and comparing names from the phonebook yielded only a dozen names from Mannix's list of doctors, and I'd eliminated nine of them based on the pictures that accompanied their yellow page ads. The remaining three were listed in the book as names only, with no big bucks wasted on flashy, half-page ads. I set those three aside as possibles, but with so many more still listed in the yellow pages and no more left from the list Mannix had compiled for me, the odds of one of those three being our local madman archvillain Dr. Cohen were pretty remote.

Most P.I. work is just this kind of glamorous, dead-end slog, like trying to swim up the Ganges but with fewer dead fakirs. I figured the previous three-quarters of an hour would have been more rewarding if I'd spent them trying to nail a hammer into the wall with my forehead, which at least reminded me of something I had to do

I'd gotten up to stretch my legs and to collect the recently framed photo of Johnny J. Johnson from the wall over the water cooler when Mannix reentered the room.

"I finished as fast as I could, Mr. Crag," the elf announced, hustling over with the stack of newly developed photos.

He'd scarcely planted them in my hand than the phone began to ring, and with Mannix-like efficiency he didn't even stop, spinning sharply on one heel and racing back into the outer office to answer it.

"If that's Doris, I want to talk to her!" I hollered after him.

I left Mannix to deal with the shock of this sharp reversal in standing office protocol and headed back to my desk with the picture frame in one hand and the stack of photos in the other.

I wasn't interested in the pictures from that morning of Johnny Johnson trudging to the doors of the Panhandler Federal Ameribank and slumping down behind his desk. The only photo that interested me was the single shot I'd managed to squeeze off inside the Johnson home.

As requested, Mannix had blown up every object on the side of Gwendolyn Johnson's fridge. There was an enlarged copy of a photograph of Client #1 herself quietly suffering in a lime green bridesmaid outfit at somebody's wedding. The picture was held in place by a banana magnet, and Mannix had dutifully blown up both banana and wedding photo in separate photos.

There was a promotional magnet from my own insurance company, which I was apparently privileged to share with the Mr. and Mrs. Johnny Johnsons of the West Side.

There was a magnet apple, a magnet pear, a magnet

bunch of grapes, and enough goddamn fruit magnets to populate magnetic Provincetown.

With the final blowup, I hit pay dirt.

I hadn't been one hundred percent sure from a distance. Plus at the time I'd been getting perp-walked more-or-less backwards as I was being delicately shoved out the front door by Gwendolyn Johnson. Turns out my eyes hadn't lied and the camera had taken crystal clear evidence of that fact.

Under the enlarged shape of a plastic magnet shaped like a bunch of cherries was a doctor's appointment card. The card sported a unique O with a bunch of bumps arranged around inside it which I now knew were supposed to represent teeth. The goddamn cherries covered the first name as well as the address, but I could clearly read "Cohen" along with the last letters of a word that could only have been "orthodontia."

Doris had gone through a phase a couple of years back where bleaching her teeth to near-transparency wasn't enough, and she'd insisted on getting a set of adult braces, having missed out as a teenager on all the fun of looking like somebody had dumped out the silverware drawer in her mouth. All this time I'd been remembering that specialized O was because of Doris waving a business card under my nose for a year insisting she needed yet another afternoon off to get her mouth hardware realigned. If I'd cared one scintilla about how she wasted all the money I didn't pay her, I'd have remembered where I'd seen that card right away. The orthodontist Doris had gone to was Dr. Cohen.

"Orthodontia. Cohen," I said aloud. "Oh," I added.

Mannix stuck his head in the door, but not to see why I was talking to myself like a maniac.

"It's Miss Senorita on the phone, Mr. Crag," the elf

said. "She wants you to come over to her apartment. She says it's important."

"Tell her there's important, and then there's *important*, which might sufficiently confuse her to keep her from throttling you through the phone," I absently told Mannix. "Only don't make the mistake of telling it to her in Spanish because she won't understand a word of it."

I was too busy to get involved in Senorita Tamale's day-after recriminations.

At that moment, my semiconscious brain was wondering why the word 'zero' was suddenly as important as, unbeknownst to me, my unconscious brain apparently seemed to have been yelling for a while that it was. Usually my two primary levels of consciousness -- semi- and un- -- couldn't even agree on where I should pass out for the night, which is why I so often awoke in interesting and unexpected places.

The gears were turning in my sleep-deprived, marginally stewed brain, and I didn't have time for the distraction of being screamed at by a crazed lady telephone operator who was fluent only in the international language of shoes.

Operator, I thought.

"Operator," I repeated out loud, just in case my mouth hadn't heard what my brain had just said..

Operator, I thought again, because it really seemed like something my brain wanted to obsess over at that particular moment, and who was I to argue with a long overdue nervous breakdown?

There was a spark somewhere. I could feel it flickering on and off at the back of my skull like some punk kid playing with the hallway light switch. A single synapse was firing in a lone gray fold where those Three Musketeers of liquor, middle age and exhaustion had clearly failed in the only job the bastard trio was supposed to be good at.

Somehow the word "operator" was triggering something, even though I had zero idea what the hell that something could possibly be.

Zero, you goddamn moron! my brain screamed at me.

"Zero," I announced to my office. "Dial zero. Get an operator."

Okay, so we'd gotten to the point of my mental collapse where my unconscious mind was taking complete control of my mouth in order to state the obvious to an empty room. I wondered how long it'd be before I was standing outside the bus station begging for loose change and screaming about Martian brainwaves which, career-wise, would have been a significant step up from private detective.

"The New Year's countdown clock," I said to myself.

That one came out of left field even for me, and I decided to let my unconscious mind take over without a fight just to see where the hell it was going with all this.

My hijacking brain grabbed my hand and lifted it up as I tried to visualize the clock on top of the Sonny Bono Building counting down to zero.

Zero.

Even my conscious brain, which hardly ever involved itself in my life, got in on the act.

Zero for operator.

Dr. Cohen's first scheme.

The New Year's clock counting down to zero.

The mad doctor's second crazy plot of the day.

And there it suddenly was, lying wide open across my consciousness like a Triple-A map of the USA unfolded on the hood of a station wagon, and wondering why I hadn't been quick enough on the uptake to have spotted the last exit to Yellowstone before now.

I flipped open the white pages to the last handful of Dr. Cohens and found once more a name that I'd passed over as I was wearily slogging through the book at O'Hale's Bar in the company of a despondent Grim Reaper twenty-four hours ago.

Dr. Zeroth Cohen, Orthodontist.

Zeroth, of course, coming first in a series before one, which would be the same as goddamn "zero." (Yeah, okay, I didn't know this at the time. I read it in the paper ex post facto. I figure it was a homerun enough for me to have remembered at the time that there was some asshole dentist in the book whose parents had hated him enough at birth that he came two letters away from being named "Zero.")

"If it will stop Senorita Tamale from screeching at you, tell her I found Dr. Cohen!" I hollered out to Mannix.

I'd hardly spit the words out when the papers in my office were flying around as if a deeply disoriented tornado had gone horribly off course and accidentally set down near my file cabinet. A hundred mug shots of the many Drs. Cohen that Mannix had collected were flying off my desk, something whizzed past my shoulder from the direction of the open window, and there was suddenly a yellow-and-purple-clad creep standing like a slab of granite in the middle of the room.

"I heard you call," Minus announced, breathless, excited, and with the photo of a Dr. Armand Cohen, psychiatrist, stuck to the heel of his boot like a piece of public men's room toilet paper. "Did you *really* find him, Mr. Banyon?"

I'd forgotten the lummox could hear people yelling around town like my ex-wife could hone in like an Airedale on the sound of my wallet opening.

"--" was all I could manage, which was essentially me opening my mouth like first tenor in the sea bass choir, before his eyes went wide.

Minus was staring at the stuff that hadn't blown off my desk during his latest dramatic, unwelcome appearance.

"I...that is...I should..."

He was a man of few words and no complete sentences.

His mouth clamped shut, the wind tunnel effect abruptly reversed itself, and the yellow blur was zooming back by my desk at hypersonic speed.

This time, Minus either failed to clear the fire escape and hooked the toe of a boot on the railing or the thing was so loose already that he inadvertently drew it along in his wake. Either way, the outcome was the same.

There was a terrible metallic groan and a series of sharp pop-pop-pops from launching rivets, screws, chunks of calcified chewing gum, and whatever the hell else had been holding the network of rusted, fatigued metal together and fastened to the wall.

I glanced back in time to see the slow shadow of doom descend from the floors above, bend in half before my eyes, and plunge forward like a drunk who'd just dropped his car keys down a storm drain. The fire escape slammed the wall of the building across the street, tearing bricks from crumbling mortar and shattering windows as it skipped over sills and ledges on its boomerang-shaped crawl to the ground.

It got wedged for a moment between the first and second floors, which gave gawkers the opportunity to snap pictures with camera phones. It also gave drivers time to remove their cars from the field of danger which, of course, they didn't. The vehicles in the line of fire sat under the ominous shadow, accepted the bricks that dented their hoods, and laid on their horns in a fit of misguided road rage that apparently expected the fire escape to defy gravity and back itself right back up the wall.

There was another massive groan, and the fire escape snapped at its fresh elbow bend, exposing jagged chunks of gleaming silver and showering the street with a hail of rust. It plunged the final story to the ground, collapsing the roofs of at least five cars that I could see from where I was backing strategically away from the window.

I noted that this time, unlike before, there were no shouted apologies and promises to pay for the damage floating down from the clouds.

The racket like a battleship being dropped from the roof of the building and the subsequent bedlam in the street below brought Mannix charging into my office wearing a look of panic on his ruddy face.

"Are you all right, Mr. Crag?" he cried. "What happened?"

I was the very picture of innocence over by my thread-bare sofa as I calmly pulled on my coat and hat.

"Beats me, and I'll swear to that fact on a stack of insurance investigators. If you need me, I'll be at the dentist."

14

I could write a handbook on all the clichés you run into in the P.I. business.

You've got your baby-faced client who turns out to be a Mob enforcer; the missing accountant who you think at first is a swindler for stealing a bundle out of some church charity, but it winds up the church is crooked and the poor slob stole only to save his crippled kid's life; and, of course, the hooker with the heart of gold. All of these are bullshit. Baby faces usually are as innocent as they look, Mafia hitmen look like gorillas and need to shave their knuckles daily, accountants who steal from churches are bastards to a man, and hookers hearts exist only as part of an internal meth delivery system and the only gold they ever see is welded to a pimp's mouth.

There is one cliché that deserves to endure, however, because ninety-nine times out of a hundred the son of a bitch proves true. To wit: if you simultaneously take on one goddamn small case and one goddamn high-profile one, you can take it to the bank that the two seemingly unconnected clients are going to be sharing a sardine can by the time the whole mess finally shakes out.

"Gwendolyn Johnson is tied in with Dr. Cohen," I explained to Mannix as we hustled out of the elevator and along the downstairs hallway past the row of mailboxes to the front door. "The pair of them are coiled up together like those AMA snakes, which I realize Cohen doesn't belong to but I have no idea what kind of intertwined animals comprise the official ADA logo. Possibly beavers."

I hadn't even asked the elf how he had managed the heretofore impossible feat of politely extricating himself from a firing squad of quasi-Spanish.

The phone had been on the hook in the outer office. Mannix was too polite to have hung up on her, so Senorita Tamale had apparently disengaged voluntarily. She was no doubt off somewhere sharpening her larynx, and so Mannix had been free to lock up the joint for his half-day Saturday to follow me out to the street.

"Are you going to call Mr. Minus to help you?" the elf asked as I plowed through the door and the two of us marched into the weak sunlight.

I took a right to avoid the pile of collapsed fire escape that blocked the street. Vincetti was out in his apron waving an ineffectual fascist fist at the pile of rubble.

"I get the sense that Mr. Minus will not be of much assistance in dealing with the villainous Dr. Cohen," I said. "Not that he has been of great assistance thus far. Except, if you want to split hairs, for hauling that atomic bomb into outer space before it could Hiroshima all our asses. But that was more flash than substance."

At least I'd laid one suspicion to rest. Minus and his archnemesis -- Doctor-Orthodontist-Major-League-Nutbar Cohen -- were not one in the same jerk.

"There is a strong temptation, Mannix, to buy us a couple of plane tickets out of this dump and leave it to the cops and our pathetic, local superhero to sort out what I figured out after only one day of half-in-the-bag snooping." I paused on the sidewalk in front of a crappy Eskimo restaurant that sold only whale blubber sandwiches and baby seal soufflés. "Okay, let's say that's my point, to which you're right now going to give me your counterpoint. Tell me why you and I aren't lamming out of here and letting these great forces of good versus evil crash all of this down around everybody's ears, including this bastard Eskimo restaurateur who is staring greedily at us through his filthy front window like I am actually considering purchasing one of his eight foot-long party-sub humpbacks on rye with a free liter of Pepsi-Cola?"

Mannix answered first with his trademark doe-eyed look that informed me, as if I needed informing, that I was being naughtier than all hell.

"Mr. Crag," Mannix said.

It wasn't the words, it was the tone. Not admonishing, not quite disappointed. But somehow both of those things as well as encouraging in the way an old Nazi-bashing newsreel got Spanky and Alfalfa to run out and collect tin cans in their Radio Flyer.

"Okay, you win," I sighed. "Even though it'd save me a bundle in alimony I'll save this goddamn hellhole of a city. *Again*."

I looked into the expectant Eskimo face pressed up against his window pane. Behind the sandwich shop owner, his wife had already lugged a loaf of bread the size of a cetacean coffin out on the counter and was hacking it up the middle with a Ginsu.

"No sale, Nanook," I mouthed into the window.

The panicked Eskimo raced over waving his mittens over his head to stop his overly enthusiastic wife from gutting the massive loaf of rye like a pregnant gray whale.

Mannix and I resumed our stroll down the sidewalk, which perambulation would now, I was reasonably certain, end in my death at best, my dismemberment at worst. It was only a question of which of my members would be first to get the ax, and as we walked along I was running through in my head, like a wistful dead celebrity Oscar montage, a short list of favorites that would be missed in the coming calendar year.

"At least maybe I won't have to save this ungrateful burg at the thrilling last minute this time," I mused. "After all, it's nearly ten-thirty and the decaying skyline is still more-or-less standing. Maybe I can head off Dr. Zeroth Cohen before he unleashes his next zero-themed scheme, assuming the bastard is even planning a third act."

My ill-chosen challenge to fate was answered by a whip-sharp crack over the roofs of the city far above our heads.

It was as if every cloud in the sky had been turned to blocks of floating ice and then dropped in a heavenly glass of vodka, which I could have used a double of given what ensued. The February cold deepened with a whoosh, and my hat was nearly blown off by the gust of gale force wind that attacked the tenements and cheap office buildings, rattling loose window panes and flinging dirty bed sheets from rooftop clotheslines, tossing them through the winter air like tattered, urine-stained French flags.

I glanced up in time to see a blue streak as wide as a four-lane highway tear across the sky. It soared over our heads, back in the direction of my office building.

The sudden deep chill flooded down the back of my collar, freezing my spine and raising the fine hairs on the back of my neck.

When it touched down a block behind us, the sound that thundered back to our ears was that of the coffin lid being dropped on our frigid, final doom.

The blue wave shimmered as it brushed the roof of

my building. As I watched, weird, undulating waves raced down the sides of the building, engulfing brick and windows, dropping from floor to floor. It quickly passed over the open window with my shingle painted on it and rolled down the next two floors until it completely coated the windows of Vincetti's For the Halibut Fish Market. The old fishmonger unwisely ran into the wave, the fist he'd been impotently shaking at the collapsed fire escape in the street now redirecting its wrath at the mysterious blue glow.

Vincetti instantly froze as solid as the statue of Raymond Burr at the Number 2 highway rest stop just before the exit to the Rooster Museum.

As quickly as it had descended, the beam ascended once more, leaving in its wake a building entirely encased in the shimmering crystal glow of a five-story block of ice. Somewhere an unseen switch must have been thrown, because the blue streak that had continued to bisect the sky throughout the process bled away like rapidly dying contrails. All that remained in its wake was the cold shiver up my back, as well as a couple of unfortunate pigeons that had been trapped in the beam and which, once it was turned off, plummeted like dropped rocks and shattered to glistening shards of frozen red entrails on the pavement at my feet.

"All right, so maybe air travel is unfeasible," I suggested to Mannix. "But I'm willing to take Amtrack's word that there's something about a train that's magic."

The elf didn't have time to scold/encourage me with a glance. A ringing abruptly issued from his pocket. The shrill sound was simultaneously shared by pretty much every pedestrian loitering on the street around us. Traffic was backed up as a result of the fallen fire escape, and I saw people in parked cars lay off their horns long enough to rummage around in their pockets and haul out their cell phones.

"*This is Dr. Cohen!*" a voice boomed from every electronic device in the neighborhood and, I assumed, the entire city. "*I gave you the chance to meet my modest demands, but your officials have chosen to unite with my sworn enemy. In so doing, they have condemned you all to death. Think of that next time you vote, people. I mean, God, it's not just all about the horse race and a bunch of TV commercials. There are real issues out there as well. Anyway, to make a long story short, I gave you the opportunity to die quickly in nuclear flame, but now you will all perish slowly, horribly at absolute zero. You are all doomed! Doomed!*" His voice cut out, but immediately returned. "*And if Mrs. Ida Shapiro is listening, I'm canceling your eleven o'clock. The girl at the desk will reschedule. The rest of you, remember what I said. Doomed, and so forth.*"

With a feedback shriek like some asshole calling up a sports radio show and not remembering to turn down his radio on the kitchen counter, all the phones shut down simultaneously.

"It would appear that we are well and rightly screwed," I informed Mannix.

To punctuate that point -- as if there hadn't been enough goddamn punctuation going on in the neighborhood already -- we were nearly plowed over in the crosswalk we had just made the mistake of stepping out into by a taxicab that came flying up from a side street between a pair of decrepit buildings.

I grabbed Mannix by the collar and yanked him back to the curb, and the move twisted me around so that I nearly fell face first into the road. I barely managed to jump back, and I felt the whiff of air of a bruised yellow fender as it came a fraction of an inch away from launching my kneecap across the street like a bloodied hockey puck.

The cab flew past us and nearly T-boned a van that was bottled up in stalled traffic thanks to a collapsed fire escape some jerk had left in the middle of the street a block down the road. The taxi slammed on the brakes, twin streaks of rubber squealing up the pavement as it slid to one side until it was abreast with the van (but not in the sexy way), and spun out to a stop. The taxi did an alarming twelve-point turn in about three seconds, slamming into three parked cars and a mailbox in the process, and then flew back at us for a second attempt.

I was about to grab Mannix to attempt to shot-put him up to a second story awning, but the cab slammed on its brakes again, shrieking to a stop before us. The tires somehow kept on shrieking even while parked, and it was only when Senorita Tamale popped out of the back door that I realized her mouthful of steel-belted radials were screaming streaks of burned rubber at the driver.

"*I tell ju he was here!*" she hollered at the guy. "Why ju no stopses when I tell ju to stopses the first time round before? God, ju es estupido!"

I turned to my elf pal. "Mannix, if you are able to get out of town, go."

There was another crack from the blue ice highway in the sky. Although I couldn't see it this time it was evident that it had touched down only a couple of blocks away, because I could hear the sounds of people screaming in panic accompanied by the sudden crazy honking of worthless car horns.

Mannix, Senorita Tamale and I were still craning to see where the latest action was when a third crack assaulted the air. This one was less loud, less harsh. Wherever the beam had landed, it was somewhere far away from us. I managed to catch a glimpse of a narrow blue streak between the last pair of buildings on the block, and I guessed it had touched down somewhere in the Fudgepacking District.

"I'm not kidding about not going by air," I told Mannix. "These freeze ray things look random. I don't want you getting hit with one two minutes after your plane lifts off. Take the subway as far out of town as you can, then rent a car. Most important of all, don't pay out of pocket. Bill it to one of our worthless current clients. Either will do, since I hate both of them pretty much equally right about now."

The elf shook his head firmly. "I'm coming with you, Mr. Crag," he stated, with the kind of matter-of-fact, pig-headed heroism that invariably gets a guy killed.

For the second time in less than a half-hour, I opened my mouth and only managed to get out, "--."

Another word would have been a waste of time, because Mannix had already hustled straight past Senorita Tamale and scampered up into the back of the waiting cab.

"Vamanos, Banyon-san," the senorita snapped impatiently, slipping in a little out-of-the-blue pseudo-Japanese as icing on her mangled Spanish cake, possibly because it wasn't fulfilling enough for her to be illiterate in only two languages.

She was already sitting back in the rear of the cab when I tumbled in beside her. The cab's interior reeked like a Denny's waitress I'd dated for the free hash browns a couple of years back, and as a first-rate detective I expertly honed in on the source of the reasonably-priced breakfast stench.

In the rearview mirror, the goddamn cabbie I'd unloaded barely an hour before was scowling at me from within his perpetual five o'clock even as he fried up strips of bacon on the sputtering, grease-smeared dashboard vents.

"You're paying," I informed Senorita Tamale.

I gave our epicure hack the address of Dr. Zeroth Cohen's orthodontia practice, and Senorita Tamale, Mannix and I were flattened to our seats like the pancakes I was sure our driver would soon be spooning out for himself on the engine block, assuming we weren't all encased in an impenetrable slab of ice before his brunch shift was over.

15

"I needed to speaks with ju, Banyon," Senorita Tamale insisted as we tore down side streets, bounced curbs, raced up the double-yellow line on Main Street between two lanes of traffic, blew through stop signs, held up both literal and metaphorical middle fingers to red lights, and otherwise enjoyed a typical, leisurely taxi ride across town.

"Do you feel all right, Miss Senorita?" Mannix asked, deeply concerned. "I think, Mr. Crag, that we should bring the nice lady to the hospital."

"My buddy here might be right, Senorita Tamale," I said. "You don't look so good. Not that you don't look as effortlessly spectacular as always in the facial and rack regions even with the flu. Assuming it *is* the flu that's got you bright red and sweating like a fat taxi driver slipping strips of bacon between his chapped lips like a non-diabetic feeds dollar bills into a vending machine." I battled the intense G-forces of our million mile per hour rocket ride up the front lawns of Sycamore Terrace and leaned forward. "That simile wasn't inspired in any way by you," I confided in our cabbie, who was in the process of slobbering down his third strip of semi-raw pig ribbon.

(When a rapacious glutton cab driver, who is already

ticked at you for cheaping out on an earlier tip, has your life in the one greasy hand he's steering with, it's an incredibly smart strategic move to stay on his good side.)

"I was referring to a completely different disgusting, fat, gluttonous slob," I concluded. "You? You're just swell. Keep up the fantastic work. Hey, there's a swing set next to that wading pool you don't want to miss. "

We flew off a lawn, shedding the remnants of the swing set he'd managed to blast apart with a spectacular, last-minute Kentucky bluegrass swerve. The cab cleared the retaining wall adjacent to the driveway and touched down with a bounce of protesting shocks out in the street and directly in the path of a mail truck. The USPS vehicle cut sharply to get out of our way, and the last I saw of it, it had flown into an open garage door and came crashing out the side along with a bouncing slew of half-used paint cans.

"Ju remembers that Geiger encounters they was waving round me last night when ju was talking to Minus and that estupido policia-man?" Senorita Tamale asked. "The ambulance people tells me the readings was funny, and I should see my doctors."

"That's a fascinating tale," I said, as I jammed myself as far into the corner of the seat as was humanly possible without popping the back door and falling out into the gutter at a hundred miles an hour. "Speaking of fascinating tails, Mannix, unless you don't want to grow one and your boxers aren't lead-lined, I suggest you cram yourself away from the lovely, irradiated senorita."

"I am not giving off the radiation, Banyon," she snarled. "God, ju are the worst. I can't believe ju actually loved me."

"I think you misunderstood the basis of our brief and fiery relationship," I informed her. "In point of fact,

I've only ever really loved me. It was a particular bone of contention with my ex-wife, but she made up for it by loving everyone else as frequently as the shock absorbers on her Sealy Posturepedic permitted."

"Whatever ju say, I do not care," she said, waving a dismissive hand. I noted a fresh stink in the back of the cab and looked over to see that the plastic cover on the driver's headrest had melted a couple of bubbling slag streaks across the back.

"You're sure you're not throwing off radiation?" I asked.

"They did not know what it was they were finding on their machines, but they assured me that I was not active with the radiation."

I started to peel myself off the side of the cab, but the driver chose that moment to take a corner on two wheels and my back was replanted against the door. When I tumbled back down at the next hairpin curve I thought momentarily that I had sprouted a few extra arms and legs until I realized that Senorita and Mannix had formed a pig pile on top of my rumpled trench coat. The three of us collapsed back across the seat for an instant, then launched hard into the seat behind us before finally flying forward into the bulletproof shield that blocked us from the restaurant in the front of the cab.

When we scurried up from the floor mats, we were parked in front of an old Victorian-era whitewashed clapboard two-story number that had been converted to office use. There was a sign out front for a second floor acupuncturist, and a larger sign that read:

Dr. Zeroth Cohen, Orthodontist, D.D.S.,
All Who Do Not Yield Will Die.
Mon - Fri. Appts. Only.

The middle bit about the yielding and the consequences

of not doing so was so new that the sign painter's truck was still parked in the narrow driveway that ran up the side of the building to the backyard parking lot. The sign truck was backing out of the driveway as the three of us piled out of the back seat of the cab.

I'd tried as best I could to keep tabs on the occasional frozen blue streaks that blasted across the sky while I was bouncing around the rear of the cab like a ping-pong ball in a Lotto cage. I'd caught sight of only five more, but in fairness it wasn't like my attention was capable of laser-like focus, what with a demented Latina dame shooting off radioactive isotopes in the direction of my lap, as well as a bent seat cushion spring that had been spearing my right ass cheek for half the ride. One thing I knew for certain was that the freezing rays weren't coming from Dr. Cohen's dental practice. They got farther away the closer we got to his building, and while we were hanging around outside the cab, a distant crackle rose high into the clouds and arced across the sky, slamming silently down somewhere near the waterfront.

"Mannix, reconnoiter around back," I instructed my assistant. "That freeze ray might not be on the premises, but Cohen is still dangerous, and not just because he ropes in vain, insecure, middle-aged dames and convinces them they'll be Farrah Fawcett if they'll let him wrap a million bucks worth of barbed wire around their choppers."

"Yes, sir, Mr. Crag," Mannix replied.

"Just stay beneath the windows and be careful. Run like hell at the first sign of trouble. Don't be a hero. The pay stinks. You know that better than anybody, since you write and sign your own payroll checks. Got it?" The elf nodded, then darted up the side of the building opposite the driveway. He was the perfect choice to sneak through the bushes, around the porch, and beneath the wide picture window with the blinds drawn tight. He vanished around the corner.

"So, if you're not dying," I asked Senorita Tamale as she settled up with the rancid-smelling taxi driver, "what the hell is so urgent that you've got to bug me while I'm working? In fact, if you give me ten minutes, nothing about me will be working since I'll most likely be dead. Whatever it is, you can pester me about it then. I'll be a captive audience, and if anybody can screech through six feet of dirt, it's you."

Another blue blast attacked the pale February sky. This one landed somewhere nearby, no more than a mile away. An instant later, a frigid wall of displaced air chased over the landscape around us as the wide streak of blue melted to nothingness high above. I guesstimated from the angle it came in that the Clown Cemetery and the adjoining Three Ring Chapel were now encased in an impenetrable block of ice.

"I needs to talk to Minus," Senorita Tamale insisted. "He's jour clients. Ju can find him." The cab driver sped off, abandoning us on the sidewalk.

"Yeah, he's still a client, since he paid in advance and there's no way in hell he's getting a penny of that money back at this point. But I don't think we're going to be seeing much of him in the last-minute-rescue department."

"Ju have gotten in touch with him in the past," she insisted.

"Actually, he gets in touch with me. Which is to say that he mostly just flies through my window and breaks things. Excuse me, there's an elf signaling to me from that rhododendron, and I really need to take this call."

Mannix had poked his head up out of the bushes next to the front walk. I had to hand it to the little guy for being stealthy as all hell.

"There are five cars in the back parking lot," Mannix said. "There's a garage, but the windows are painted black and I couldn't see inside. I didn't see any people. The blinds are all down on the first floor of the building, so I couldn't see in there either."

"Thanks, kid. Now make yourself scarce. If I need you, I'll holler. If I don't holler, there is a high probability that I'm dead, so all I'll need you for at that point is to identify the body and iron my suit for the wake. My dying wish is that you don't run out and get a job working for another P.I. They're assholes to a man."

Mannix ducked into the bushes and disappeared, but for a momentary rustling around the hedges at the corner of the building a moment later.

I turned to Senorita Tamale. "Thanks for the lift, sister. It would be in the interest of all of us if you would kindly and, ideally, *quietly* buzz off. I stress that 'quietly' because even when you're calm you tend to be louder than an earthquake, and the way your head is bright red and steam appears to be escaping from your ears right now I'm afraid we've got a volcanic situation on our hands of Pompeii proportions."

She was redder than mere anger, and the faint puffs of steam rising from the sides of her head might have been -- but probably wasn't -- the result of the change in temperature from the heat of the taxi to the curbside February cold.

"I'm going in with ju, Banyon," she insisted. "I need to talk to Minus."

"He isn't in there," I insisted. "Expensive adult braces and impending death are. The former looks moronic on grown humans, so I'm here for the latter. Why don't you keep your tongue idling out here by the curb? If I'm not dead in ten minutes I'll be back, and if I'm not back in ten minutes, you and the elf beat a hasty (albeit not so hasty because it will have been delayed by ten minutes) retreat."

I left her on the sidewalk and headed up onto the porch.

Any hope I had for a great stealthy incursion into the enemy's camp was dissolved the moment I heard the thunderous pounding of a cattle stampede at my six o'clock. Senorita Tamale was clomping up the steps immediately in my wake, and I understood that I had only imagined that her massive soles were loud the previous night now that she was treating the neighborhood to the percussion solo from Mozart's Lost Symphony for Ludicrous Footwear on Porch Stairs.

There was no sense telling her to turn around at that point, since I was reasonably certain every living creature on the face of the planet was holding out palm, paw, hoof and fin to feel for the raindrops to which the high-heeled thunder was precursor.

"Just follow my lead," I suggested as she tailed me across the porch like Trigger stomping up Blackbeard's gangplank.

There was a welcome mat in front of the door and a gold sign which read "WELCOME" stuck over the mail slot. I accepted the kind invitations of the psychotic supervillain (whose freeze ray I'd heard blast across the sky two more times since I'd headed up the walk and mounted the stairs), and entered the orthodontic lair of Dr. Zeroth Cohen, D.D.S., Zero-Themed Disaster Engineer and All-Around Maniac Crackpot.

16

"Wipe your feet," snarled the old bat at the counter.

She was maybe in her early sixties, or could even have been a young seventy. She was the kind of nurse/receptionist/hygienist/whatever who looked like she'd arrived inside an Acme Dental Practice starter kit along with a vinyl recliner, molar-shaped desktop pencil holder and spit sink. She'd probably been with Cohen forever, and so could afford to be surly and bored because of the job security that came along with sitting her aging ass in the same goddamn chair for forty years.

The dame had a severe black dye job and Moe Howard bangs. She fidgeted the glasses that were leashed to the end of her nose as she fiddled with her free hand behind the counter where she roosted. As the old bag struggled with the twin burdens of creeping dementia and being a nasty hag, a brunette in her thirties with a teenaged daughter in tow appeared down the hallway behind the reception desk.

I could see the tips of a row of perfect white teeth jutting out from underneath the daughter's mouthful of unnecessary, absurdly extravagant braces. A silver hula hoop had been shoved halfway down her face and encircled her head like a displaced halo.

"See you next week, Mrs. Wycopf," the mother ventured timidly, as if used to having her head bitten off on the way out the door.

"Well, you're going to have to call first," Bag Wycopf furiously snapped without looking at the mother or her heavy metal daughter.

The daughter with next year's mortgage payments fastened to her choppers let loose a histrionic sigh of impatience with her mother's gross stupidity that would have brought the house down in front of her cheerleader pals, but made middle-aged me want to yank the stainless steel pin on a bicuspid and stand back while her ingrate head blew forty pounds of silver shrapnel into the suspended tile ceiling.

The mother apologized to everybody in the world on her way out the door, which the daughter not only failed to hold open for her, but let deliberately slam in her face.

There was nobody else in the waiting room adjacent to the reception desk, and I heard not a sound coming from up the hallway.

The bag behind the counter finally finished the excavation of her pile of paperwork, and her arthritis-gnarled mitt slapped down a clipboard with a dangling, attached pen.

"Fill this out," the delightful Mrs. Wycopf commanded. "No major insurance accepted. No financing. Cash. Up front."

I eschewed the tethered pen for an implement of my own which, admittedly, was shit for writing but was pretty good for blasting periods through all kinds of forms, including cold legal as well as the warm-blooded forms of malevolent dental receptionists.

I tapped the barrel of my gat on the clipboard and held a silencing finger up to my lips. I also ripped the pen off the clipboard and stuffed it in my pocket because I was still running low back at the block of ice that used to be my office.

"Tie her up," I whispered to Senorita Tamale.

My loudmouth telephone operator companion hustled behind the counter and used the old dame's own powder blue sweater to bind her hands to her chair. The gag was a handful of surgical masks stuffed in her mouth, held in place with dental floss that completed the journey around the equator of her aging head about a hundred times.

I noted that once Senorita Tamale was through, the sleeves of the sweater where they were knotted around the old bat's wrists were smoking.

I am the opposite of heroic which, for anybody keeping track at home, is cowardly. Bravery is for suicidal idiots who don't mind the heart palpitations and nervous rash that comes along with feats of derring-do. The few times in my life that I've been called on to be heroic have ended with a cardiologist's appointment and about a gallon of calamine lotion. But the good news was that Senorita Tamale had managed to keep the cork in for the preceding two minutes, which had to be a personal record, and so far I hadn't heard a single peep from the rest of the first floor offices of Dr. Cohen.

The senorita came back out and the two of us crept up a hallway beside the reception desk from which six doors led into various small rooms.

Fortunately, the entire joint was carpeted, so there wasn't a repeat of the clomping show pony act from the front porch. Unfortunately, it didn't matter because out of three of the six doors stepped three people who simultaneously got the drop on us.

The one directly in front of us was a white-haired bastard wearing a surgical mask, thick glasses, a white smock, and chewed-up brown leather shoes which he'd probably been wearing for the past twenty years. He pulled down the mask and I finally came face to face with the recently-minted archvillain Dr. Cohen.

"Mr. Crag Banyon, private detective extraordinaire," Dr. Cohen announced, twirling a mirrored dental probe airily and flashing a wicked grin.

"I'll see your meaningless, bullshit, victory-lap preening and raise you a 'physician heal thyself,'" I replied. "By which I mean, your goddamn mouth is a horror show. It is, quite frankly, something over which a rock-eating dog would have nightmares. I'm deadly serious, and you have to know that's true because your thug just took my gat so I have nothing with which to defend myself. I once saw an M.E. pull a plastic comb out of a cadaver that was half-eaten away by stomach acid, and it had better teeth than you. I'll bet middle-aged women from Quebec laugh at your teeth. Honest to God, from goddamn *Quebec*. Give me an hour and I'll round up some hippo-toothed expatriate Quebecker dames so we can all point and laugh."

Dr. Cohen's sneering smile changed over to a closed-mouth sneer, which was the greatest gift short of death the son of a bitch could bestow on anybody who'd ever had the misfortune to look him straight in the mouth. I could see now why he'd opted for the camera shy approach to all his villainous efforts. His dental horror show was like a rotting picket fence on an abandoned house where the kids from the neighborhood had kicked out half the pickets and the other half had been installed crooked and painted with a sealing coat of Sherman-Williams gingivitis.

"Are you quite finished, Mr. Banyon?" the evil orthodontist snarled.

"Yes," I said, "but I reserve the right to return to the topic because, if I haven't made it clear, your teeth are an abomination of nature that I'm afraid strongly suggests that militant atheists might actually be on to something."

The first of his companions held one of those ray guns that the bastards had used on the roof of the telephone company. He was the mook who'd relieved me of my piece and handed it off to the shadowy figure who'd appeared to my left.

I recognized the first son of a bitch as the guy I'd winged inside the roof door of the opera house. It looked like Dr. Cohen himself had dug out the bullet, judging by the massive stain seeping out through the shoulder of the scumbag's white hospital scrubs and bloodying a sling that had been fashioned from a pair of drool bibs.

The second of his henchmen might have come as a surprise twenty-four hours before, but now that all the pieces of the puzzle had comfortably dropped into place it wasn't the shock which, judging by the insufferably superior look on her face, she very clearly needed it to be.

"Hello, Mrs. Gwendolyn Johnson," I said. "It's probably gauche to talk shop to a treacherous dame who has my own gat aimed at my forehead, but it's important at this juncture that I remind you that Banyon Investigations doesn't give refunds."

"Ju?" said Senorita Tamale from somewhere in the no-man's land between furious and confused. "What is this, Banyon? This womans is jour client, isn't she?"

"Jes," I replied in her native tongue, whatever the hell it was. "But she hasn't been on the level since the first day she sashayed her pretty little derriere into my office, parked said attractive diminutive kiester in a chair, and asked me to tail her non-philandering bank manager husband. As for you, Mrs. Johnson, I've been expecting you to show up, so you're pretty much right on schedule. Although, granted, I didn't expect you'd be pointing my piece at me when you made your grand entrance."

"Oh, don't pretend you knew I was in league with Dr. Cohen, *Mr. Banyon*," said Client #1. She said my name like it was a goddamn curse word which, in most of the bars around town, in my ex-wife's apartment and in Norway, it was. (They know why.)

"I didn't know you two were bosom pals most of the time, although I can understand why he'd want to be given the bosom in question," I said. "However, I pretty much knew it since late yesterday. This morning, when I got a package back from the FBI, I confirmed my suspicion."

"This is all well and good," Dr. Cohen interjected, since he was the kind of bloviating asshole who, when people weren't paying enough attention to him and his ego, wasted everybody's time by saying things like "this is all well and good."

The mad orthodontist produced one of those little silver squirt guns on a narrow hose that dentists use to water down smoking molars, and with a little twist of the wrist beckoned us all to join him in the room from which he'd exited.

It was a tight fit with the patients' chair, the x-ray stand and the wall of TV monitors which at a glance appeared to cover every major area of the city.

Most of the town was still the shitty dump I was used to seeing in my waking, sleeping and rare detoxing night-mares, but here and there I could see random patches of glistening ice where Dr. Cohen's freezing ray had turned buildings and the occasional whole city block into glistening blocks of ice. As we entered the room I saw that one of the blue beams was in the process of attacking city hall. The blue glow faded to nothingness, but in its wake the seat of corrupt, incompetent city government was transformed into a towering bureaucratic glacier.

Dr. Cohen marched over to the wall of flickering

screens, twirling around and throwing out both hands.

"Amazing, is it not? Frozen at absolute zero. A special formula of my own invention. That is not ordinary ice, Mr. Banyon. It won't melt for centuries. The delivery system employs a computer program that selects random targets, so there is no way for our fine city's leaders to see from where the next attack is coming,"

"It's possible this is all a case of mistaken identity," I ventured, "since our city and its leaders are the polar opposite of fine. They're time-serving kleptocratic hacks, and the city they're running into the ground is pretty much a crap-heap on wheels. That's not me being cynical, that's the first line in our *World Book Encyclopedia* entry."

Dr. Cohen ignored me, demonstrating that he was discourteous as well as a raving batshit loon.

"Your office building wasn't random, of course," the fiendish Dr. Cohen informed me. "I can override the system if I wish. Gwendolyn here suggested it as a target."

Gwendolyn Johnson and the henchman with the sling and the ray gun had followed Senorita Tamale and me into the room. She flashed a wicked smile, which glinted like the front grille on a Peterbilt tractor-trailer.

"I see you got your payment, sister." I nodded to her brand-new mouth hardware.

"One hand scratches the other," she said, obliviously mangling the axiom. "I wanted to be rid of my husband. Dr. Cohen here -- Zeroth -- fronted the money I paid you. You tailing Johnny to that hotel would have worked out nicely *if* you'd been halfway competent. But when you went all civic minded and just had to pitch in to stop both of Zeroth's schemes yesterday, there was a little change in plans. Oh, and no matter what you think, I *will* be getting that refund. Posthumously, of course."

"You think this is the first divorce dance I've ever

waltzed into the middle of?" I asked. "Think again, kitten. And while you're wasting all that energy thinking, check the fine print in your contract. I only had to prove infidelity on the part of one Johnson spouse. You being Dr. Cohen's squeeze fits the bill, and that mouthful of shiny slag and no invoice from the diabolical doctor to go along with it is all the proof a jury'll need."

She held my gun steady, although it was self-evident to anybody with eyes that she'd never held a piece before. As she spoke, she kept one baby blue trained past my shoulder and on the wall of monitors at which stood her maniac boyfriend.

"He's here, Zeroth, darling," she said through a mouthful of pricey chicken wire.

Cohen glanced around the monitors. I'd already spotted the thing Gwendolyn Johnson was pointing out to the white-haired old bastard.

Zipping through the pale white sky over the post office was a little figure in a garish yellow and purple ensemble. Minus vanished from the first monitor and made an encore appearance on another TV screen toward the middle of the wall, this one in the vicinity of the Moderate to Heavy Petting Zoo and heading toward Connie Sellecca Lake.

Dr. Cohen attacked a keyboard on a counter in front of the monitors like a demented concert pianist who'd lost his last dime between the ivories, which he really needed because it was the dime he'd planned to use to call back in time to warn his younger self to pick a career that paid better than professional goddamn pianist, like grocery store cashier or gas station attendant.

Crazy Cohen was a traditionalist when it came to computer design. As he typed, a bank of retro, NASA-inspired mini-mainframes over near his ergonomic stool blinked multicolored lights, spit out a strand of paper, and spooled a couple of reel-to-reels.

"It's an easy enough matter to target my freeze ray," Dr. Cohen explained as he worked. "Of course, that's only if you're a genius, as I am, Mr. Banyon. Third in my class at dental school, so don't even try to follow my virtuoso moves because you don't have a chance of figuring out how it works, and neither you nor your lovely companion have a chance of stopping me before I have you both killed. I simply thought before I dealt with the two of you that you'd appreciate witnessing the end of the man you've been assisting and the greatest thorn in my side."

All the monitors suddenly switched to a single image: that of Minus tearing up the sky over the lake on the east side of town.

A blue beam flashed from the right side of every screen and caught every image of the flying superhero in midair.

The block of ice that instantaneously formed around Minus was so thick that he virtually disappeared. All I could make out once the blue beam vanished was a faint yellow discoloration at the heart of the rock-hard chunk of ice.

Forward momentum carried him only a little further along before gravity remembered it had a say in how this story would play out. The block of ice quickly slowed into a majestic arc and then all forward movement arrested and it was rocketing in a deadly straight line down to Earth.

The slab of ice in which Minus was buried vanished from every monitor simultaneously.

A few keystrokes from the mad maestro and we were suddenly looking at an entire wall of monitors on which was the same distant image of Connie Sellecca Lake. The video was being shot somewhere on the eastern shore, and from a distance I saw a small, yellow-tinged block of ice splash quietly, with no fanfare, into the lake.

Before the ice cube had a chance to bob to the surface, the blue ray returned. The black waters of the wind-churned winter lake froze up first at the center, with the sheet of freshly-formed ice crackling across white-capped waves in all directions to the frosty shore. In a matter of seconds, the entire lake was a mile-deep slab of impenetrable ice.

The blue beam faded to nothingness, and the bastard Dr. Zeroth Cohen twirled from his bank of monitors with a look of triumph on his face and a bunch of pastrami stuck between his spectacularly revolting teeth.

"Not a very *ice* way to die," Dr. Cohen announced, wearing the pinched smirk of a smug ice-hole who actually thought he'd just said something genuinely clever.

"I'm not loaded enough either to endure or engage in juvenile wordplay," I replied with an honest shrug, so instead I socked Cohen's henchman in the bullet wound.

The thug with the ray gun howled like a coyote in a bear trap, and the clumsily stitched-up wound immediately burst apart. His hand sprang open and the ray gun slipped from his fingers and bounced to the beige carpet. I dropped right along with it, grabbed it up, wheeled while kneeling on one knee and fired at the bank of computers.

The ensuing explosion ripped a hole straight through the blinking mainframes and took out half the wall behind them. Sheets of exterior siding collapsed on the far side of a haze of sparking circuits and rising smoke. The ugly wallpaper caught fire and all the monitors went to static for a split-second before winking out to dead black screens.

Dr. Cohen toppled backwards, upending a tray that sent dental implements flying through the air and scattering around the room.

Throughout the chaos, Mrs. Gwendolyn Johnson

remained the ice queen I'd pegged her to be. The instant I'd socked the punk in the shoulder, the dame jumped back and started yanking hard on my trigger.

Mrs. Johnny J. Johnson's hand was so steady she'd missed her calling as a surgeon, and if she'd pursued that alternative career she might even have been able to stitch together the fragments of my head which she was evidently frustrated weren't blowing off my shoulders. Too bad for her I'd flipped on the safety before I handed the gun off to the goon who'd then passed it over to her. She'd never flipped the safety off. The dame had the heart of a homicidal loon, but she didn't know shit about gats.

While Client #1 was focusing all her murderous energy on me, she had made the tragic mistake of underestimating the attack dog that was Senorita Tamale. The Latina spitfire suddenly came screaming out of nowhere, launching up from a hidden crouch in the growing wall of choking smoke. Her face was bright red as she tackled Gwendolyn Johnson. My piece went flying out of Mrs. Johnson's hand, and the two dames rolled out into the hallway in a display I hoped was being picked up by some office security camera so I could play it back at my leisure when I wasn't busy saving the goddamn city.

"*No!*" Dr. Cohen's voice cried from somewhere beyond the cloud of smoke that had enveloped the entire office.

The fire raced up the tooth-themed wallpaper and spread across the yellowed suspended ceiling tiles.

I could see Dr. Cohen's silhouette rising against the backdrop of the open hole I'd blown through the side wall of the room. He held an object in his hand, and for an instant I was afraid he'd gotten his mitts on my piece. When I realized it was the same shape as the rinse-and-spit number he'd been waving around moments before, I made the fortuitous mistake of relaxing enough to look around for my gun.

I saw the butt sticking out from under the mad dentist's chair, and the precise moment I leaned down to grab it up, Dr. Cohen pulled the trigger on his squirt gun.

The stream of directed water sliced through the wall like a Ginsu knife through a tin can in the spot directly behind where my neck had been one second before.

"A cutting tool, Mr. Banyon!" Dr. Cohen cackled maniacally. "Another product of my incredible genius. Focused water. More precise than a laser, stronger than a diamond-tipped drill. It took millennia for water to carve the Grand Canyon. I rather think it will take considerably less time with you."

I rather thought he was rather goddamn right, except that the asshole couldn't rather rein it in. Cohen simply had to give me a grand, sweeping, supervillainous gesture with both arms in order to show just exactly how dead I was about to be. Too bad for the criminal genius that his finger was still on the trigger, and as his arms swept out, so too did the concentrated stream from his water laser. The insane orthodontist went wide with his aim and sliced straight through a supporting beam.

There was a split second where Dr. Cohen appeared to realize his moronic mistake, indicated by the fact that the dark figure that I could barely make out through the fog of smoke stopped firing and muttered, "Oops."

Next came a great creak of wounded, shifting wood which was followed by an unholy crash. All at once, the upstairs acupuncturist's office was relocating into Dr. Cohen's first-floor practice in a cascade of needles, massage tables, scented candles, and one startled Chinese dame in a silk bathrobe and flammable slippers.

I dived out into the hallway just in time to avoid the avalanche of some pasty slob who came dumping down into the room with a porcupine's worth of needles sticking out of an acre of pale, jiggling back fat.

I inadvertently plowed into Senorita Tamale, who had Mrs. Gwendolyn Johnson pinned to the smoking hallway carpeting. The two of us tumbled into Cohen's office, which afforded Mrs. Johnson the opportunity to scamper to her feet and run like hell.

"Ju idiots, Banyon!" Senorita Tamale erupted.

"Erupted" was the go-to word there, since twin puffs of smoke launched from her nostrils and a couple of streams of flame shot out of the top of her head and set fire to the ceiling of Dr. Cohen's personal office. The flames raced quickly down to his desk and file cabinets.

"What the hells was that?" Senorita Tamale demanded, aware of the bright flash but apparently unaware that it had launched from out her glorious mane of smoking hair.

"Remember at the opera house how I told you that one in a million people who get exposed to radiation develop super abilities, while all the rest of us drop dead? It would appear, Senorita Tamale, that you're one in a million. Although I suspect you figured something was up already or you wouldn't have been looking for Minus, who no doubt exposed you to massive levels undetected by authorities because you thoughtfully absorbed them all before they killed the rest of us. Thanks for that, by the way."

I wrapped an arm around her shoulder and led her out into the hallway, although gingerly since she was giving off a great deal of heat and I didn't feel like having my arm cooked like a slab of bacon on a taxicab dashboard vent.

There was nobody left in the room across the hall. I figured Dr. Cohen had ducked out the convenient hole I'd blasted through the wall. Smoke was pouring out of the small room and flooding the ceiling in the corridor, and we had to duck low as we ran.

The fatso covered in needles and the Chinese acupuncturist dame from upstairs were scrambling for the exit ahead of us, and the door out back hung open wide, indicating that Gwendolyn Johnson had already made good her escape.

I was worried about an ambush as we burst out onto the back porch, but it wasn't like we had much of a choice what with the whole house going up in flames behind us, so I just made sure we stayed tucked in behind the panicked team from the acupuncturist's, in particular the pile of jiggling flab who was shedding needles like a dry Christmas tree and running for a parked Hyundai as fast as blind terror and morbid obesity permitted.

Senorita Tamale was a braver man than I am, and as we ran she stuck her head around a flabby, naked, hairy shoulder.

"The garage!" she shouted.

The garage out back was actually a converted two-story nineteenth century Victorian carriage house, with several stalls and a cupola with a rooster weathervane perched high up on the slate roof.

One of the garage doors was open, and inside, I saw the silver escape pod Dr. Cohen had used to flee the telephone company building. The worthless henchman with the bloody shoulder had crawled out as far as the capsule, but had passed out facedown on the garage floor.

Cohen was already inside the pod, and Gwendolyn Johnson was standing on the back of the unconscious henchman as if he were a Sir Walter Raleigh-inspired coach stool and was attempting to squish her various feminine attributes inside the dome of the one-seater. A foot shod in cracked leather popped out of the dome and gave her a shove between the knobs, and the dame fell to her ass on the garage floor. She scrambled back up, but the dome was already snapped shut.

"Where are you going? Take me with you!" Mrs. Johnson hollered, pounding with both fists on the dome of the escape pod.

"I'm afraid there is room only for one, my dear!" Dr. Cohen shouted back, and his reverberating voice was so loud I looked around as I ran and spotted some speakers mounted on the roof of the garage. "You damaged my equipment inside, Mr. Banyon, but I've redirected a freezing beam by remote control. It will arrive here any second. You can try to run. I'll enjoy watching that from the sky. You will not survive. In a minute, this entire neighborhood will be encased in ice for all eternity. Goodbye, forever."

There was a rumble that shook the ground. Gwendolyn Johnson fell backwards from the thrust of the rocket as the escape pod lifted off the floor of the garage.

Senorita Tamale and I hadn't the time to cover the ground between burning house and rattling-apart garage, but I still had the ray gun clutched in my hand. I whipped it up and took aim on the silver teardrop as it rose into the air.

The gun failed to fire, naturally, but it didn't fail to spring apart in a million goddamn pieces in my hand as the escape pod blasted through the roof. Timbers and slate shingles above the far left garage stall exploded in every direction, and I had to grab Senorita Tamale by the wrist and swing her around to get myself between her and the exploding garage.

The pile of junk scattered fast, my trench coat came through the blast unscathed, and I turned back in time to see the escape pod rise with slow-motion majesty into the air.

It got about sixty feet up before the engine spluttered and died. The thing did an ungraceful midair turn and crashed straight back through the middle front part of the garage roof that hadn't been busted to kindling on its way out five seconds before.

As the second garage door in line burst open and vomited the silver capsule out into the driveway, there was suddenly a panting elf standing at my side holding a bunch of multicolored wires in his little hands.

"I went back to the garage and found that machine inside," Mannix announced with breathless exuberance. "That naughty man escaped in it from the telephone company according to the newspaper, so I thought I'd fix it so it wouldn't work right. I hope I did the right thing, Mr. Crag."

Dr. Cohen popped the half-shattered dome lid of his escape pod and dumped out in a bloodied heap into the driveway onto the scattered ruins of his garage. The jilted and abandoned Mrs. Gwendolyn Johnson was revved up and itching to kick his face like a soccer ball, which she promptly did. Crooked, rotten teeth flew everywhere.

"Yeah, I would say it's a pretty safe bet that you did the right thing, Mannix. Spectacularly, unreservedly, the one hundred percent absolute right thing."

The elf's face only had a second to beam with pride before we all heard an ominous crackle somewhere to the east. Even Mrs. Johnson stopped planting her foot in Dr. Cohen's mouth to join the rest of us as we looked up at the blue streak tearing across the sky. Clouds disintegrated and unfortunate birds caught at the leading edge popped apart, raining half-frozen meat and feathers on houses far below.

It would be on us in seconds. Gwendolyn Johnson

watched ashen-faced, while wounded Dr. Cohen tried to crawl back up the side of his busted escape pod.

"Hands above your head, Senorita Tamale, palms aimed up," I snapped.

There wasn't time for her to be as confused as she was, so I grabbed her wrists and arranged her in the necessary pose.

"Now think of how I abandoned you on that ferry and how you were subsequently stuck in Canada without anyone to screech at but Canadians for an entire week. Hell, toss in that time I got drunk at your brother's wedding. Not at the reception, mind you, which is traditional, but at the actual wedding. I passed out in the confessional, in case you were wondering where I was for the next three days."

As I figured, the dame turned bright red. Redder than the red she'd first exhibited in the cab. An inhuman, boiled-lobster red: brilliant, glowing like a string of chili pepper Christmas lights, and hopefully not spitting out radiation like a quasar or a microwave oven with a busted door. She reached the apex of being fired up just in time.

The blue superhighway-in-the-sky freeze ray was on us.

The world winked out, and an evil darkness descended. There was a monstrous sound, like the roar of a train inside a mountain tunnel. It was a typhoon, a tornado, and Mount St. Helens tossed in a food processor set on "puree."

As the world ended, I grabbed Mannix in close and we did what all brave he-men do in times of crisis and gallantly hid behind a dame's skirts.

Senorita Tamale came through like the hot-tempered trouper a thousand unsatisfied telephone customers already knew her to be. She remained standing, unbowed as the concentrated ice storm raged down on all our heads.

The red glow slid from her face like a rat negotiating its way through a snake's digestive system. It vanished down her throat and disappeared below her collar. It found its way across her shoulders and down her arms, because a moment later it joined forces with the bright red glow that illuminated her hands. The light emanating from her palms grew in intensity, doubling, tripling, then going completely off the scale.

I could hear the crackle of ice forming all around us, but the area in which we stood was an oasis of warmth in a rapidly freezing wasteland. The ground froze first, then layers of ice rapidly added to layers.

Gwendolyn Johnson turned to give Dr. Cohen one final swift kick but was frozen in place like a furious mannequin advertising infidelity in a downtown store window. Dr. Zeroth Cohen became a fly in amber, glued for eternity like a rotten-toothed hood ornament on the crumpled nose of his silver escape pod.

The ice rose higher, covering cars, garage remnants, and flash-freezing the burning Victorian building that housed Dr. Cohen's late orthodontics practice.

The beam lasted for eight of the longest seconds since that one episode of *Wings* I got stuck watching with my brother-in-law, and when it was finished it shut down as if somebody in some remote location had flipped a switch.

It was on, then it was off, and when it was over I found that I was not, in fact, something for future archaeologists to chip out of ancient ice to prove to the world of tomorrow just how handsome and incredibly well assembled humans of the past were.

I was surprised at how relieved I was that we weren't all dead, but I chalked most of that up to the fact that Mannix had pulled through, since there wasn't anybody else out there I could trust to make sure there were postage stamps and Seagrams in stock at the office at all times and that the gas bill got paid on time.

"That was amazing, Miss Senorita," the elf enthused.

The dame was staring in shock at her own glowing hands. Luckily she had them aimed at the block of ice that had formed to her left and not at me, since I had a new lease on life (or at least a down payment on wanting to get loaded within the next hour), and I didn't feel like doing my impression of a rotisserie chicken.

I noted that an awful lot of ice was continuing to melt instantly as she held her hands to the wall. The ice was evaporating before it could transform into so much as a single water droplet, which was great news for those of us who had just narrowly avoided being frozen like a fish stick and didn't want to enjoy the victory of one narrow escape while drowning to death in a tide of rising ice water two seconds later.

"Only partly amazing, Mannix," I said. "In case you haven't noticed, we are currently standing at the bottom of an ice shaft that I would estimate is a good forty feet deep. As an ex-North Pole elf, you might be able to climb out for help--"

"Easily, Mr. Crag," the elf announced, and started up the wall.

"--except the town's emergency services are tied in knots right now," I finished, plucking the plucky elf off the wall of the ice shaft in which we were trapped. "And with the ice machine of sinister Dr. Cohen (who is suspended in ice over there and staring glassily at me at this very moment) still presumably firing random bursts out there somewhere, I think I'd probably freeze to death before help arrived."

"I could throw down a rope," Mannix suggested.

"I'm a delicate flower. I blister. Besides, I have a better idea."

I reminded Senorita Tamale once more of our trip to Canada, admitting for the first time that her car which I'd borrowed hadn't been stolen from me by Serbian hobos as I'd informed her, but that I'd sold it for scrap to buy a Greyhound ticket home.

I told her that her sister had attempted to seduce me.

I told her that her brother had attempted to seduce me.

I told her that her mother and three of her aunts had attempted to seduce me.

I told her that the telephone company refused to give her a raise for seven years because of customer complaints. They all worked, but that last one was the difference between a kernel of popped popcorn and an atomic bomb.

The wall around us had been melting and evaporating to steam, rolling back by feet at a time, but just mentioning the telephone company customers Senorita Tamale so despised sent a burst of heat from the fiery dame's scorching paws that wiped out almost in an instant the entire glacier that had formed around the entire neighborhood.

I'd forgotten about the fat slob acupuncture client who, while we were across the driveway saving the world, had apparently been in the process of attempting to start his Hyundai. Time had stood still for him and his foreign piece of shit, but the instant the ice vanished his engine kicked on and he tore off down the driveway, oblivious to the fact that the crisis was over. The Chinese acupuncurist dame was hanging in through the passenger side window, kicking her feet and screaming her pork fried head off as the car bounced out into the road and shrieked a pair of rubber stripes in a hasty, naked getaway.

I was grateful at least that we'd missed the part of the show where the fatso's massive towel had dropped off. The terrycloth bed sheet had been abandoned in haste in the middle of the driveway amongst the remains of the busted-up garage.

The towel wasn't the only thing left in the wake of all the excitement.

Senorita Tamale had already started to get the hang of her newfound superheroine abilities. All the ice was gone but for two blocks, the perimeters of which she had very carefully carved even while she was disintegrating the rest of the massive ice slab.

Mrs. Gwendolyn Johnson was a furious, frozen statue of marital betrayal. Her teeth had been bared when she'd been flash-frozen, and the expensive orthodontia that had been partial payment for the affair she'd been having with the menacing Dr. Cohen glinted beneath a half-foot of ice that was as clear as Windexed glass.

Frozen in a permanent crawl away from the rigid feet of Client #1 was Dr. Zeroth Cohen; craven, bloodied, defeated, and with the most horrifying mouthful of teeth this side of a royal wedding.

I noticed for the first time that the very tip of his escape cone was decorated with the stylized O of his logo, and if that thing could be piloted around the city I had a pretty good idea what he'd used to run down the bike messenger in the street outside my office.

"Very good work, Senorita Tamale," I told the dame, who was still a little confused, but was already getting an early hint of that look of female empowerment that was never a good sign for any guy within piano stool-hurtling range. "There's a lot more crap around this town to thaw out, starting with the world headquarters of Banyon Investigations. Just make sure you let me act as your agent. At, of course, a twenty-five percent fee per building, park, monument, lake, superhero, etcetera. If the cops don't manage to track down his freeze ray machine, we could be set for life."

I was afraid I spoke too soon, and that the sound of tires in the driveway heralded the arrival of Dr. Cohen's freeze machine, desirous of another go at finishing what the sinister dentist had started. But when the three of us who weren't already ice statues turned, we found a scrawny figure pedaling toward us on a ten-speed bike.

The bike messenger wore a knitted scarf, an asshole Che T-shirt, a pair of skintight black jeans, and a stoned expression within irregular clumps of a beard that stubbornly refused to take root on his pasty face.

"Dr. Zeroth Cohen?" the college dropout asked.

I identified as same, and plucked the offered note from his hand. He pedaled closer to the garage to inspect the figures frozen in ice.

"Whoa, dude," said the fascinated bike messenger.

"Whoa, indeed," I replied, since I'd already opened the envelope and perused its contents.

Inside was like an evil orthodontist's Christmas wish list come true. I held up the items in turn to Mannix and Senorita Tamale.

"A five hundred million dollar money order," I announced, "made out to The Whole Tooth, LLC. A pair of season tickets to the opera. A notarized letter from the opera board awarding a perpetual parking space out front as soon as the Luciano Mankowitz Opera House is repaired. Ah, and our tax dollars have been deployed to pay off the maniac dentist's student loans. Tell me again, Mannix, why you started making me pay taxes? And don't mention Doris' problems with the IRS, because you'll only be right and I'm not in the goddamn mood."

"I'm sorry, Mr. Crag?" Mannix asked, fishing for the response that would make me happy while allowing him to continue to keep my ass out of jail by paying all my taxes, tickets, fines, fees, tabs and ex-marital obligations.

"Damn right," I said.

"Gngngaang!" interjected the stoned pervert bike messenger, who'd somehow managed to get his tongue stuck to the Gwendolyn Johnson ice sculpture.

It was the last semi-language he would ever utter, since the instant the gibberish had passed his lips there came a sudden reverse-sucking sound directly beside him, which was followed by the surprising appearance of a black-robed figure who promptly touched the kid on the shoulder. The remaining walls of the Victorian carriage house abruptly collapsed, dragging the wobbly, thousand pound cupola along with them. The cupola and nearest wall squashed flat the messenger and most of his bike.

The Grim Reaper held the handle of his scythe in the crook of his elbow and hitched up his belt, Barney Fife-like. He suddenly noticed me standing two feet away.

"Oh. Banyon," Death said, his skull face unreadable but his voice deeply bored. "Jaublowski said you wanted to see me. What do you want? I'm a busy man."

"It matters a lot less now than last night," I said. "I was only wondering how you were tied up in this Dr. Cohen affair. You first took out the messenger who brought me the photographs I'd taken for the case of frozen Mrs. Gwendolyn Johnson over there. Then you wiped out the one who delivered the warning from Cohen for me to watch it, as well as the one from Cohen for Johnny Johnson to watch it. I figured whoever was getting you to take them all out was paying you to cover his nefarious tracks. However, this last unfortunate human shit stain currently twitching under that pile of garage debris appears to have dispelled my concerns. I assume now this coincidental vendetta is something altogether different from the pair of cases I've been working."

Death shrugged his bony shoulders. "Bike messengers. I just hate the goddamn little pricks," the Grim Reaper said.

He gave the jutting wheel of the dead kid's bike a vicious kick that sent it spinning like mad before he and his long, crooked scythe vanished in the reverse of the reverse-sucking pop that had heralded the Grim Reaper's auspicious arrival.

"He is cute," mused smoking Senorita Tamale. "Do ju have his numbers?"

"Three sixes," I replied. "But he's never at home, so you'd have to leave a message with his service, and we all know how crummy operators are. In the meantime, those of us who survived, unfortunately, still have work to do."

With a well-earned weary sigh, I trudged into the remains of the garage to see if I could scrape up a car in stealable condition.

17

Fifty-four hours of semi-lucidity later found me on Monday evening gently swaying under a spluttering streetlight near the corner newsstand outside Bottomless Joe's Diner. Across the street in the Happy Hobo Motel, the girl whose old man owned the joint was sitting glumly at her post behind the counter under a shock of pink hair.

I didn't see any sign of the ogre housekeeper who'd tried to plant me like a tulip bulb through the asphalt behind the crummy philanderer's paradise.

It looked like management had found a cheap Mexican import to do the job American ogres just wouldn't do, probably after the lying dame at the counter blamed the attack on the telephone pole out back and the subsequent power outage entirely on the poor, dumb ogre bastard who was only following orders. The middle-aged maid dozed beside her laundry cart on the second floor as randy guests came and went.

I'd trailed Johnny J. Johnson from work, and I watched from my post under the weak streetlight as the bank manager approached the counter, paid in cash, and accepted a room key. Same routine as all the nights I'd tailed him the previous week, except this time I was off the clock, I hadn't brought my camera, and Johnson looked like more of a pathetic loser than ever. That last point might have had something to do with the fact that news of his wife's infidelity had been broadcast nationwide for the previous two days.

The chunk of ice in which Gwendolyn Johnson was entombed had been hauled to police lockup, along with the frozen slab containing Dr. Zeroth Cohen, criminal mastermind and rotten-toothed orthodontist bastard extraordinaire.

A special police unit had been assigned to thaw out the masterminds of a laundry list of supervillainous acts, the fallout from which the city would be cleaning up for months. Detective Daniel Jenkins was on the front page of Sunday's *Gazette* leading the charge against the accused with a scowl and a hair dryer.

The cops could afford to waste time defrosting the evil duo. Dr. Cohen's freeze machine had been discovered Saturday afternoon, thanks to a busted taillight. The diabolical dentist had mounted the device in the back of an old ambulance, which had been driving around town with the lights on and siren blaring. It was actually pretty clever, except Cohen didn't take into account the fact that local cops were morons who'd stop a speeding ambulance just because of a burned-out twenty-cent bulb.

With the freeze ray no longer sending out random blasts around town, it was a simple matter to cart Senorita Tamale to the edge of every ice field to work her magic. When she'd thawed the ice on Connie Sellecca Lake, Minus had launched himself from the black depths through about a million boiled trout (Senorita Tamale was still getting the hang of things), and tore off across the sky without so much as an apologetic glance for dragging the two of us into his goddamn mess.

"He could say *gracias*," the senorita with the glowing

red hands had groused.

"Given your limited command of Spanish Lite, or whatever the hell it is you speak, I am, frankly, surprised that *you* can say it," I'd replied, which had kept her sufficiently furious that she was able to free my building, along with Vincetti the fishmonger and whatever other pathetic souls toiled within its four sandstone walls.

I hadn't told Senorita Tamale on the lakeshore two days before that Minus probably had a lot more on his tiny mind than even she could imagine.

I watched Johnny Johnson exit the lobby of the Happy Hobo Motel. He disappeared for a few seconds on the elevator, and reappeared in the open hallway on the second floor. He swiped a keycard and entered room 218.

Only once the door had shut behind him did I hustle across the street. I made sure to keep out of range of the counter at Bottomless Joe's at my back. I didn't want a repeat of last week, with the angry waitress screaming from the alley behind the hotel. Likewise, I kept a keen eye out for the dame at the counter of the Happy Hobo.

The only eyes that saw me cross over to the far sidewalk belonged to a little elf loitering half a block down. I nodded to him as I stepped up from the curb, and as I headed around the side of the building I saw my diminutive assistant slip through the front door of the Happy Hobo.

I made it around back at a trot, counted windows down from the corner until I was standing beneath room 218, and mounted the nearest convenient telephone pole to the second floor. I noted that the busted pole had been replaced, but that the upper half that was still strung with wires had been chainsawed halfway up and fastened to the new pole.

I was waiting for only a few seconds when I heard a muffled knock inside the room. A moment after Mannix rapped on the door of room 218, the window opened and a figure climbed out onto the sill carrying an armload of folded clothes.

The big goon launched himself off the sill, but rather than perform the traditional belly flop on the pavement two stories down, he began to float quietly up to the roof. He kept his back close to the wall for some stupid reason that I assumed had to do with stealth, which is pretty hard to manage when you're dressed like a banana and wrapped in a purple cape with matching boots, mask and gauntlets.

"Psst. Hey, genius," I called over to Minus, who hadn't noticed me watching every moment of his pathetic escape attempt from my perch glued to the telephone pole that was positioned between his room and the next. He was so shocked that he nearly dropped his suit, necktie and dress shoes which were tucked carefully in the crook of his arm. "Mr. Gwendolyn Johnson, we need to talk."

* * *

Two minutes later, we were both inside Minus' crummy motel room. The hero of the hour had flown me in through the window, and had immediately taken off his mask and sat morosely on the edge of the bed. As far as I could tell, he was trying to stare the color out of the toes of his purple boots which, for all I knew, might have been one of his hitherto unknown super-abilities.

The folded clothes of his not-so secret identity were piled beside him. I was over at the door, which I'd opened a crack to find a nervous elf loitering in the hallway.

Mannix need not have been anxious, since the only sentry on duty was the snoozing Mexican chambermaid, who was a hell of a lot less intimidating than the ogre the Happy Hobo had previously employed to terrify patrons into not straying outside the broad range of what the sleazy dump regarded as acceptable behavior.

"Hit the bricks, Mannix," I said. "I'll take it from here."

The elf turned on a pointy-toed shoe and hustled to the exit.

I shut and locked the door and took a seat at the desk across from the bed. The surface of the desk had been carved up by hundreds of romantics who'd wanted to memorialize the five minutes they'd spent at the Happy Hobo. There was no heart-shaped scar to mark any of the nights Minus, nee Johnny J. Johnson, had spent there.

"I suppose you want bribe money," Minus announced glumly.

"I'd be insulted if I were in any other profession," I replied. "But as it happens, I take everybody's low opinion of private detectives in stride, mainly because I know a lot of them so, frankly, my informed opinion is far lower than the typical layman's. In point of fact, you paid me plenty. But you're not getting a partial refund, since you nearly got me killed multiple times, so the multiple death clause in our contract kicked in. Plus, I had to save the city, for which you and Senorita Tamale are getting credit. Or blame, if you prefer. I'm vacillating between the two. It's pretty much thirty-seventy right now."

"So what are you doing here?" Minus asked.

"A few things. First, to clear up your case. I thought we might be able to do it at your house while you were still Johnny Johnson, mild-mannered bank manager, but thanks to your wife's extramarital adventures in the dental chair of the fiendish Dr. Zeroth Cohen, there are TV camera crews parked all over your neighborhood."

Minus sighed and covered his eyes with one purple glove. "I can't believe Gwendolyn was cheating on me."

"Yes, I'm sure it was quite a shock to you and that one blind, deaf monk living in an underground cage on Jupiter. For the rest of the human race, it wasn't quite the same bolt from the blue. On an astonishment scale of one to a billion, I'd say I put my personal amazement at about one. Wait. Less than one. I just remembered that hot-to-trot strapless number she was shoehorned into on the day she hired me."

He looked out from around his glove. "Wait. Gwendolyn hired *you*?"

"Funny story. She claimed *you* were cheating on *her*, so she had me tail you. Mostly to this dump, as a matter of fact. Since she's frozen in ice at the police station right now, I can't really ask her, so most of this is conjecture. I figure she figured out your double life. Somehow you do that thing superheroes do where you put on a pair of tights and nobody recognizes you. But maybe a wife knows. Maybe you talked in your sleep. Maybe she tailed you here one night before me. Who knows? But once she knew your secret, she needed to expose you. She wanted dental work. She didn't need it, mind you, since her teeth were perfect. But she was a dame for whom perfection isn't perfect enough, and she decided she was going to use every tool at her disposal, including the two of us, to join that expanding legion of adult skirts who think fastening a chain link fence to their choppers is a goddamn status symbol. She couldn't afford the braces, so she'd been trying to romance a set out of Dr. Cohen, who, ironically, was himself terrified of all dental procedures. He planned to end all dental work as we know it. They found a manifesto tucked away in a hidden compartment in the ruins of his spit sink."

"How long was she having an affair with him?" Minus asked.

"Three weeks, ten years, who cares? Well, I expect *you* might, but as far as your intertwined cases are concerned the duration of her horizontal exploits with the demented Dr. Cohen are as immaterial as they are stomach-turning. She was Cohen's dame, and she sold you over to him for the dental work she craved."

"I told her we couldn't afford it," Minus insisted morosely. "She'd been nagging me for years, but she has such expensive tastes. I told her maybe, if we could save up the money, but she spent it as soon as I could make it."

"If I'm right about that, as I'm reasonably sure I am since cheating spouse cases practically write themselves, the rest is simple. She was a front. She hired me for Dr. Cohen in order to expose you. This *new* you. You, the flashy dresser, not the two-piece blue suit you. She was very specific about me taking pictures. She wanted me to have photographic evidence of you going into this dump as Johnny Johnson and coming out as Minus. Of course, she couldn't tell me exactly why. She needed me to uncover it myself. I never actually got a picture of you in the room because the one time I tried you'd already flown off, which is why I only managed to get a couple of snapshots of an empty motel room before I was viciously assaulted with a telephone pole by an ogre chambermaid."

"I saw the damage when I flew back later that night. That was you?"

"It was me who nearly got killed, it was the staff of the Happy Hobo who knocked out power for ten blocks around this dump. Try to keep up. As I was saying, your wife wanted you exposed, and that's not the definition of the word you usually get around the Happy Hobo. Public knowledge of your true identity would ruin your ability to work as a freelance crime fighter in town, which would be fine with Cohen, who decided he was your sworn enemy since there weren't any other superheroes in town he could level his crazy rage against. It would also wreak havoc on your personal life, and your wife would clean you out in the divorce. Nice and neat, in addition to being ruthless and diabolical. That dame you manacled yourself to really is the whole package."

"That's why you had the picture of me on your desk," Minus said. "The one where I was wearing--" He picked up the sleeve of his suit jacket and let it slip from his fingertips.

"Yeah. That was a misunderstanding on the part of my staff. I didn't know that you were, in reality, the you who you actually are until I got the FBI report on the pen you'd signed your contract with. You'd removed your glove, so I had your fingerprints."

Minus moaned. "The FBI knows who I am?"

"No one does," I said. "Except me, your wife and Dr. Cohen. How you deal with them is your business, but if you're interested I happen to know a minor superhero from Baton Rouge who can wipe their memories. Memory-Man. Crummy name, and his abilities are pretty limited. He can help you remember or forget stuff, which can pretty much be accomplished with a self-help library book on improving your memory or a gallon of vodka, respectively. The guy's also retired, but I'm sure he'd do a special for a fellow traveler." I pulled a scrap of paper from my pocket and handed over the phone number. "He doesn't have to come here, he can handle it over the phone. Just call the police station -- they'll definitely take your call -- and have idiot Detective Daniel Jenkins hold the receiver up to their respective blocks of ice. When you call Jenkins, by the way, don't mention me. He thinks I was crank calling him the other day when I asked him to track a couple of calls that came through the police switchboard. They were calls you'd placed from here as Minus. It was for your wife's case, before I knew you were Minus, so Jenkins understandably thought I was yanking his chain."

"What about you?" Minus asked. "You know who I am."

"Yes, but the part of my brain that knows that fact will no doubt succumb to a shaken Etch-a-Sketch variety of wood alcohol poisoning by week's end. By night's end, if I really roll up my sleeves and get to inebriated work." I could see the poor bastard was worried that I'd blab the truth to somebody. "Look, you're welcome to have Memory-Man (which really is a pathetic superhero name) work his magic on me as well. Hell, if you really want to waste money, have him wipe out the last ten years of my life as a P.I. However, my ingrate pal at the FBI only knows that he ran a set of fingerprints and came up with Johnny J. Johnson, boring bank manager. He has no idea why I asked him, and he made it clear he never wants to hear from me again, despite the fact that he owes his current parking space to me. So that's a dead end. My assistant doesn't even know the truth. He only knocked on the door. He didn't know he was flushing you out the window so I could nab you out back before you could take off on me again, and he didn't see you fly me in here. It won't go in any official files at my office, since most of the paperwork in my case files consists of unpaid I.O.U.'s, losing slips from the track and notes to myself to climb into the bathtub with a radio in my lap."

"Somebody else will figure it out," Minus said.

"Probably not. People are, since you apparently were never told this, idiots. You just need to be more careful. For instance, when you were passing out on the roof of the telephone company, you asked something about me having an account. I know now that in your delirium you had reverted to the banking side of your life. Same as the 'animal yields' you were babbling about after getting hit by the nuke at the opera house, which clearly was 'annual yield.' You were also apologizing about not wiping your feet, which very clearly suggests that you are subconsciously terrified of that shrew wife of yours even after you've been blown up by a nuclear bomb. I've met her. It's justified."

Minus picked up his mask from the bed and let it slip from his fingers. "So as an ethical man who apparently pulls no punches, how about a little advice, Mr. Banyon? Where would you suggest I go from here?"

"I'd suggest you run to a dictionary and look up 'ethical,'" I replied. "But first…"

I fished in my pocket and pulled out an envelope, which I tossed over to him.

Minus tore it open, and as he scanned the official letter inside, a look of confusion settled comfortably on his chiseled, dimwit face.

"I'm so goddamn ethical, I didn't read it," I said. "I didn't have to. Senorita Tamale told me what was in hers." When he glanced up at me, I nodded. I also stood, since I was pretty much done. "They do this all the time with superheroes. The city headhunts them, gives them all kinds of perks to relocate, sets them up with the local superhero leagues, gives them caves or fortresses to hide out in on their off hours. It's up to you if you want to stay or go. Once the senorita got on their radar, she told them she'd get that note to you, but since she didn't know how she gave it to me."

Minus shook his head. "New York wants *me*?"

"In point of fact, New York doesn't give a shit about you. They just like to boast the highest superhero per capita rate in the world. That's why you find so few everywhere else in the country, and why their city is such a paradise. A hero on every block gives them the lowest crime rate in the world. Senorita Tamale already left. Although they've already got a fight on their hands with her. She wants to call herself either the Mexican Firecracker or Hot Tamale. The usual groups are calling her racist. She's calling them things back, but no one can quite understand exactly what those things are since she speaks a language that is uniquely incomprehensible."

I left him sitting on the edge of the bed and I headed for the door.

"It's not my business, but there's no point you staying here for a cheating wife. And with Senorita Tamale gone, it'll take months to thaw her out using the police union-approved Conair method. If you try doing it with heat breath and brute strength, you're liable to snap that ice cube she's in in half, which I wouldn't object much to, but which the cops and courts might. Panhandler Federal Ameribank's world headquarters is in New York. Put in for a transfer. Either way, it's up to you. See you around, pal."

I pulled open the door, then shoved it closed.

"One last thing. How the hell did you come up with 'Minus?'"

He was suddenly sheepish. "Well, this all happened really suddenly, this superpower craziness. I was accidentally bombarded by gamma rays from a shipment of radioactive Susan B. Anthony dollars. Long story. Well, all of a sudden I had to come up with this, you know, *big* name. I couldn't use my real name, obviously, and, well, I just can't make snap decisions like that." He pointed to the badge on his chest. "I didn't have a name yet, I was just dash-Man. Temporarily, of course. It was going to be *something*-dash-Man. I actually had it narrowed down to Magnificent-Man or Spectacular-Man."

"Humility-Man having already been taken," I said.

(It had been, by a superhero in Chicago so unassuming he was afraid to interrupt bank robberies because he thought it was impolite. I read in one of those Sunday *Parade* inserts somebody left in a booth at O'Hale's that he quit super-heroing after the survivors of Bloomington tried to lynch him for not warning the city about the impending robot invasion back in '98. He said afterwards that it was so early in the morning that he thought it would be too "show-offy" to fly around waking everybody up. *Where are they now? Parade* asked. Apparently selling used Crown Victorias in Peoria. Maybe there are worse things than being a P.I. after all.)

"I had the dash there on my chest as a sort of place-holder. But then some shopkeeper over on 122nd Street who saw the...you know, the *this*--" He pointed hastily again and a little shamefaced at the symbol lounging between his impressive pectorals. "--and he yelled 'thanks, Minus-Man' for foiling a robbery, and there was a reporter from the *Gazette* in the store, and Minus-Man became Minus, and there you are."

There he was all right. And there I left him.

This time, I shut the door behind me and headed down the hall.

I was surprised to see Mannix standing in front of a barely open door on the first floor of the motel. The elf was handing over a takeout bag from Bottomless Joe's Diner.

I caught a glimpse of bleached hair and a pair of mascara trails streaking a couple of pasty cheeks below a set of bloodshot eyes. When she saw me, the dame hiding out in the room squeaked and slammed the door, as if she thought that by slamming it loudly and fast enough she could slam it straight back through time so that the previous five seconds during which I'd seen her loud and clear had never happened. Who knows? She was such a prize-winning dingbat she might actually have believed it was possible.

Mannix joined me on my stroll through the lobby. The counter dame recognized me and was swearing a blue streak and flapping her flaming red fingernails in the air as we exited to the street.

"So how long has Doris been hiding out here?" I asked the elf.

"Since last Friday," Mannix replied. "She phoned me on Saturday to tell me. I've mostly been bringing her makeup and those entertainment magazines she likes. Also a little food too, but she isn't eating much."

"Our Doris prioritizes. Food comes and goes, but lip gloss and *Entertainment Weekly* are forever. Does she grasp that you're scrupulously honest and that if the IRS directly asks you if you know where she is, you won't lie?"

"Gee, I don't know if she knows that, Mr. Crag, but it's funny you mention it because a very nice IRS agent phoned the office and asked me that just before we left."

Three official-looking sedans selected that moment to come tearing around the corner near the newsstand next to Bottomless Joe's, squealing with the reckless abandon of government officials who go in for the dramatic and don't care how many tires they wreck as long as they don't have to foot the bill. The three cars slid in crazy arcs to sideways stops in front of the Happy Hobo Motel. A phalanx of armed IRS agents rolled out of the cars and stormed through the front door through which we had just beat a hasty retreat. The dame at the counter screamed something about discretion, and toppling telephone poles, and her old man murdering the lot of them, and the last I saw she was getting handcuffed by a Fed for gallantly defending her citadel to human libido run amok.

"Do you think I should I go back and tell Miss Doris I spoke to the nice man?" Mannix asked.

"Save it," I said. "You'll need something to talk about on visiting days."

As we headed for the bus stop, I noticed a brilliant streak of yellow, tinged with purple, tearing across the night sky in the direction of New York. There was the clap of a sonic boom, and the multicolored stripe vanished with the reverberating sound.

The fading memory of the racket and light show was quickly replaced by the exhaust stink and the squeal of the opening door of a cross town bus.

Mannix and I climbed inside, and as the elf fished around in his pocket for the exact change, my bored eye fell across a little billboard ad above the long seat behind the driver: Dr. Zeroth Cohen, Orthodontia. Put your teeth in my hands.

The good doctor had posed for his own poster. He was depicted wearing a white mask over his mouth and nose. A pair of wild eyes glared out at the world from underneath a shock of insane white hair.

Thanks to the strategic placement of Cohen's surgical mask, invisible was his entire mouthful of horrifying, rotten, crazy-orthodontist archvillain choppers.

Mannix could deal with our fare. The artist inside me had a far more important task, and after many days I at last had in my possession the one tool I needed. I rummaged in my trench coat and, like a knight of old unsheathing a sword, I drew the pen I'd swiped from the mad doctor's reception area.

"Take care of business, Mannix," I instructed resolutely, as I struck off alone down the aisle. "I've got some vital graffiti to attend to."

About the author

James Mullaney is a Shamus Award-nominated author of nearly 50 books, as well as comics, short stories, novellas, and screenplays. His work has been published by New American Library, Gold Eagle/Harlequin, Marvel Comics, Tor, Moonstone Books, and Bold Venture Press.

He was ghostwriter and later credited writer of 26 novels in The Destroyer series, and wrote the series companion guide *The Assassin's Handbook 2*. He is currently the author of *The Red Menace* action series as well as the comic-fantasy *Crag Banyon Mysteries* detective series.

He was born in Taxachusetts and wishes he were an only child, save one.

Other books by Jim Mullaney

The Crag Banyon Mysteries series:

- One Horse Open Slay
- Devil May Care
- Royal Flush
- Sea No Evil
- Bum Luck
- Flying Blind
- Shoot the Moon
- The Butler Did I.T.
- X Is for Banyon
- Habeas a Nice Corpus
- Banyon Investigations: A Crag Banyon Mysteries Anthology

The Red Menace series:

- #1 Red and Buried
- #2 Drowning in Red Ink
- #3 Red the Riot Act
- #4 A Red Letter Day
- #5 Red on the Menu
- #6 Red Devil
- #7 Ruses Are Red

Printed in Great Britain
by Amazon